BLIND
VIGIL

BLIND VIGIL

A RICK CAHILL NOVEL

MATT COYLE

OCEANVIEW PUBLISHING
SARASOTA, FLORIDA

ISBN 978-1-60809-469-1

Published in the United States of America by Oceanview Publishing

Sarasota, Florida

www.oceanviewpub.com

10 9 8 7 6 5 4 3 2

PRINTED IN THE UNITED STATES OF AMERICA

For Ariel Amavisca,
a courageous woman who tackles life head-on

ACKNOWLEDGMENTS

This book would not have been possible without the help of many people.

My sincerest thanks to Kimberley Cameron for her continued support and sharing my vision.

The crew at Oceanview, Bob and Pat Gussin, Lee Randall, Lisa Daily, and Kat Daue for always listening.

Ken Wilson, Jane Ubell-Meyer, and Jennifer Vance for ABM, Always Be Marketing.

Carolyn Wheat, Penne Horn, Carl Vonderau, and Becca Jenkins of the Saturday Writers Group for always making me think twice.

My family, Jan and Gene Wolfchief, Tim and Sue Coyle, Pam and Jorge Helmer, and Jennifer and Tom Cunningham for word-of-mouth marketing and responding to "look at me" emails.

Bob Buckley for a wide variety of legal and criminal defense issues.

Nancy Denton for a vital early read.

David Putnam for police procedure and all-around cop stuff.

Assistant Marshall Mynde Heil for Bellevue, Idaho, specific law enforcement information.

D. P. Lyle M.D. and Paul J. Wesling O.D. for medical information.

Jim O' Donnell for hedge fund information.

A woman behind the glass in the lobby of the San Diego Central Jail for information on the jail's inner workings.

Darlene Young and Bobby Hunter for information on life in Idaho.

Jan Moran for expertise on perfumes and scents.

Kelly McLaurin for information on computer programs.

And to Ariel Amavisca and Kristin MacDonald for gracious insight into living with vision impairment.

Any errors regarding legal and criminal defense issues, law enforcement, medical situations, hedge funds, the San Diego Central Jail, Idaho, perfumes, computer programs, or living life visually impaired are solely the author's.

BLIND
VIGIL

CHAPTER ONE

DARKNESS. I OPENED my eyes and still couldn't see. Every day started and ended the same. In a dark void. Ever since my life ended and started all over again. I touched the cylindrical scar hollowed out below my left eye. Still tender. Its damage still raw.

Still blind.

The only time I saw clearly now was in my dreams.

I reached to my right and felt the cool sheets of my bed. Not Leah's warm skin. Gone. The fourth morning into her two-week trip back up to Santa Barbara. The longest we'd been apart in nine months.

Since a killer shot me in the face and stole my vision.

Leah had been by my side during the weeks and weeks of grueling physical and cognitive rehabilitation. Praising, cajoling, prodding me up the next rung of the rehab ladder. She'd put her life on hold the last three months, living with me back in San Diego, and making weekend trips to Santa Barbara to keep her interior design business afloat.

Leah was gone, but I wasn't alone. Midnight, my nine-year-old black Lab, stirred from the foot of the bed. I heard his license tink against his metal nametag as he rose from the floor, his muscles unfurl under his skin, and his paws push off the carpet. I swung my legs over the edge of the bed and felt warm breath on my right knee.

I found Midnight's head and scratched it. He licked my face. I got out of bed and walked the ten steps to the master bathroom. Last year, the trek would have been only eight or nine steps. My strides were shorter now. More regimented.

And always numbered.

I showered and walked the five steps from the bathroom to the dresser against the wall.

Midnight at my side. I opened the top drawer. Underwear and socks. All folded into neat little packages. I never used to fold my clothes or even care what drawer I put them in.

Now it mattered.

I grabbed a pair of athletic socks from the left side of the drawer and a pair of underwear from the right. I could tell the difference between athletic and dress socks by the thickness and cushion of the fabric. But I still separated them. Everything had its place. T-shirts next drawer down, blue jeans in the bottom. Tennis shoes snug against the dresser around the right side. Dress shoes, slacks, jackets, coats, and button-down shirts were in the closet.

Along with a gun safe I no longer opened. But I still kept a .357 magnum in the nightstand next to my bed. Old habits die hard.

I only went into the closet for my bomber jacket these days. There wasn't a reason to get dressed up or have a quick change of clothes that I could stuff into the duffle bag in the trunk of my car for stakeouts.

My private investigator's license was still good for another year. After that, I'd let it lapse. I didn't want to return to my old life. At least, not that part of it.

I dressed and headed downstairs with Midnight at my left thigh. Six steps out of the bedroom, fifteen down the hall, and fourteen stairs descending onto the landing. Another step down into the living room.

Midnight had sensed something different about me after my injury. He'd always been dedicated to me and an excellent guard dog, but now he rarely left my side.

We walked the sixteen steps from the staircase to the sliding glass door to the backyard and I let him outside.

The first couple weeks after I got home from Santa Barbara, I spent hours and hours walking off distances from every conceivable option in the house. Bedroom to kitchen. Front door to back door. Office to living room. And dozens of others. Over and over. So many repetitions that I didn't consciously count the steps anymore. My subconscious did that for me and directed me where I had to go. I saw where I was going inside my head. The logistics of my house still fresh in my mind's eye. The only time I didn't envision my surroundings was when I was in the bathroom at the sink brushing my teeth or shaving. I knew there was a mirror in front of me, but I didn't visualize myself in it. Just a blank space.

I followed the map in my head to Midnight's food bowl, then slid two wide steps to my right and opened the door to the pantry. I found the sealed sixty-quart storage container that housed hard kibble dog food. The good stuff. I took off the lid and felt for the measuring cup inside and doled out two cups into the bowl. Breakfast.

I reversed my trek and set Midnight's bowl down on the hardwood floor. Found his water dish next to it and checked the water level with my fingers. Still full from last night. I traversed my way back to the sliding glass door and let Midnight inside. A sense of movement in a dark background. I felt a faint vibration along the hardwood floor in my feet when he sat on his haunches.

"Breakfast, big boy," I said and heard his toenails clatter atop the kitchen floor, then kibble crunching between his teeth.

I navigated my way back into the kitchen and got eggs, bacon, and orange juice from their established areas in the refrigerator, a skillet from an undercounter storage drawer, and made myself breakfast.

I took the food out to the round table on the deck in my backyard. Twenty-three steps from the kitchen door. I angled my head toward the sliver of a view of the ocean two miles away as the seagull flies. The view was one of the chief selling points for me when I bought the house six years ago. It would still be today, even though the view was just a memory. I felt the ocean's cooling breeze feather my face and whiffed a hint of salty tang hidden behind the exhaust fumes and road grease from Interstate 5 between me and the beach.

At least, I convinced myself I could smell it from my sanctuary in the dark.

The morning sun crawled up the back of my neck. Its warmth spread throughout my body. I pictured it climbing over the roof of my house on its journey to the sea. I turned and faced it. Shards of light, not really light, but something less than dark, danced around the edges of my nothing. This was fairly new.

I first noticed it two and a half weeks ago. I didn't know what it meant but let my imagination off its leash and allowed myself to dream that my sight was coming back. But just for an instant. I didn't tell Leah about it because I didn't want her hopes to soar up there with mine until I knew what the occasional lightening bursts in my endless night meant.

Doctor Kim, my ophthalmologist, dashed my escaped dreams. She thought what I was experiencing was a visual hallucination or CBS. Charles Bonnet Syndrome. The brain's stored memories of sight playing tricks. Kind of like an amputee still feeling his lost appendage. A visual phantom limb.

I turned away from the sun.

The surgeon who saved my life in Santa Barbara, along with the ophthalmologist he consulted, thought that the swelling near the optic chiasm caused by the bullet fragments he removed from my brain would eventually go down and I might regain my sight.

Nine months. Still blind. Nothing had changed except my mind now played visual tricks on me.

My vision was gone, but the pit below my eye from the bullet that exploded my cheekbone remained. A nasty reminder that wasn't fixed at the time of surgery because the surgeon was just trying to keep me alive. Facial reconstruction surgery was an option that I couldn't afford now, even if my insurance covered most of it.

I'd lived. That was enough. For now.

My voicemail pinged at 8:00 a.m. I found my phone and listened to the message.

Leah.

"Rick, my miracle man. Each trip north without you is harder than the last. This one is especially difficult. I pray for a time when I can live under one roof with you forever. And Midnight, of course! You two are my family and my heart aches for you when I'm away. I'm excited for our future together and know better times are ahead. I'm proud of the man you are and love you more every day. I'm counting the hours until I can see you again. Love you."

The emptiness in me filled with warmth. It always did when Leah left me a straight-to-voicemail message on a Santa Barbara trip. A verbal love note left under the pillow. Each message reminded me how lucky I was. I lost my eyesight in Santa Barbara, but I found Leah. Yet, each recorded message from her was also a tacit reminder that such deep professions of love were rarely verbalized by me.

I did love Leah. More than I'd been able to express.

* * *

I spent the rest of the morning listening to cable news on the TV in my living room. I knew a lot more about what was going on in Iran, China, and North Korea than I did about anything just outside my front door.

Midnight growled and a second later the doorbell bonged. I walked to the front door with Midnight at my side and tapped my hand along the bench in the foyer and found my sunglasses. Right next to my collapsible white cane.

The sunglasses had frames that dipped below my scar. The lenses were extra dark so neither my eyes nor my scar were visible. They weren't for my vanity. I didn't have any. Protection for my guests. I often wore them in the house for Leah's sake. Sometimes she'd take them off me and kiss my scar. Sometimes she left them on.

In my old life, I would have grabbed the Glock 19 I kept in the hall closet and peeked through the peephole before I greeted an unexpected visitor at the front door. Now I put on sunglasses and saw nothing. There might still be evil waiting on the other side, but it might be an Amazon delivery driver, too. I had to face the world without seeing it.

And I had eighty-five pounds of muscle and teeth right next to me.

I opened the door and knew instantly that my guest wasn't unexpected. The scent of Degree deodorant floated underneath a coconut shampoo fragrance and danced under my nose.

Moira MacFarlane.

The best private investigator I knew and occasional associate in my old life. Reluctant best friend in my before and after lives. I should have figured that Leah would conspire with Moira to check up on me. Or she may be checking on her own.

"Hi, Moira." I spoke quickly before she could, showing off. After I lost my sight, my other senses became more acute. I concentrated on each one intensely, like a scientist examining cells under a microscope.

"Dammit, Rick. It still freaks me out when you do that." The machine-gun voice on full auto hit me about chest high. Moira was five feet even, a hundred nothing pounds. Brown hair in a bob cut, the last I'd seen. Brown eyes too big for her face, lips the same. But everything came together to form exotic beauty.

"You're hard to forget." Midnight's wagging tail banged off the back of my leg.

"Shut up and let me in." At first glance, or listen, Moira still treated me with the indulgent disdain of a mother to a teenage son, even though she was only a few years older than me. But something had changed since I'd gone blind. Her words remained mostly harsh like before, but her tone had softened a degree. I didn't like the change. I feared there was pity hiding in the new tone.

I preferred disdain to pity.

I stepped back from the door to let Moira in and give her space to bend down and greet Midnight. They had an ongoing love affair. The door closed, and I walked into the living room, Midnight tracking beside me. I heard the woomph of Moira sitting down on the sofa.

"Leah's idea or yours to check up on me?" I sat down on the chair opposite the sofa and faced Moira.

"You think you're so clever."

"Just moderately clever." I scratched Midnight's head.

"I'm not here to check up on you."

"But you two talked." That hint of pity in her voice, real or imagined, made me want to get under Moira's skin. To get her mad at me so, for an instant, I'd be worthy of her anger.

"You're still an asshole, Cahill. That hasn't changed."

Better. "What has?"

"Shut up, Rick." Hard snap in her voice. "I came here because I could use your help on a case."

My stomach knotted up and walls I couldn't see closed in on me.

"I'm not a P.I. anymore." I took off my sunglasses. "Lost my skill at surveillance."

I'd already sworn off private investigating even before I was shot in the face. The physical damage it did to me was obvious as soon as the sunglasses came off. The emotional scars were harder to see, but just as deep.

Deeper.

Moira hadn't seen me without my sunglasses before. Hadn't seen the pit under my eye. An image I could only feel through my fingers and didn't have to see. Disfigured. But better than dead, which I would have been if I hadn't snapped my head away from the gun before it fired.

No gasp came from the couch upon seeing me unmasked.

"So, what *do* you want to do now?" Moira's tone wasn't mocking or combative, but she made her point.

I didn't know what I wanted to do, only what I did. I counted steps inside my house, worked out, and listened to the television. I was living off disability insurance and a mortgage refi. I had minimal marketable skills. Ex-P.I., ex-cop, ex–restaurant manager. Enough Xs to win at tic-tac-toe, but not much else. There was a possible book deal in the offing about what happened in Santa Barbara. And before. But I didn't know where to put the truth or where to hide the lies.

"What I don't want to do is work cases anymore." I'd chased my last ghost. I'd finally learned the one truth in Santa Barbara that I'd pursued for fourteen years. It hadn't given me closure, just an ending. I couldn't help strangers find truths that might destroy their lives anymore. People had died on my watch. People I cared about. And people I killed.

"Turk Muldoon wants to hire me and I need your help."

Shit.

CHAPTER TWO

Turk. My onetime best friend.

The man who saved my life.

He owned Muldoon's Steak House, the restaurant I once had a sliver of ownership in and managed for seven years. My limited partnership didn't end well and neither did our friendship. Still, Turk had let me use a booth in the restaurant to meet clients as a private investigator since I never had a real office.

He didn't have to worry about me taking up space anymore.

"Turk emailed me a couple days ago for a recommendation for a good P.I. I gave him your name and contact info. I figured he wanted a background check on a new hire." I hunched my shoulders. "Why do you need my help on something so simple?"

"It's not that simple." Moira's voice lost its rattle. Her inborn confidence gone. "He wants me to surveil his girlfriend."

That didn't sound right. Turk had always been laissez faire about relationships. He'd never been married and had at least nine or ten girlfriends during the time I worked with him at Muldoon's. Ninety percent of the time, the breakups were amicable. Everyone remained friends and Turk would be dating someone else within a month. Every once in a while, there'd be drama during a breakup, but it was usually short lived and never on Turk's end. Everybody liked Turk. Even his exes.

"That surprises me. The Turk I knew wouldn't spy on a girlfriend, but we're not close anymore." I put my sunglasses back on. My face had made its point. "Either way, you certainly don't need my help for the job."

"Yes, I do. But only for the initial meeting." Regaining her natural confidence. "I want you to listen to his voice when I talk to him. To hear if he's being truthful."

"Why wouldn't he be?"

"You know as well as I do that people who hire P.I.s to check up on loved ones are desperate. Sometimes they hide their true intentions. I'm not going to take a case where someone could get hurt."

"Turk's not like that." I shook my head. "He'd never get violent. Not unless he had to defend himself. And never with a woman."

"People can surprise you, Rick. You know that better than anyone."

Turk had surprised me. A surprise that caused the end of our friendship seven years ago. Still, violence against a woman? Never.

"Not in that way." I said.

"Well, then come with me and let him prove it. I'm not taking the case without you there. I don't do domestics anymore, anyway."

"Since when?"

"I took a domestic while you were in Santa Barbara. Doctor John Donnelly. My son's pediatrician until he outgrew him. He was a nice man. Gentle with Luke. Never got impatient with me when I asked him question after question." An ache in her voice. "His first wife died six years ago. He hired me to find out if his new wife, Rachel, was having an affair. She was."

"It's always hard giving bad news to a client, especially a friend, but Turk will be able to handle it. He won't hold it against you."

"John Donnelly murdered his wife, Rachel, and killed himself the day after I told him she was cheating on him. The doctor who I entrusted with my son's health for eighteen years. A man I liked very much. Revered in the community. Bad news turned him into a murderer."

I didn't know what to say. Moira wasn't big on receiving sympathy, and I wasn't great at giving it. Still. "That's awful, but it's not your fault. If it hadn't been you, it would have been some other P.I. who gave him the information."

"I know, but I should have read the situation better. Maybe if I had, he wouldn't have killed his wife. And himself."

"There's nothing you could have done, but if you're that concerned, why even take Turk's case? You don't owe him anything."

"I know, but now I owe the woman who's going to be investigated by me or someone else. If I take the case and think she'll be in any kind of danger, I'm going to warn her. I'm the only P.I. who has a friend who can get a read on Turk. If I agree to take the case, I'll investigate Shay Sommers, but she'll be my responsibility as well as the target of the investigation."

In the six years I'd known her, I'd never seen Moira get emotionally involved in a case. I'd been the one who crossed over the line from dispassionate investigator to unbalanced zealot. She'd always been on the outside trying to rein me in. Seems the wrong side of me rubbed off on her. Not a good development. I'd have to play out of character and be the cautionary voice.

"When do you want to meet with him?"

"Now."

"I guess you drive." I stood up. Ready to help Moira. And Turk. And ready to venture back into my old life for at least one day.

CHAPTER THREE

MULDOON'S STEAK HOUSE was in La Jolla, a wealthy enclave and tourist magnet, clinging to the coastline just north of San Diego. The chilled mist on my face told me the sun hadn't yet pierced through the winter morning haze. Only five miles from my home in Bay Ho, but a completely different microclimate.

I hadn't been to Muldoon's in almost a year. Before Santa Barbara. A different lifetime ago. I had my service cane with me, but let Moira guide me from her car, along the sidewalk, and down the stairs to the restaurant.

At the bottom of the staircase, Moira angled slightly to the right and stopped after a few steps. The front door.

"It's locked," I said. Muldoon's only served dinner and didn't open until five p.m. "The back door will be open for deliveries."

I heard a muted clack when Moira tried the handle.

"Told you." I smiled.

"Shut up."

Just like old times. Progress.

We walked toward the back of the building, then Moira turned me to the right. A few more strides and we stopped again. The creak of door hinges. Latin music spilled out through the doorway.

"Watch your step." Moira grabbed my arm.

But I'd already stepped over the raised threshold and entered the short hall. A tiny office would be on the right and the kitchen straight ahead. My memory kicked in with images I remembered of a restaurant I spent years traversing.

I hoped Turk hadn't moved any of the furnishings around. We headed into the back of the kitchen and Moira turned me to the right around the wire shelving that held cookware. A quick left and we were in the main kitchen. A knife working on a cutting board behind the shelving. No, two knives. Prep cooks chopping vegetables on the metal prep table.

Where it started for me.

Turk's father gave me a job cutting veggies and mopping floors the summer I was fourteen. My father, once a proud and distinguished member of the La Jolla Police Department, had been kicked off the force four years earlier amidst rumors that he was a bag man for the mob. Shame, misplaced honor, and the bottle finally beat him down until he could no longer hold a steady job. I had to pitch in to help pay the bills.

I hid my father's shame under a chip on my shoulder and a quick temper. Turk didn't care about my father's reputation, he only cared about his own father's restaurant. Either I put the success of Muldoon's and the team that made it run ahead of my own insecurities or I had to find a new job. I quickly learned how to be a good teammate.

Life had forced me to become an adult at an early age. That summer, Turk Muldoon taught me how to become a man.

Turk stood at the butcher block table cutting meat across from the prep cooks. Or someone else did. The smell of raw meat that had just been unwrapped from its packaging. A slight metallic smell from the meat's bloody juice floated in the air.

The scent of blood. I first smelled it in this kitchen cutting meat. Later, as a cop and as a private investigator, I'd smell it again with dire consequences.

"Veronica Mars and Magnum P.I." Turk's voice bellowed from a few feet away. I could almost feel his physical presence.

That presence was as large as his personality. At six foot three, two-hundred-fifty pounds, he'd been an All-Pac 12 linebacker at UCLA three years ahead of me. His curly red hair bushing out the back of his helmet as he raced from sideline to sideline making tackles. I'd followed him to UCLA and we'd played together my freshman year when I was a starting safety.

"Sirloins?" I asked.

"How the hell?" His baritone.

"Sirloin butts were always the most pungent." I cut meat while I managed Muldoon's. Sirloins took much more labor than striploins and tenderloins. And they had the most meat juice to sop up with a cloth towel.

"Are you two a team now?" Clatter of a knife set down on the butcher block. "Am I getting a two for one?"

"I thought it would be nice for you two to see each other since I was coming down here anyway." Moira's voice had a forced cheer to it. If she'd brought me as a lie detector, her voice was the first lie I detected. Of course, her words were lie number two. "Plus, Rick and I have worked a lot of cases together. Consider him a consultant."

There was some truth in that, but only to hide the lie. I rethought my decision to meet Turk with Moira. I was lie number three. When I worked with Turk, I would have asked him if he was out of his mind hiring a P.I. to follow his girlfriend. But our friendship had changed since then.

And I hadn't yet met Moira then, either. She was my best friend now. She'd asked for my help, an unusual thing for her to do. I owed her. Even more than I owed Turk.

"I guess that's okay as long as I'm only paying one of you." Turk had meant it as a joke, but his voice was tight and stuck in the back of his throat. He was uncomfortable. A rare situation for him. At least the him I used to know.

"As we discussed on the phone yesterday, I have a few questions for you." Moira, back to her confident, professional self. "Do you want to talk here or . . ." She paused and may have glanced at the prep cooks, an unexpected audience.

"Rick, your office or mine?" Ease returned to Turk's voice. I doubted he'd meant to be cruel or ironic referring to the booth I'd never be able to use as an office again.

"Booth four," I said and took a step forward.

Moira grabbed my arm and I let her lead me through the kitchen door into the dining room, past the large open grill on the right, women's restroom on the left, and a right turn around the busboy station straight ahead. The hint of cooked steak and sautéed garlic hung in the air from last night's service.

I heard Turk behind us on the cement kitchen floor, then the tile in the grill area, and finally, the carpet in the dining room. Hard footstep, thunk of the cane, and drag of his right leg. Over and over again. The fact that he could walk at all was a miracle. The lead fragment lodged against his spine from the bullet he took saving my life put him in a wheelchair for almost a year. Willpower, athleticism, and modern science had gotten him out of it.

We made our way across the dining room, two men forever changed. Turk a little ahead in the recovery process. Both physically and emotionally. I heard the click of Turk pushing the dimmer switch for the lights over the booths. Moira led me up the two steps onto the platform that held the booths. Number four was on the left. I found the edge of the table and slid in. Moira next to me, Turk across the way.

"Are your questions about the information I emailed you yesterday after we talked on the phone?" Turk, voice tight again. "You got all of it, right? The photo, address, social security number?"

"Social security number?" I said. "Why the hell would you have someone you're dating's social security number?"

One hundred and eighty degrees from the Turk I used to know.

"Rick." Moira elongated my name like a mother scolding a child.

I guess I was supposed to be mute as well as blind. She should have thought more carefully before she invited me to come along. She knew me well enough to know that I wouldn't sit quietly when something didn't sound right.

"That's okay. I got Shay's social security number when I hired her, just like I would for any other employee." Turk's voice more defensive than his words.

"But you don't date every employee you hire," I said.

"Rick! Enough." Moira.

The rule at Muldoon's when I ran it was that management didn't date the staff. I'd upheld that rule and so had Turk while I was there.

"She's not an employee anymore." Still defensive. "Are these your questions, Miss MacFarlane?"

"You can call me Moira, and no, they're not." I could almost feel Moira's glare burning into the side of my face. "I apologize for Rick. I guess holing himself up in his house the last few months has made him even more antisocial. If that's possible."

"No need to apologize." Turk beat me to my own defense. "That's just Rick being himself. He likes to get right to the point. And be an asshole doing it." A forced chuckle.

"Why do you want Miss Sommers followed?" Moira asked.

"I have my reasons." No chuckle. "I didn't realize that was something you needed to know. I'm hiring you to follow Shay and report back on what she does and who she sees. Those are the parameters."

"You're hiring me to follow your girlfriend, Mr. Muldoon." Moira, full command presence. "I have my own parameters. If you can't give me reasons why, I can't take your case."

Turk let go a long sigh, but didn't say anything. I stared at nothing.

Finally. "I think she's seeing someone else." Voice tight again. From sadness or shame that his girlfriend was cheating on him or something else. I couldn't tell, yet. I wished I could see his face.

"How long have you and Miss Sommers been dating?" Moira.

"A little over a year. We met when I hired her as a hostess. I work the reservation station on the weekends with the hostesses." The tenor of his voice went lower like he dropped his chin and shortened his neck. Maybe staring down at the table. "One thing led to another and . . ."

Six months was about the average length of a Turk relationship when we worked together. I couldn't remember him ever dating someone for a whole year. Should be time for him to move on to the next woman, anyway. Shay Sommers must be special.

"And you two are still in an active relationship?" Moira.

"Yes."

"Do you love her?" Moira, dispassionate like a questionnaire you'd fill out for a doctor's appointment.

Silence. I couldn't tell if Turk was thinking or turning red with anger.

"Yes." A slight hiss at the end.

"When was the last time you made love?"

"What kind of a question is that?" An edge in Turk's voice now. One you didn't want to be on the other side of if you were an unruly customer in his bar.

"You know the rules." I jumped in before Moira could. "Answer Moira's questions or we walk."

"A couple nights ago." Clipped.

"Why do you think she's seeing someone else?"

"She's been a little distant the last month." A hint of shame. "Sometimes she's hard to reach and it takes her a while to reply to my texts."

"To be honest, Mr. Muldoon, that just sounds like your relationship is finding a new level or nearing its end."

"Call me Turk. If you're going to ask me how often I make love to my girlfriend and who's on top, we might as well be on a first-name basis." A little more at ease. Closer to the Turk I used to know. "But I understand your point. By distant, I mean more preoccupied than uninterested. And to advance your point about making love, we still do it as often as before and with the same passion."

"Then why do you think she's having an affair?" I couldn't help myself.

Another pause. Anger or thinking? Moira had a better view than I did.

"I followed her twice last week after she left the restaurant, and both times she went to the La Valencia Hotel." Sad. "She told me she'd gone home when I asked her what she'd done after work."

"I thought she didn't work for you anymore?" Moira.

"She doesn't. I got her a job at Eddie V's up the street. She hostesses there and usually gets off around nine or nine thirty, then stops by here before she heads home." His voice dropped again. "Or wherever she goes at night."

"Did you see Shay meet anyone at the hotel?" I asked.

"No. I didn't follow her inside. I didn't want to risk her seeing me."

"Maybe she stopped at the bar for a drink to unwind after work." Moira.

"Shay rarely drinks. Only on her birthday and sometimes at parties. But never alone at a bar."

"Maybe she has a drink once in a while and doesn't want you to know," I said. Everybody has secrets. Some innocuous, some dangerous.

"I doubt that's it." Confident without being dismissive.

"Did you confront her about La Valencia after she lied to you?" I asked.

"No." Barely audible.

"Why not?"

"Because I accused her of lying about something trivial once. Turned out I was wrong. She broke up with me for almost a month. I don't want to go through that again." A tremble in his voice. "Trust is very important to Shay. Her father abandoned her and her mom when she was three years old. Her mom died a few years ago. She doesn't really have anyone else."

I kept my mouth shut for a change and didn't mention that by hiring someone to spy on Shay, Turk was betraying her trust. This wasn't the Turk I knew. For many reasons. An unsteadiness to his emotions I'd never seen before. Felt before. Shay Sommers mattered to him. Maybe more than any girlfriend ever had.

But the Turk I used to know didn't walk with a cane and almost bleed out below the cross on Mount Soledad seven years ago. That kind of incident can change you. Forever.

It did me.

This was why I decided to quit my P.I. gig even before I lost my eyesight. Too many people in pain acting out of desperation. And sometimes those people were friends. Or used to be.

"What are you going to do if we find out she's seeing someone else?" Moira, devoid of any sentimentality. Another trait that made her such a good private investigator. She didn't get personally involved in her cases. That's why she had less scars than me. Inside and out. But her son's pediatrician murder/suicide had scarred her and she didn't want to get hurt again. Or anyone else to on her watch.

"I guess I'll have to move on with my life." Melancholy.

As Moira and I knew, it was never as easy as that.

CHAPTER FOUR

I HELD ONTO Moira's left arm as we walked down Prospect Street. She stayed on the outside of the sidewalk, the buffer between cars on the road and me. I'd always taken that position when I walked with a woman before I was shot in the face. An anachronistic blast from the chivalrous past my father drummed into me as a kid. I'd learned his lessons well. So much so that I always took the outside position whenever I was with anyone, man or woman. I felt comfortable out there. Being able to recognize potential danger and react to it instantly.

I didn't feel comfortable holding onto Moira and being led. Not by her or anyone. But it was either that or the cane. The cane worked fine, but it made me stick out. After over a decade of being the main suspect in my wife's murder and seven years as a private investigator, I'd worked hard to blend in. Now it was second nature and my comfort zone. Hidden in plain sight. The cane was a neon sign. "Look at me."

I didn't like to be looked at. Ever. I especially didn't like being looked at when I couldn't see who was doing the looking. I'd made some enemies during my time as a P.I. None of whom I wanted to bump into on the street. Or walk in front of at a crosswalk as they sat in their cars revving their engines.

Female voices approached on my left. Two women. Perfume commingling. More spicy than floral. Younger women. Probably thirties. The swish of a plastic shopping bag.

No threat.

Outdoors, away from the sanctuary of my home guarded by Midnight, my life morphed into constant threat-level assessment. Blind vigilance. Like animals hunting in the wild, criminals look for the weak and vulnerable to prey on. And I'd never been more vulnerable. Attitude and physical projection were the first line of defense. Head and chest high, confident walk. Even when I couldn't see where I was walking.

And that was just for random criminals whom I'd never come across before. If any enemies from my past were on the hunt, I wouldn't be able to see them coming. I had to find other ways to spot them. Or hear them. Or smell them. Even if I could, what then? Start shooting in the dark? Lock myself in my house twenty-four seven? Arm whoever I was with and tell them to shoot anyone I thought smelled suspicious?

There wasn't a good answer. Nonetheless, I continued to use my heightened senses. If the day ever came, I intended to make it as difficult as possible for whoever tried to harm me.

"You get what you needed out of me?" I asked Moira as we walked at half speed down the sidewalk. Really three-quarter for me, half for her. Her short, sturdy legs fast twitched like an NFL running back's. The speed of her gait was matched by the speed of her intellect.

"I won't know until you give me your read on Turk." Her voice trailed back to me from her slight forward position. A breeze pushed briny ocean air up from La Jolla Cove a quarter mile away.

"I'd like to, but it's in braille."

"Clever." Her tone conveyed an opposite opinion.

"How stupid do you think I am?" I asked as we passed two sets of footsteps going in the other direction. A man and a woman, by their sound.

"Moderately. Why?"

"You asked me to be at your meeting with Turk because you knew I'd call him out on any bullshit and get under his skin."

"Why would I do that?" I wished I could see the smirk on Moira's face.

"So you could see how he'd react when pushed. You got to keep your distance but still have a bird's-eye view while I did your dirty work."

"Like I told you, my main reason was for your read on Turk. Deception or truth in his voice. The fact that you would probably antagonize him, like you do to just about everyone, was an added bonus. We can discuss it in the car. Right now, I need to focus on keeping you from getting run over."

"Glad my disposition is a benefit to you."

"It's certainly not a benefit to you. Wait." Moira stopped walking. The whoosh of cars passed by on the street. We'd come to the end of the sidewalk on the west side of Prospect. A railing was straight ahead. Cave Street circled below on its journey to Coast Boulevard. Moira turned us to the right. "Damn. I forgot there wasn't a crosswalk here."

"I can tap my way out into the middle of the street. That might stop traffic."

"Don't give me any ideas." More car sounds. Prospect was one of the busiest streets in La Jolla and our stay at Muldoon's now put us into early afternoon. Rush hour for shoppers and tourists.

Footsteps shuffled to a stop directly behind us. Single person. Long strides. Athletic. Something slightly heavier than tennis or running shoes, with a soft Vibram-type sole. Like a cop or military tactical boot. A silent stop to all but the blind.

The breeze off the ocean died, and I caught a deodorant scent mixed with a hint of sweat, and human musk. I knew the deodorant. Dove for Men. A brand I used when I had to fly and needed a travel-size antiperspirant. The person behind us was a man. Probably my age or younger.

Complete silence behind me against the sound of traffic on the street. An unnerving stillness. When I was a street cop, I learned to sense danger in the stillness of silence. I used that skill as a private investigator. Did I still have it? The tingle along my spine told me, yes. I turned my head to glance at the man. To spot the danger and let it know I was aware. But of course, I could only see shades of darkness.

"Okay." Moira. "It's clear. Step down. Let's hustle."

We stepped off the curb and walked at a speed that would have been about my normal gait before I lost my eyesight. I heard the soft-soled footsteps behind us. The Dove wearer was close. Moira stopped me after step twenty-one.

"Curb."

We stepped up onto the sidewalk and Moira waited on the corner. Mr. Dove passed behind us as particles of his scent floated in the air. Again, my instincts forced me to turn in his direction.

"Did you see that guy?" I said in a low tone to Moira.

"What guy?"

"The guy who just passed behind us. Thirties, athletic. Maybe a cop, or a soldier?" I realized how stupid the cop or soldier reference sounded, but I didn't care. I was riding adrenaline and instinct.

Moira's arm shifted to the right like she turned her upper body.

"I don't see a cop or a soldier or anyone like that. How can you tell what he looks like?"

"An educated guess. You didn't see the guy behind us before we crossed the street?"

"No. I was watching traffic so you didn't become a hood ornament. Is there a problem?"

"No." Maybe. Probably not. I hadn't been down to La Jolla since I was shot. Maybe the trip to my old haunts had put me on instinct overload.

Moira led me across another street. We walked for three or four minutes until she stopped and opened the door to her Honda Accord for me.

"I should have valeted the damn car and expensed Turk for it," she said and waited for me to get into the passenger seat. I listened for her to enter through the driver's door.

"Does that mean you're taking the case?" I asked.

"I need to hear what you have to say first." She started the car and pulled away from the curb. "Did you believe Turk when he said he loved Shay?"

"I think so, but I've never seen him in love. Maybe this is what being in love looks like for him."

"Do you believe that he'd just move on with his life if he found out that Shay was seeing someone else?"

"The old Turk wouldn't have blinked." Inertia tried to pull me to the left and then pushed me back into the seat as Moira turned right and climbed the hill before Prospect bisected Torrey Pines Road. We stopped at the light at a forty-five-degree angle in astronaut blastoff position. "But he's changed."

"Do you believe him or not? Would he just move on with this life?" Terse. The old Moira.

"I don't think so. He might be trying to convince himself that he would, but the guy I just listened to doesn't want to lose his girlfriend." Push to the right as Moira turned left onto Torrey Pines. "If your real question is would he hurt Shay or himself if we found out she's cheating on him, the answer is no. Turk's changed, but not in that way. If anything, he seems gentler."

"You said if we found out she's cheating on him." She rode out the "e" sound of "we."

"I don't know what you're talking about." But I heard it, too. My subconscious had forced "we" out of my mouth instead of "you." It told me, and Moira, what I didn't want to, but needed to, hear.

"I'll split the retainer sixty-forty." The tommy-gun delivery. "After all, I'm doing all the driving."

Despite my subconscious interjection, I didn't want to be a private investigator anymore. To get tangled up in other people's problems. Make a bad decision, or even a good one, and have people get hurt.

But I couldn't avoid the fact that getting out of the house today and trying to solve the puzzle of Turk Muldoon's emotions had given me a lift. A rare lightness. A purpose. My only purpose since I lost my eyesight had been to learn how to cope and adapt. I'd been isolated by my situation, but even more so by my own narrow goals.

I needed something new, even if it was something old. And even if it was a charity case. Moira didn't really need my help. I couldn't be part of a two-person surveillance team. The best I could hope for was not to be a liability. But I could live with that. Losing my eyesight had forced me to be more dependent upon other people. At least it had so far. I was slowly regaining a sense of independence but couldn't lie to myself that I was all the way back. I'd take the charity because I needed it to move forward. I wouldn't even bother to swallow my pride.

Plus, I didn't have to worry about the effect my decisions would have on other people's lives. I wouldn't be making any decisions. Moira would. My goal was to aid her however I could to help Turk. And be a friend to him again if we had to deliver bad news.

"Deal." I shifted in my seat and thrust my right hand toward Moira. Her small hand grabbed mine and gave it one firm shake.

"I'm the Boss." Punctuation on the end of the handshake.

"When haven't you been?"

"Smart ass."

"What's the plan for Shay Sommers, boss?"

"I'll pick you up at eight fifteen tonight, and we'll drive down to La Jolla and park somewhere within view of Eddie V's. If Shay follows the routine Turk mentioned after she gets off work, she'll stop at Muldoon's to see him and then go to La Valencia."

"And you'll be following her on foot?" A statement more than a question

"Yep." We slowed to a stop. Had to be at the stoplight at Torrey Pines and La Jolla Shores Drive.

Moira's response made me think back to working cases as a P.I. Tailing targets on foot used to be my favorite part of the job. Blending into the background. Following the mouse to the cheese. A lot of the time, there was no cheese, no payoff. The target was just out for a day of shopping or a night out on the town. Still, my body dosed me with a jolt of adrenaline every time I followed someone on foot. Even more so than in a car.

As much as I'd sworn off private investigative work, and couldn't continue to do it anymore even if I wanted to, I knew I'd be envious as soon as Moira left the car tonight and tracked Shay Sommers on foot.

Reverberations from a life that wasn't anymore.

CHAPTER FIVE

My phone rang as I sat on my deck and convinced myself I could smell the ocean miles away. Midnight stirred against my leg when I picked up the phone from the table.

"Rick?" Turk.

"Yeah." A call I didn't expect to get after our talk in Muldoon's.

"I just wanted . . ." Uncertainty. A side he rarely me showed when I used to know him. "I didn't expect you to show up with Moira MacFarlane today."

"I can quit if it's a problem."

"No, that's not what I meant." He paused. I didn't fill the silence. Turk had something to say, but hadn't figured out how to say it yet. I had time. A lot of it. "I should have visited you in the hospital in Santa Barbara or dropped by your house when you came back to San Diego."

"No worries." I wasn't sure what to say. We hadn't been close for a long time. I hardly ever saw him the last few years. Even when I'd used Muldoon's as a meeting place for clients, Turk and I seldom went beyond hellos or head nods, if we saw each other at all. "I never gave it a thought, but thanks for mentioning it. We're good."

"I actually didn't call to apologize." A nervous chuckle. "I am sorry about not visiting you, but I really called to . . . to explain things about Shay."

"Explain what?" I kept my voice light. I didn't want him to reconsider talking to me about her.

"I know you don't understand why I hired Moira. I can barely understand it myself."

Another pause. I let the silence fill the void.

Turk finally continued, "Shay's different from anyone I've ever dated. I . . . You remember the uilleann pipes hanging above the bar?"

Irish bagpipes handed down to Turk from his father. Turk took them off the wall every St. Patrick's Day and played "Danny Boy." Just like his father before him.

"Of course."

"When I turned forty, I gave up on the idea of passing those down to a child. Gave up on the idea of keeping the restaurant in the family. My time for children had passed while I played the field like I was a twenty-year-old. I hadn't given the idea of having children much thought when I was younger. I should have."

The image of Colleen, my late wife, floated into my head. She often did. Still, fifteen years after her death. This time a memory. We were on Stearns Wharf in Santa Barbara eating ice cream cones and trying to one-up each other with goofy names we'd give our kids. I thought I had all the time in the world back then.

"It's not too late," I said. Unconvinced about my own timetable.

"You're right. Shay made me see that. We've talked about having children. She's changed my life." His voice quavered. "That's why deciding to hire a private investigator was so hard. It's a shitty thing to do. The worst thing I've ever done, but . . . I have to do it."

"We'll find the truth." Emotion I didn't expect filled my voice. "Moira is the best private investigator there is in San Diego. We'll get you what you need."

I didn't know how I could help Moira find the truth about Shay Sommers. Only that I had to try.

CHAPTER SIX

I took Midnight for a walk around the neighborhood in the late afternoon. My cane in my right hand and the leash in my left. I lived on a cul-de-sac and we only walked around the block so we wouldn't have to cross a street or venture up or downhill. Midnight stayed close to my side. He never went too far ahead or lagged too far behind like he sometimes did before Santa Barbara. He seemed to know that I now had limitations. I'd considered getting him guide dog training but was told he was too old. I decided to learn to use the cane, so the guide dog question was moot.

Somehow Midnight seemed to pick up some of the training on his own. Two weeks ago, he stopped me in front of a driveway when a car started to back out without seeing us. The driver apologized effusively once she realized that she could have hit us. Without Midnight, I might have been roadkill. Or, at least, road-injured.

We did five horseshoe laps, then retreated back home. I took off my sunglasses and set them down onto the bench next to the front door when I entered my house. Nobody but Midnight there to see my face and he didn't seem to care.

I led him through the laundry room into the two-car garage that still had one car parked in it. My Honda Accord. I'd bought an Accord for P.I. work years ago. It was the most popular car in Southern

California and blended into the background on a stakeout or tail. I guess I'd kept it because I hadn't yet given up on the dream of getting my sight back.

I never had to look at the car, but knew it was there every time I went into the garage to work out on the used universal gym I got cheap from a former client. The ten to twelve grand I could get for the Accord would only buy me another two or three months of figuring things out before I found a new job. Whatever the hell that might be. The Accord stayed. For now.

I'd spent a lot of time in the garage the last few months. I hadn't only worked hard to strengthen my other senses in an effort to offset my loss of eyesight, I'd strengthened my body, too. Instinct told me to fortify all my defenses and assets now that I'd lost my most important sense. I'd even cut way back on alcohol and sugar. The sugar was the hardest, but I had to admit I felt better physically than I had in a long time. Probably looked better too.

The strength of my mind was still up for debate, but I'd been working on that, too. Deciding to help Moira with Turk's case was part of that work. A small step toward the light.

* * *

Leah called me at 7:00 p.m.

"How was your day?" The sweet voice I'd learned to rely on over the last nine months.

"Good. Moira came by today. We went down to La Jolla and saw Turk Muldoon."

"Wow. Great." Light, pleased voice, like I'd made her proud. "But I thought Muldoon's didn't serve lunch."

"We didn't meet for lunch. Turk hired Moira to work a case."

"Really? Why?"

"I'm not at liberty to say, but I'm helping out." All the work I did as a P.I. was confidential. Even to the woman I loved.

"You're helping her out?" Her voice went up at the end. "I don't understand."

"She asked me to help because I know Turk." And to throw me a financial bone.

"Is this a dangerous case? How can *you* help?"

There it was. How could *I* help?

"I can trip bad guys with my white cane or hold up a tin cup for quarters in case we need to buy some gumballs." I wanted to pull back the words as soon as they left my mouth.

"You know I didn't mean it like that." Sad.

"I apologize. Reflex." A situation where I *should* have swallowed my pride. My mind and my pride still needed a lot of work. "I'm going to help Moira in any way she thinks I can. She's paying me and we both know I need the money."

"We've talked about this, Rick. I can help you out with bills until you decide what you're going to do."

Charity from Leah or a somewhat charitable paycheck from Moira. Leah's business had suffered since she'd taken up dual citizenship with me in San Diego. Her heart was bigger than her bank account, and I didn't want to sap either.

"I know. I appreciate that, but Moira asked for my help." If I took the money from Moira, I could feel that I'd somewhat earned it. With Leah, I'd be a burden.

"But you're not a private investigator anymore." Adamant. "That job almost got you killed, for God sake. I don't want you to get hurt again. Physically or emotionally. I know what that job does to you."

I told Leah things I'd never told anyone else. She showed me all of who she was, the good and the bad. That's why I loved her. I showed her as much of me as I could. But not everything. No one knew all the bad. And no one ever would.

"There's no danger." Although in domestics, as Moira sadly lived through, there's always the chance that someone will break and get violent. But that wouldn't happen with Turk. "I'm going to help Moira and then find that next thing in this new phase."

We ended the call with stilted "I miss yous" and "I love yous." I did miss her. And love her. She'd slept in my hospital room on a cot for a month while I recovered from the gunshot wound. She held my hand while I tried to adjust to a sightless world. She'd uprooted her life to move down to San Diego to be with me. Her parents and brother were in Santa Barbara. Her home, her interior design business, everything important in her life was in Santa Barbara.

Except me.

My former life was in San Diego. I could have started the new one anywhere. Grab Midnight and get on a plane or into the back of a car. Anywhere. Santa Barbara was anywhere. But I'd lost too much there. My wife. My reputation. My eyesight.

San Diego was home, even if that was only Midnight, Moira, and a house with a view I could no longer see. I didn't ask Leah to leave her life and come with me to San Diego, even though I wanted her to. I didn't want her to feel obligated to be my nursemaid, but I knew she wouldn't want me to be alone as I learned how to live my new life. I just needed to be home, which was selfish enough.

Maybe the cracks from that decision were starting to wear on both of us.

Moira called at 7:30 p.m.

"Change of plans for tonight." Her rapid-fire staccato in my ear.

"Leah called you."

"Huh?" Moira had never learned to lie as well as I did. The only skill I was better at and used more often than her as a private investigator.

"I know she called you and talked you out of taking me with you." Time for the baby chick to leave the nest. Leah wouldn't be happy, but

I wouldn't be either if I stayed home. "Pick me up in forty-five minutes as agreed upon or I'll take an Uber down to La Jolla and white cane all over your surveillance."

"I promised Leah I wouldn't take you with me." Slower cadence than her normal voice. "I'm still going to send you a check for five hundred. You earned it. I wouldn't have taken the case without your assurances about Turk."

It wasn't fair of Leah to put Moira in the middle of our tug-of-war. Not to Moira and not to me. But it wasn't fair of Moira to take her side, either. I might have told Leah things I'd never told anyone else, but Moira knew me viscerally. She'd killed a man to save my life. She knew I'd done things that I couldn't tell Leah about and things I couldn't even tell her about. She knew who I really was.

"The money's secondary." Although I needed it. "If you think I'll be a distraction or a hinderance, then go without me. The case comes first. But if you think I can be any type of asset, I want to help. I need to help."

"I'll pick you up at eight fifteen." She hung up.

I walked from my recliner to the sliding glass door to the backyard and opened it. Midnight pranced inside. The sound of his paws on the hardwood floor was always quicker coming in than going out. His wagging tail banged against my leg.

I took a step to the right and found the dimmer switch on the wall for the chandelier in the living room. I made a habit of turning on a couple lights in the house at night for Midnight. Just because I walked around in the dark didn't mean he had to.

I pushed the dimmer and the border of my dark lightened like the edge of a solar eclipse. My mind playing tricks on me again. More CBS. Charles Bonnet Syndrome. I turned and looked up where I thought the chandelier would be. The rim around the darkness brightened.

My breath quickened along with my heart. I closed my eyes. The bright edge was still there. CBS. Dirty mind trick. It told me to imagine what I might see if a light shone. I kept my eyes closed and the rim of fire faded. I opened them and the circle of light returned. I pushed the dimmer and the light faded again. Back on, circle brighter. Dimmer all the way up, even brighter circle. One eye at a time, open and close. Much brighter in each opened eye. I steadied my breath and slid down along the wall to the floor. Midnight licked my face.

More mind games or the return of a fraction of my eyesight? Hope and dread wrestled in my stomach. What if it was true? Was this just the beginning or a slightly higher cement ceiling? A final joke to buoy my spirits only so they could be drowned again? I pushed down on the hope and swallowed the dread. My ophthalmologist had diagnosed my first flashes of light as CBS. I'd give it another week or so before I went back to her. For now, I'd keep the light show to myself. I couldn't tell Leah and raise her hopes for an uncertain outcome. The same with Moira. A secret.

I hugged Midnight and got back to my feet, ready for whatever the the night might bring.

CHAPTER SEVEN

MOIRA CIRCLED PROSPECT Street for a few minutes before a spot opened up near Eddie V's Prime Seafood Restaurant. She pulled into one of the angled parking spaces in front of the sidewalk. We each cracked our windows to keep the car from fogging up if we had to sit for a while. The salty funk of the ocean a street below floated into the car.

"How far are we away from Eddie V's?" I asked, sorting through my memories of Prospect. A street I knew better than any other in La Jolla. Except for the one I grew up on in the tract home section of town.

"About five spaces north of Eddie V's. Between it and the entrance to the Crab Catcher." I appreciated Moira's specificity. She understood my need to picture what I couldn't see. "I have a good view of Eddie V's from here."

The restaurant was set back from the sidewalk and had magnificent ocean views. It opened a couple years before I left Muldoon's and was its biggest competitor. Higher end and advantaged by a view that Muldoon's didn't have, it was winning the battle. The restaurant biz was brutal, especially in La Jolla, but Muldoon's had managed to keep its doors open for almost fifty years since Turk's late father first staked his claim on Restaurant Row.

"Did you learn anything else about Shay?" I asked Moira and stared in her direction through my blackout sunglasses.

"Twenty-nine. Lives in Bird Rock. Born in Bellevue, Idaho. Her mother, June, died three years ago at the age of fifty-three. Mother and father never married. The father, Colt Benson, died in 1997 at the age of forty-six." Moira's rapid-fire professionalism. "Shay went to college at Portland State. Graduated with a degree in Business Management in 2013. Worked in a Hilton hotel in Portland until she moved to San Diego eighteen months ago. Has held four restaurant and hotel jobs in San Diego since then. Hostess, waitress, front desk."

"Twenty-nine. Fourteen years younger than Turk." Just an observation. He'd dated younger women back when I knew him, but never that much separation.

"Very pretty from the photo Turk gave me and the ones I've seen on her limited social media footprint. Blond hair, blue eyes. Kind of a girl next door who blossomed into a beautiful woman. There's a sweetness to her . . ."

Moira's voice drifted off as if in thought. Maybe thinking about Rachel Donnelly, murdered by her physician husband after Moira reported to him that she was having an affair.

"Limited social media? No leads there?" I wanted to bring her back to the present.

"No. All of her posts are from her years in Portland."

"You seem to have everything covered. What's my role in this partnership?"

I'd avoided the elephant in the car up until now. Even as I realized how much I needed this gig with Moira to regain a sense of usefulness in my life, I needed to believe that she really thought I could be of use even more.

"What do you mean?" A bad liar. She knew what I meant.

"How can I help with the case?"

"As I said before, you already have helped with your read on Turk. Going forward, I'll run things by you for your opinion. And if we have to give him bad news, I want you to be there with me." A wavering exhale. "I need to know how he'll react."

Moira did need me. The fiasco with Doctor Donnelly had really shaken her. She didn't want to make the decision alone about how to handle Shay Sommers if we had to tell Turk she was cheating on him. A familiar roil that I hadn't felt since Santa Barbara filled my gut. What if I misread Turk and gave Moira bad advice? Shay Sommers was my responsibility now, too. Her life could be affected by a decision I made. The kind of decisions I thought I'd never have to make again. Decisions I didn't want to make anymore, but knew I'd have to one more time. Moira needed me. And even with the turmoil in my gut, I needed to be needed.

"You got it, Boss."

I angled my head away from Moira and toward the windshield. I'd made a habit of facing people that I talked to since I lost my eyesight and started wearing sunglasses at night. A faint shimmer of light haloed out the corner of my right eye, possibly above the thick temple of my sunglasses frame. I turned my head toward the light. It disappeared through the blackout lenses.

"Are we parked near a streetlight?" I asked.

"Yes, there's one to your right about fifteen feet away." Business staccato. A pause, then a slight lilt of optimism. "Why?"

"Just trying to get my bearings and adjust my memories of the street accordingly." I couldn't tell her about my light revelation. If it even really was that. Not yet. I wasn't ready yet to say it out loud and make it real. Not until I was sure that the glimmer of light I could now see was some sort of path to regaining at least some eyesight. "Any action down at Eddie's?"

I wanted to be sure Moira was looking in the other direction. I turned toward the passenger window and took off my sunglasses. There it was again. A circle of light around the dark ball was just like I saw when I looked at the chandelier at my house. The streetlight. I did the individual eye tests. Both registered the dim halo. A flicker of hope accelerated my heartbeat. I rubbed my eyes and put the sunglasses back on in case Moira had looked over at me. Even blind eyes get itchy.

"You know, you don't have to wear the sunglasses on my account." A gentle tone of voice she rarely used with me. "The scar is not as bad as you think it is. You're the same Rick to me. Still a major pain in the ass. But's that's okay, I'm used to it."

Moira had definitely softened to me since Santa Barbara. But I didn't hear the faint pity I thought I'd heard in her voice this morning. This was affection. Comfort from a friend. The change still had me a little off balance.

"Thanks, but you have to admit they do make me look like the Terminator. I even have the same damaged face." I turned toward her and did my best Arnold robot impression. "I'll be back."

"Yep. Still the same asshole."

We sat silently for a while and the minutes ticked by.

"Bingo." Moira broke the silence.

"She headed this way or toward Muldoon's?"

"Muldoon's." The sound of her door clicking open. "I'm pursuing on foot. If she follows her routine, I'll tail her to Muldoon's and then to La Valencia. Maybe we can rap this up tonight."

"Text me every fifteen minutes with updates."

"Half hour."

"I'll be sitting in the car staring at nothing while you're outside in the world tailing a target." A little of the desperation I felt seeped into my voice. "Play along so I can, too."

"Roger. Fifteen minutes." The swish of Moira getting out of the car, then the thunk of the closed door.

An adrenal rush spiked my body, then bled out and left me hollow. The chase. And I couldn't participate. A sounding board left behind waiting for updates and the opportunity to give an opinion.

I wanted back in the game.

The game that had broken me and nearly taken my life now beckoned me to reenter. To rejoin the quest for the truth that was in my blood. It hadn't ended with the truth I found in Santa Barbara.

I just had to find a new way.

A smell folded in under the ocean brine through the window. Familiar. My heart double-tapped. Dove for Men deodorant coupled with a distinct human musk. The same scent I'd smelled today on this very street. The man who Moira didn't notice, but I knew had been there. I faced the window. The scent hovered. Then a soft shuffle of footsteps toward the sidewalk.

The Invisible Man.

CHAPTER EIGHT

IT HAD TO be the same man. And he'd been standing outside my car window. Staring at me? Why? A coincidence that I'd come across him twice in the same day? But I hadn't. He'd come across me. From behind each time. If I wasn't blind, would I have even noticed him? No. I wouldn't have smelled him, because I wouldn't have fine-tuned my olfactory senses to use them as sight and his footsteps would have been lost in background noise.

If I'd seen him tonight, I wouldn't have known that he'd been right behind me on the sidewalk today. How many people pass by us every day of our life that we never notice? Maybe it wasn't even the same man. Could I really be sure? Maybe alone in the dark, I was just being paranoid.

Except he'd stood next to my open window and looked at me. I knew it. He'd come from across the street, paused, and stared at me through the window before he got onto the sidewalk. It was him. Why was he here now? Following me?

If he was following me, why take a chance by getting so close? Because he knew I was blind. I wasn't a threat to him. He was taunting me without me even knowing. Playing a sick game with himself. With me. But he'd left. Why?

Moira.

He was following Moira.

I pulled out my phone and told it to call Moira. Straight to voicemail. I left a message.

"Call me. I think someone's following you."

I whipped open the car door. It banged against the car next to me. I got out, slammed the door shut, pulled my collapsible support cane from the inside pocket of my bomber jacket, and snapped it into a straight line.

I tapped the cane back and forth in front of me. It bumped off the front tires of Moira's car and the one next to it. Two steps forward and the tip found the curb. I got on the sidewalk and asked my phone for directions to Muldoon's Steak House so I'd be alerted when I arrived. Siri voiced directions and I started three-legging toward the restaurant as fast as I could. I audibly sniffed the air for the man's scent like a bloodhound on the chase. Gone. Only the piquant scent of the ocean and wisps of perfume and cologne as people shuffled out of my way.

"Whoa." Male voice. Twenties.

"Watch out for the blind dude. He's in a hurry." Another. Same age.

I felt the ground with my feet and the vibrations through the cane into my hand. Smooth sidewalk. Distant voices on my right. Must have been the inlet of bricks and grass where Eddie V's was set back from the sidewalk. Muldoon's had to be only thirty or forty more yards down the street. But what would I do when I got there? Barge into the restaurant and shout Moira's name, blowing her cover?

I'd figure it out when I got there.

I moved up closer to the outside edge of the sidewalk away from the street and made wider arcs with the cane. The surface changed from hard cement to something more giving on the far-right edge of each arc. The lawn next to the Morten Gallery. A couple more strides, the lawn ended and the cane tip banged off something hard on the right arc that gave off a dull echo. The door to the odd little garage

structure of the health supplement business next to the gallery. A few
more strides and Siri told me Muldoon's was to my right.

The staircase down to the courtyard that led to Muldoon's was set
back from the sidewalk. I turned right and the cane found open space.
A couple more steps and I found the handrail to the staircase. Thirteen.
The number that popped into my mind after taking them by rote for
so many years. I hadn't counted the stairs this morning when Moira
led me down them, but my mind said thirteen steps

I transferred my cane to my left hand and held onto the rail as I
hurried down the stairs, counting off in my head with each step. A
man and woman talking below me to the left. Strangers. I set my
right foot down on the fourteenth count, let go of the rail, and followed with my left foot. Air. My left foot finally found ground, jar-
ring my body off balance. I stumbled left, caught my leg on something,
and heard a woman's scream as I hit the ground, hands first, then left
side of my head, then my shoulder. My cane clattered away on the
adobe bricks.

Fourteen steps.

"Kira, are you alright?" Male voice. Thirties. Ruffle of clothing like
someone being helped off the ground.

I crawled forward searching for my cane. A half-moon of light at
the bottom of my left eye.

"Yeah, but what's wrong with that guy?" Female. Twenties. Angry.

"Hey, asshole, are you even going to apologize?" Same male. A couple steps closer, standing over me.

I abandoned my search for the cane, stood up, and faced the direction of the voice. The half-moon of light was broken by a dark vertical
rectangle.

"Whoa." The man, surprised.

"I'm sorry, ma'am," I said in the direction I'd heard the woman's
voice.

I suddenly realized the light was visible because my sunglasses had been knocked askew on my face in the fall. I could feel the left earpiece slightly higher against my head raising the left lens higher. Exposing the hole in my face.

I righted the frames.

"That's okay." The woman. Apologetic. "I didn't know you ... Here, let me get your cane."

"Yeah." The man.

Two sets of footsteps around, then behind me. I turned to face the pair.

"Here." The woman. "Your cane."

I held out my right hand. The handle of the cane pressed against my palm and I circled my fingers around it.

"Thank you. Are you okay?" I asked embarrassed. Exposed. Vulnerable.

"Yes, I'm fine. Are *you* okay?"

I'd scraped my hand, my ear felt on fire, and my shoulder was sore. But my pride hurt more. And the confidence that I could somehow find a new path back to my old life cracked hollow.

"Yes. Thank you."

"Your ear's bleeding, dude." The man.

I reached up and touched my ear and felt warm liquid on my fingers. The edge of my ear had been scraped when I landed on it.

I heard the buzz of a zipper.

"Here." The woman. "A Kleenex for your ear. I don't have any Band-Aids."

A tissue pressed into my hand. I folded it a couple times and pressed it against the scrape.

"Thank you."

"Can we help you find someone?" The woman. A sigh from the man. He needn't worry.

"No thanks."

I turned to face where I thought Muldoon's was. The sound of footsteps on the staircase to my right confirmed that I'd made the correct guess.

Now what?

Could I really be of any help to Moira in the field? Would it be better for both of us if I stayed home in my middle-class mortgaged prison, staring at halos of chandelier light and waiting for Moira's phone call so I could give her my opinion? How long could she afford to pay me for my thoughts and how long could I live with getting paid for them?

No good answers, but the wrong questions for tonight. Moira needed me on *this* case. And there might be someone following her.

Muldoon's was straight ahead. I tapped the cane in an arc in front of me until it made contact with the outside of the building. A left turn, a few more tapped steps, and I found the metal threshold to the front door.

The sound of jazz from the bar pulsed through the closed door. I put the bloody tissue in my pocket and entered the restaurant. Stimuli overload assaulted my working senses. The music, customers' conversations battling to get above it, smells of cooking meat and vegetables wafting back from the grill area mixing with perfume and cologne of people in the hallway.

I stood in the doorway and tried to separate and categorize each sound and scent to get a sense of what I couldn't see. Too much static to get a clear vision.

"Excuse me?" Irritated male voice from behind. Forties or fifties. I realized I was blocking the entrance to the narrow hall. "Can we get by?"

"Sorry." I turned sideways.

"It's okay. I didn't . . ." Voice calm now. Slight vibration of two sets of footsteps passed by me.

Everybody's disposition toward me changed when they saw I was blind. All perceived trespasses forgiven. I hadn't been on the receiving end of grace much in my life. Had been on the giving end even less. I hadn't yet gotten used to it and at that moment regretted it. Because to receive grace I had to be seen as blind. Seen. Noticed. A fatal flaw in a covert op. Yet here I was, stumbling in the dark, seen by everyone.

I waited a couple beats after the people passed, then worked my cane down the hallway, bumping the tip against someone's foot sitting on a sofa. Apologies. Grace.

"Can I help you?" A young woman's voice I didn't recognize in front of me to the left. I'd made it to the hostess station.

"Is Turk working tonight?"

"Yes. He just took some customers to their seats. He'll be back in a minute. Would you like to have a seat and wait for him?"

White cane and sunglasses sitting in the hallway. Flashing neon sign. If Shay Sommers was in the restaurant or leaving, she'd notice me. And remember me if she saw me again. A coincidence for someone going about their normal life.

"I'll wait outside, thanks. Could you tell Turk that Rick is waiting for him?"

"Sure." The hostess. "Rick." She said my name like she was reminding herself.

I wanded myself outside into the courtyard, which had a ceramic tiled planter box that housed an elm tree. I found the back end of the structure, sat down on its eighteen-inch tiled rim, and folded up my service cane.

The muffled thrum of jazz music from the bar inside Muldoon's competed with the street sounds of night in downtown La Jolla. Up the stairs on Restaurant Row, cars passed by and parked in front by valets, conversations and laughter on the sidewalk. All easier to separate than the cacophony rebounding inside the closed space of the restaurant.

Discordant noise assaulted me on my right. Someone opened the door to Muldoon's. The noise faded as the door closed.

"What are you doing out here?" Turk. Footstep, thunk, drag. Repeated a couple times. I stood up.

"Waiting for you."

"I know. But . . . hey, your ear's bleeding and your sunglasses are scratched up." Concern.

Shit. Even more of a neon sign. I grabbed the Kleenex out of my pocket and pressed it against my ear. Pain shot through my shoulder with the movement.

"I had a little mishap. I'm fine."

"You want a Band-Aid out of the first aid kit?"

"I'm good. Thanks." I put the Kleenex back in my pocket.

"What's going on? Where's Moira?"

"Did Shay stop in after she got off work?"

"No. She texted me that she was going straight home." Urgent. "Why?"

I'd made a private investigator 101 rookie mistake. Worried the client needlessly by involving him before adequate information was available. Now Turk was concerned and I didn't have information to calm his nerves or even confirm his worries.

I didn't know anything. Only that Moira had spotted Shay leaving Eddie V's and she'd headed in the direction of Muldoon's and La Valencia. And that she hadn't returned my phone call.

"I was with Moira staking out Eddie V's. Shay left work and Moira followed her on foot. I'm sure she followed her to her car and that Shay is now on her way home."

"But why are *you* here?" Emphasis on "you."

I didn't like to lie to clients. Especially ones who were friends. But sometimes it was better to fudge the truth until you knew all the facts. I wasn't going to further panic Turk and tell him about the Invisible Man and my concern for Moira. Especially when the Invisible Man might not even exist.

"I got bored sitting in the car so I ventured out."

"But you asked me if Moira was here. If you don't know where she is, why don't you call her and find out."

"Radio silence on surveillance." I tried to sound believable.

"Yet, you're clomping around out on the street. Shay knows I have a friend who's blind and used to be a private detective. If she saw you, she might wonder what you're doing here."

"Seeing an old friend."

"You're lying about something, Rick." Now angry. "What's going on?"

"I told you." I should have stayed in the damn car.

"Why would Moira be following Shay down here? Shay parks her car over on Cave Street in the other direction." Then it hit him. "She left work and came this way, didn't she? You thought she was coming by here like she usually does. Shit. She went to La Valencia again."

"We don't know that." I was ninety percent certain she did.

"Have Moira call me tonight when you find her. Or when she finds you."

Step, thunk, drag until the rush of sound from Turk opening the door to his restaurant.

Shit. Turk was mad and Moira would be, too, when I told her about my encounter with him.

But I could take having Moira mad at me over not having her at all.

CHAPTER NINE

I CALLED MOIRA again. No answer. Texted her. Nothing. I tapped my way to the staircase and used the handrail to ascend it. Fourteen steps. Once I made it to the top, I realized I'd made a critical error when I left the car. I hadn't counted the steps from the car to the staircase. I could start walking but I wouldn't be able to find the car.

I'd acted on impulse and ignored necessary details, a bad habit from my before life. Details mattered. Now more than ever. The number of steps from one place to another mattered.

Everything mattered.

I asked my phone the time. 9:19 p.m. Only fifteen or so minutes since Moira left me in the car and followed Shay Sommers. It felt like an hour. Every fifteen minutes was our agreed-upon time for her to check in so she wasn't even late yet. But I'd called and texted her and gotten no response. I couldn't go back to the car and wait for her to return. I couldn't go down to La Valencia and try to find her. A walking road flare.

All I could do was wait and do nothing. Like I should have done in the car.

I walked ahead and found the covered brick walkway next to the garage in front of the supplement company. The business was closed at night and set back forty or fifty feet from the sidewalk, if my memory was correct. I took a couple steps down the walkway, turned to face the sidewalk, folded up my aluminum cane, and shoved it back into my inside coat pocket. The neon sign that was me would be less visable than when I was on the sidewalk.

I pushed my sunglasses down on my nose. A circle of light appeared in my upper vision. Another streetlight on the sidewalk? Must have been. I edged a few more feet down the walkway until the upper half of the halo disappeared. There was still a half-moon of gauzy light on the bottom. Slight shifts of darkness in the void passed in front of the dull arc of light. Sounds and smells. Conversations. Laughter. Faint scents of perfumes and colognes. Low murmurs of car engines on the street. And rapid thumps of the valets jogging to retrieve customers' cars parked blocks away.

No return scent of the Invisible Man. And no Moira. I asked my phone the time. Nine-thirty-seven. She'd now been gone over a half hour and hadn't checked in. I called her again. Voicemail. I grew more anxious as each new minute passed. Moira was a smart, seasoned private investigator, who despite her diminutive size, knew how to handle herself. Common sense told me that nothing could have happened to her during the quarter-mile walk from her car to La Valencia on the pedestrian-populated street. Even with an invisible man present who might not even exist.

Maybe things had gotten interesting and Moira had forgotten about checking in or just ignored me. Still, my anxiety persisted. But the more I examined it, a different reason for its cause made more and more sense to me. Smelling the same scent from a man I'd smelled earlier today could give anyone pause, but the real reason I felt anxious was because without Moira by my side I felt isolated. Exposed. Vulnerable. For the last three months my home had been my cocoon, my sanctuary, my fortress. With Leah and Midnight by my side.

The truth was, despite the hours I'd spent strengthening my body and my remaining viable senses, I wasn't ready to take on the world alone. Not the world I used to inhabit. It was dangerous and the truth about people was often hidden even from those who could see.

*   *   *

A half hour into my blind vigil, I heard the rapid pulse of running feet pass in front of me. Lighter and closer together than the loping strides I'd heard from the parking valets the last thirty minutes. My antennae went up and I listened for chasing footsteps, but none came. Good. No one was being chased. Not that I could do much about it if they were.

My phone rang ten or fifteen seconds later.

"Where the hell are you?" Moira. Angry.

"On Prospect. Where are you? You were supposed to check in."

"Where on Prospect? I'm in the car. I'll pick you up."

"I'm in front of the vitamin place."

"What? Where the hell is that?"

"Thirty yards north of the entrance to Muldoon's where that little garage structure is."

"I'll be right there."

I walked out onto the sidewalk and stopped next to the curb. Footsteps behind me.

Sensory recognition jolted through my body. The scent. Dove for Men mixed with human musk.

The Invisible Man.

CHAPTER TEN

I WHIPPED MY head north toward the scent, but it dissipated on an ocean breeze. He'd walked right behind me. Moving in the same direction Moira had on her run back to her car. He was following her, but he wasn't running.

Tires compressed to a stop in front of me.

"Straight ahead." Moira muted, like she was yelling at me from her driver's seat through the open passenger window. "Get in."

I stepped down into the street and my cane found her car. I opened the door and slid into the passenger seat. The car started moving before I closed the door.

"Did you see that man walking away from me?" His scent was gone, but his aura still haunted me.

"What man?" I felt her head turn toward me.

"The same man behind us on the sidewalk today. I think he's following you." I took a deep breath to settle myself, realizing what I said next would be hard to believe. "I smelled him again tonight. Twice."

"You mean the man I couldn't find when you asked me to look for him?" Disbelief.

"I didn't imagine him, dammit!" The anger from feeling isolated and useless over the last hour bubbled out of me. "It's the guy.

He passed by the car after you got out of it. Then he walked behind me while I was waiting for you on the curb just now."

"Good."

"What?" Was she making fun of me?

"Shay met a man at La Valencia tonight. The two of them were waiting for the valet when I ran to my car. They're still there." The car slowed. "Whoa. They weren't waiting for a valet. They were waiting for the man's driver. He's driving a Mercedes Benz Maybach."

"Check your rearview mirror for headlights. Is anyone following you?"

"There are all sorts of headlights behind me, but none of them are following us. We're on Restaurant Row."

"Have you had any unsatisfied clients in the last few months? Someone angry with you? Did Rachel Donnelly's family hold you responsible for what happened?"

"Thanks for bringing that up." Hurt. "I don't have any angry clients. No one is following either one of us."

"I'm sorry. I didn't mean it like that. There's nothing you could have done to save Rachel Donnelly." I'd let my mouth run before my brain could catch up. Not for the first time. Still, that didn't change the reality of the Invisible Man. "But there *was* a man following you. The same one I sensed earlier today. Don't just blow it off."

"I appreciate your concern, but I think your imagination has gotten the better of you." Pedantic, like she was speaking to a child. I liked her angry much better. "I know your sense of smell is incredible. You show it off every time I go to your house, but you're not a bloodhound. You can't identify someone solely by their scent. You use deduction as much as smell when you recognize me. Very few people come to your house. So, when I come by, you smell a familiar, but not necessarily distinct, scent and deduce that it's me."

"You're wrong." But she'd planted a seed of doubt in my belief of my newfound capabilities.

I could pretend that I could differentiate someone's unique odor but I really didn't have any proof. The man I smelled today could have been different from the one who walked by my car window and he could have been different from the man who walked behind me a minute ago.

But my gut told me all three encounters were the same man and he'd followed Moira to and from La Valencia tonight.

"What happened to your sunglasses and why is your ear bleeding?" Moira's voice rose.

"Nothing." I took out the tissue the woman I knocked over gave me and dabbed my ear.

"Doesn't look like nothing."

"Not a big deal. I bumped into something." The truth was too painful. "Why didn't you text me updates or return my calls?"

"I turned off my phone—Wait. There they go. Down Prospect." The car accelerated then went down a slight incline. "Write down this plate number."

She called out the license plate number, and I dictated it into my phone.

A right turn down a sharper incline. A few seconds later, a left turn.

"Coast Boulevard?" I asked.

"Yep. Along the ocean."

"What happened when Shay got to La Valencia?"

"She took the elevator up to the tenth floor and was let into the Sky Suite." The car jostled over a pothole.

"Who did she meet there?"

"I can't be sure. If I'd continued down the hall, it would have been obvious that I was following her. But when she returned to the lobby forty-five minutes later, she was with the man who got into the Maybach."

"What does he look like?" But I doubted she'd describe someone I knew or knew of. I grew up in the tract home section of La Jolla and worked on Prospect Street for many years. But the world inside La Valencia Hotel was one I'd never ventured into. It was way out of my reach. The same zip code as the house I grew up in, but millions of dollars away.

"Early forties. Five-ten. Brown and brown. Decent shape, but not a gym rat. Navy blue tailored Italian suit." Her voice went up at the end of "suit" like she was going to add something, but she stopped talking.

"But what? You were going to say something else."

"He's wearing Italian, but it looks more like Canali than Brioni."

"Speak English."

"His suit is expensive, but not elite expensive. Not in the league of someone who pays $1,000 a night for a hotel suite and is driven around in a Maybach."

"I never knew you were so up on fashion and what constitutes upper elite," I said.

"I've lived in La Jolla a long time. Granted, in my late husband's family house that was paid off decades before I set foot in it. But some things rub off on you if you pay attention."

The first thing I ever learned about Moira was that she paid attention. All the time.

"Maybe he's slumming in his casual Italian suit instead of his showoff clothes."

"Maybe so." She didn't sound convinced.

"What are you going to tell Turk about what you saw tonight?"

"I'm not going to tell him anything. He'll get a report when I know exactly what's going on. There's nothing to tell, yet."

"You'd better think of something." I told her about my meeting with Turk.

"Why the hell did you go into Muldoon's? You could have blown the whole surveillance and now you've freaked out the client."

She was right, of course. I'd broken protocol. There wasn't a good explanation for why. I could tell her I was worried about her safety, but was that the real reason? Or did it have as much to do with my need to be relevant again? To show I was needed, an asset, because of the special talents I'd honed for the last nine months? All of it or the one simple truth those talents screamed at me tonight?

"The Invisible Man."

"The what?"

"I told you. I smelled the same guy I smelled today."

"You've given him a name?" Incredulous. "This man who probably doesn't even exist."

"You asked why. I told you." Moira would need more evidence to believe in the Invisible Man. I didn't know how to get it for her. Until I did, I'd live in her reality. "I know I messed up with Turk. Now we have to deal with it. What are you going to tell him?"

"I'll let you know when I figure it out." A snap in her voice.

My body suddenly shifted right, then pressed against the seatback. Moira had turned left up a hill.

"Where are we going?"

"Looks like they're probably headed back to La Valencia."

"Roger."

"Now where's he going?" Moira asked herself after a brief silence. "He drove past La Valencia and turned right onto Ivanhoe."

"He's going to drop Shay off at her car in one of the bank parking lots on Cave Street."

"What?" Moira, a hint of annoyance. "Why do you think that?"

"That's where all the restaurant workers park at night."

"Damn," Moira muttered under her breath.

"He turned left onto Cave, didn't he?"

"Yep."

"Don't follow him into the lot."

"When did you start thinking that I was stupid?" Emphasis on the *p* in stupid.

I didn't say anything, but thought back to this morning when I wished Moira would stop treating me with kid gloves. Sometimes wishes do come true. Unfortunately.

The car pulled to the right and stopped. A faint click from the dash or steering wheel like Moira turned off the headlights. She let the engine run.

"The Maybach just exited the parking lot." A trace of excitement in Moira's voice. "Probably headed back to La Valencia."

"Shay's car is a five-minute walk from La Valencia. Why the ten-minute roundabout drive to drop her by her car? Maybe the drive along the coast was a postcoital celebration."

"Get down." I heard Moira slide down in her seat. I ducked my head. The sound of a car passed by. "Okay," Moira said. "She's going down Ivanhoe towards Torrey Pines. I guess I'll follow her."

She started the car and made what felt like a three-point turn.

"Why you guess? Is there another option?"

"I'd like to follow the Maybach to see if it's going somewhere other than the La Valencia. We need to find out more about the Italian Suit." She let go an audible breath. "But Shay is the target, so we stay with her."

If I could see, we'd be in two cars. One could follow the Maybach, the other, Shay. But that wasn't an option anymore. All my *ifs* were followed by *buts* since I lost my eyesight.

I felt a turn to the right as we got onto Torrey Pines Road heading south. The car quickly accelerated.

"Gotta make the light to keep up with her."

We drove for another six or seven minutes before Moira broke the silence again.

"Strange."

"What?"

"She passed by the street that would take her to her apartment on La Jolla Hermosa."

"Shit. Not another late-night rendezvous."

A minute passed.

"This rendezvous is with Gelson's," Moira said.

"Expensive tastes." Gelson's was a high-end grocery chain from LA that had claimed turf in San Diego.

"Let's see what she buys." The car made a quick left.

"You sure you want to do that? You've already followed her on foot tonight. She may have caught a glimpse of you." I rolled down my window knowing Moira wouldn't take my advice. I wanted to be ready for the scent of the Invisible Man while I waited for Moira in the grocery store. If he showed, maybe I could get her that evidence she needed to believe me. I pulled out my phone, ready to take a picture of a man I couldn't see.

The car slowed and pulled to a stop. Moira turned off the ignition.

"I'm a Girl Scout. Always prepared." Her husky laugh. "I don't want to miss it if she buys a pregnancy test or hair dye."

I heard a shuffle like she was taking off her coat.

"Two-way jacket. White lining." Another shuffle like she put the coat back on. "Don't get freaked out, I'm going to put my hand on your seat and reach across you and get something out of the glove compartment. I'm not making a pass at you."

"Darn."

Moira got angry at me often. Luckily, the anger was usually short lived.

The edge of my seat compressed slightly and the scent of Moira's coconut shampoo grew stronger. Click of the glove compartment door. A rustle, another click, then retreat of smell. She'd undoubtedly pulled out the Padres cap with a blond wig sticking down and fake eyeglasses I'd seen her wear on a few cases we'd worked together.

"Stay in the car this time." Her door opened, slight shift of the car, then the door slammed shut.

CHAPTER ELEVEN

MOIRA HAD BEEN inside the store for almost ten minutes. I took off my sunglasses to try to see how many cars were in the lot, but only saw bright auras of lights against a dark nothingness. I put my glasses back on and abandoned the effort. My other senses were more reliable.

Car doors opened and closed six times, three cars left the parking lot and another two entered while I waited. The only scent I smelled was automobile exhaust. No Dove for Men. No Invisible Man. I didn't know whether to be happy or sad about that.

Another car door opened and closed maybe twenty feet from Moira's car. Ignition and the car left the lot. Five seconds later Moira's driver door opened and a body slid into the seat. Car door slam. Coconut shampoo scent. Ignition. Movement.

"Shay made a couple of interesting purchases," Moira said.

We backed up, made a couple turns and sped up, now on the street.

"The suspense is killing me."

"She bought a mini bottle of champagne and a small chocolate cake."

"Sounds like a celebration," I said.

"Not a cheap one either. The champagne was Moet Chandon Imperial. What could she be celebrating?"

"And who with? When's her birthday?" I asked.

"Not for three more months. If she's celebrating with someone else, he must not have a big appetite. For cake or champagne."

"Maybe champagne and chocolate cake are her after work rewards. I used to eat a pint of Häagen-Dazs after I got home from Muldoon's every night at two in the morning."

"You were younger then. You couldn't get away with that now."

"Thanks for noticing."

"There she is." Moira must have spotted Shay's car again. "She turned right on La Jolla Boulevard. Must be headed home."

Moira's car turned right a few seconds later.

"I take it she didn't buy any pregnancy tests or hair dye. Anything else of interest?"

"No. Just some veggies and guava juice."

The car made a sharp right turn, a left turn, another right and came to a stop a few seconds later.

"Where are we?"

"La Jolla Hermosa, across the street from Shay's apartment."

I knew the area. The Bird Rock section of La Jolla. La Jolla Hermosa had a slew of small, two-story hospital-green apartment buildings. The apartments may have had a retro '50s vibe but they still sat on La Jolla dirt and were only a few streets from the ocean. A one bedroom had to go for close to a couple grand a month. A big monthly nut on a hostess salary.

"Does Shay have a roommate?" I asked.

"Nope. You're thinking the same thing I am, aren't you?"

"Yep. Her apartment is probably two thousand a month. How can she afford it?"

"Actually, $1,895 for a one-bedroom. I checked after Turk gave me her address. The math doesn't add up. You used to manage a restaurant. How much does a hostess who works thirty hours a week make?"

"Not enough to cover two grand a month, unless she doesn't eat or use electricity." Back in my day, hostesses made a bit above minimum wage plus a small percentage of the waiters' tips. Couldn't have changed that much since then. "She doesn't have any family money, right?"

"Nope. Maybe Turk helps her out with the rent. Is that something he'd do?"

"It's a possibility." Turk treated money cavalierly when we worked together. His excesses, which I didn't know about until too late, caused the fracture in our friendship. "But he never did that back when I knew him. He and Shay have been together for over a year. If he has to fork out money for her rent each month, why not have her move in with him?"

"Every relationship has its own timetable."

"When are you going to call Turk?" I asked.

"I want to talk to him in person." Sotto voce. "I need to see how he reacts."

"You talk to Dr. Donnelly over the phone?" Her son's pediatrician turned murderer and the one case she wished she could get a second chance at.

"No." Quiet for a couple seconds. "I emailed him a report."

"Any P.I. would have done the same thing, Moira. You know that. Standard operating procedure."

"Not anymore. Not for me."

*   *   *

No movement in Shay Sommers' apartment over the next hour. If she was celebrating with champagne and chocolate cake, she was doing it quietly and alone. Moira and I didn't talk for the rest of our vigil. Both lost in our own thoughts. Moira was probably going over things she wished she'd done differently with Doctor Donnelly. She wasn't one to second-guess herself and she'd done nothing wrong, but I could hear in her voice how it ate away at her when she talked about the Donnelly case. Something horrible happened and she'd taken it personally. I knew all too well the damage that could do.

While Moira no doubt worried silently about how Turk would take the news she had to tell him, I sniffed the air, listened for footsteps, and pondered the existence of the Invisible Man. If he was still out there watching us tonight, he hadn't ventured close. That, again, left me with no evidence to present to Moira to prove he existed.

"The lights just went out in the apartment." Moira broke the silence. "It's 12:05. How late is Muldoon's open tonight?"

"One o'clock."

"Will Turk still be there if we drop by in the next fifteen minutes?"

"Probably. After he got back on his feet, he went from occasionally stopping by the restaurant while I still ran the place to working sixty hours a week." Even though Turk "fired" me a few days before he got shot saving my life, I worked the restaurant for one hundred-forty-nine straight days until he was able to return. "I can call him to make sure he's still there."

"No. I want to walk in cold."

"With me? You, the eyes; me, the ears?"

"Yep."

Moira found a parking space on Prospect Street a few spots down from where we parked earlier. This time I counted the steps to Muldoon's. One hundred-thirty-seven to the staircase above the restaurant. The band in the bar was on a break when we entered. No hostess because the dining room was closed.

"Wait here," Moira said. She moved away from me to the left, heading down the hall to the bar. I waited and listened and sniffed the air. No evidence of the Invisible Man.

Conversations paused when people walked by me on their way to the bathroom or outside for a quick smoke. I'd brought my cane with me and still wore the blackout sunglasses. I was noticed. My new reality.

I felt heavy vibrations in the carpeted hallway. Someone large was coming my way. Old Spice deodorant. Three-legged gait. Turk.

"Let's go to my office." His greeting.

A hand on my back. Moira. I grabbed her arm and let her lead me instead of using my cane. We entered the dining room. The aroma of steaks, garlic, and butter still clung to the air. We turned left around the salad bar, another left around the server station, passed the grill, and entered the kitchen.

"Watch your step." Turk, step-thunk-dragging his way ahead of us.

Ammonia floated up from the floor after the kitchen crew's nightly scrubbing, and each step gave off a squish sound on the wet floor. Moira guided me effortlessly, a turn here and there and then the straight walk down the hall toward Turk's office. She seemed schooled in the nuances of leading me as if she'd done it for years as opposed to one day. She led me inside the office door on the left at the end of the hallway, and I instinctively moved back to find the wall in the cramped space. Except it wasn't there. I found it two whole steps back from where it used to be.

"You expanded the office," I said.

"Yep. Too many long days and nights here not to spread out a little bit. Wish I would have done it a lot sooner. I moved the desk to the back wall. There are a couple chairs in front of it a few feet to your left."

I heard the cadence of his gait on the cement floor, a chair scrape, and then the release of air as he sat his bulk down behind the desk. I tapped my cane and found one of the chairs before Moira touched my arm. We both sat down.

"Rick told me that you followed Shay to La Valencia tonight," Turk said to Moira. Terse. Down to business. None of the hail fellow well met that made him so popular with his customers and employees. And women.

"That's not what I said." I wished I hadn't said anything.

"Close enough." This to Moira. "What happened at La Valencia?"

Moira told Turk about the Sky Suite, the man in the Italian suit, the drive along the ocean in the Mercedes Benz Maybach, Shay's stop at Gelson's, and lights out at her apartment at midnight.

"How long was she in the suite at La Valencia?"

"Roughly forty minutes." Moira in clipped professional mode.

"That's long enough." Turk's voice a surrender.

"We don't know what happened up there." Agitation slipped into my voice. Turk defeated pissed me off. Back when we were friends, he could always take a punch, literally and figuratively, and be ready for more. I didn't like seeing, hearing, this side of him.

"Did you find out who the man in the Italian suit is?" Turk asked.

"No. Hotels won't release the names of their guests. I'm hoping to get information on the owner of the Mercedes tomorrow." A rustle of clothing told me Moira shifted in her chair. "But that might not get us the name of the man in the Italian suit."

"Why not?" Turk bit the words off hard.

"Someone else was driving the Maybach. That person could be the owner or it could be a rental. Give it time." Cool, calm. Moira slowed her usual rapid-fire delivery. "We can't jump to conclusions. You gave me a check for a week's worth of work. This is day one. Let us do the job you hired us to do. We'll find the truth."

"But you have to admit, her secret meeting looks suspicious."

"I've done this job long enough not to make premature judgments. The truth will come out. You hired me because you heard I'm good at what I do. I am. So, let me do what you hired me to do."

I didn't mind Moira dropping me from the equation and going from *we* to *I* when commenting about her abilities and promise to find the truth. I was a passenger on this trip and my exit from the ride could come at any time.

"Okay, but I can't wait forever."

"Understood."

"I have a question for you." Moira maintained her reassuring voice. "Does Shay derive income from a source other than her job at Eddie V's?"

"No." Suspicious. "Why?"

"I'm just trying to gather as much information as I can to help put all the pieces together. She's living in an apartment where the rent is nineteen hundred a month. I'm wondering how she can afford it on a hostess salary."

"What's this have to do with her meeting some guy down at La Valencia?" Agitation peeking through the confusion.

"Probably nothing, but I need to know all I can about Shay's everyday life. This is how I investigate. How can she afford the rent on La Jolla Hermosa?"

An uncomfortable pause.

"I help her out." It sounded like a confession in a square white room. "She used to live in a rathole near the bar scene in Pacific Beach. I had to get her out of there. More women are raped in P. B. than anywhere else in San Diego."

"Why doesn't she just move in with you?" I jumped in again. "Save you a bunch of money."

Something struck my left ankle. Moira's foot. I'd crossed a line and broken her rhythm. The passenger is just supposed to shut up and look at the view. I'd get an earful back in the car. I didn't care. I was tired of the kid gloves. Maybe this would force Turk to start to reevaluate his relationship with Shay. If he was paying part of her rent and he couldn't trust her, was she worth all the angst and effort?

"That's none of your business, Rick!" The anger I remembered seeping out seven years ago on the roof of Muldoon's when I confronted Turk about my investment in the restaurant. He flashed from anger to violence in a breath and we went to fists and blood. Our friendship ended that day. I didn't expect the same reaction now, but my gut roiled over the memory.

"One last thing." Moira, cool soothing voice. "I know you're dealing with a lot of uncertainty and you're anxious to find out the truth about Shay and the man at La Valencia. I will find it for you. But, in the meantime, I need you to step back and take a breath. Are you planning on seeing Shay tonight?"

A half a count pause. "No."

I didn't know if the tiny pause meant he had to think about it or slipped in a lie. I hoped it was the former.

"What about tomorrow morning?" Vibration and squeak of Moira pushing her chair back and standing up.

"Why?"

"I'm going to start surveillance of Shay's apartment tomorrow morning at eight thirty. If you're going to be with her, I'll get there later."

"No. I won't be there." Turk sounded tired. Beaten. Older than his forty-three years. I suddenly regretted saying yes to joining Moira on the investigation. Even after Turk was shot and relegated to a life on a cane, he still maintained his positive attitude. Stuck on three legs instead of two? Who gives a shit? Bring on whatever's next. It saddened me that he'd lost that.

And I was pretty sure whatever else we found out about Shay Sommers wouldn't bring it back.

CHAPTER TWELVE

MOIRA DIDN'T SPEAK on the walk back to the car. I used my cane instead of holding her arm. I hadn't followed her lead in questioning Turk; wouldn't be fair to rely on her now. When we got into her car, she whipped away from the curb before I had my seat-belt fastened. Speed and silence.

Finally, after five minutes of frost. "What was the point of your move in question? To piss off the client? Make him feel like a mark?"

"No. I just wanted him to reevaluate his relationship with his girl-friend." The more I talked to Turk, the more I remembered the man who used to be my best friend and the more I learned about Shay Sommers, the more I wanted to tell Turk to run. "Maybe she's not even having an affair, but she's lying to him about something. And he's still paying for her apartment in Bird Rock."

"We weren't hired for couples' counseling." Tommy-gun delivery with acid-tipped bullets. "And remember, you are getting paid, too, so this is a job."

"Maybe I shouldn't be working it."

"Of all the stupid things I've seen you do, I've never seen you quit. Why now?"

"Turk's not a client, he's a friend." At least he used to be.

"And, I need your take on his reaction to what we told him about Shay."

Giving my impressions on Turk suddenly felt more like talking about a friend behind his back than discussing a client. I knew the gig going in. Still, I couldn't help but feel a little slimy.

"He seems beaten down and worn out. You don't have to worry about him getting violent with Shay. It's not in his nature."

"I read as much anger as I did resignation." Less acid.

"His girlfriend is lying to him, and he thinks she's cheating on him. He has a right to get angry. I'd be more concerned if he wasn't. It's usually the ones that hold things in who explode."

"Maybe. Do you think that he's beaten down and worn out enough to give up?" Solemn.

"You mean off himself?" For some reason I couldn't say *commit suicide*. Maybe I was worried that if I used the clinical term it might seem like a possibility. No. Not Turk. Not after what he'd already been through. "No way. Hopefully, he'll realize it's time to break up with Shay and move on. He's not going to hurt himself or anyone else."

My mind slid back to the roof of Muldoon's Steak House when the argument with Turk exploded into flying fists. He'd been under pressure I didn't know about at the time and he blew like a cornered mountain lion. Angry and fast.

I wondered if he was under similar pressure now.

"I hope you're right. I couldn't live with a repeat of . . . of what happened while you were in Santa Barbara." She couldn't say *suicide* either. Or *murder*. "Do you think he's telling the truth about not going by Shay's apartment tonight?"

My own short pause.

"Yes." Ninety percent.

"If you're not sure, I'm heading over there right now."

"He's not going to Shay's tonight."

"Okay." The car slowed, turned left, then stopped. My driveway. "I'll pick you up at eight fifteen tomorrow morning.

"I'll call you at seven thirty and let you know if I still want to work the case." I needed the money, but I had to balance it against my friendship with Turk. Or former friendship.

"You can't quit. I won't accept your resignation. Eight-fifteen. Don't make me wait."

CHAPTER THIRTEEN

MIDNIGHT WOKE ME the next morning with a tongue to my ear. The scraped one. The events of last night had made it hard to get to sleep. Once I did, I was a rock. I grabbed Midnight's head and turned toward him.

And saw a shadow in the dark void. A rough, blurry outline.

I sprang up and fumbled for the light on the nightstand next to the bed. An anachronism from an earlier time. When I could see. I found the switch and a blurred edged cone of light hung over the nightstand. I looked back at Midnight. Still a fuzzy blob against the void, but discernable. Differentiated from the background of nothingness. A separate entity.

I found his neck and pulled his head to my face. Still unrecognizable as a living creature. A blurred blob. But a blob I hadn't seen yesterday or anytime in the last nine months.

My vision *was* improving.

I fought the urge to call Leah. To run in the bathroom and look in the mirror. To hope.

Too early for any of that. I was still blind. Still couldn't see the floor below me. Still couldn't navigate the outside world without a white cane.

I'd wait. And test. And pray.

* * *

I dropped Midnight next door and waited for Moira in front of my house. My neighbor's seventeen-year-old daughter, Micalah, loved Midnight and she and her mom happily looked after him. He'd always been happy to go next door before Santa Barbara. This time when I dropped him off, he'd tried to leave their house with me.

I took off my sunglasses and tested my eyes while I waited for Moira. The morning was overcast. No yellow halo in the sky. I saw only shadows and dark gray. I put my blackout sunglasses back on and saw nothing.

Today was going to be a long one. Moira and I would probably tail Shay Sommers from 8:30 a.m. 'til midnight. Hopefully, Moira's cop connection would get back to her with the name of the owner of the Mercedes Benz Maybach today. That still wouldn't tell us what Shay did in the Sky Suite of La Valencia, but it might tell the name of the man she met there. Information was power and we didn't have enough of it.

Moira rolled up in her Honda Accord at 8:13 a.m. I pretended to convince myself that I could recognize the sound of her car, but realized that it was probably just hearing a midsize car and knowing she was going to pick me up.

"You want a water?" she asked. "There's a cooler behind your seat. I've got sandwiches, too."

"I'm good, thanks. I don't want to intake too much liquid if we're going to sit in the car all day. I guess I can pee into a water bottle when necessary. What are you going to do?"

"Depends."

I paused until it hit me.

"Please don't go number two."

The banter was refreshing after the tenseness of last night. I still didn't feel good about accepting the gift of working the case from

Moira or psychoanalyzing my onetime best friend. But I'd told her I'd
do it and understood its necessity from her point of view.

We drove for about ten minutes, then the car slowed to a crawl.

"Oh, God." More a moan than a statement.

"What?" I asked. The sound of her voice twisted a knot in my gut.

"Shit! Shit! Shit!" Hands pounded the steering wheel.

"What!"

"There's police cars and crime scene tape in front of Shay's apartment. And a coroner's van." Dread in her voice. The car moved to the
right and came to a stop. She turned off the ignition.

"Oh, no." The dread I'd heard in Moira's voice tightened my throat.

"There's a woman talking to a detective on Shay's front lawn. She's
crying." Moira's voice thick with emotion. "Turk drives a blue Ford
Escape, doesn't he?"

"What?" I couldn't comprehend the question right away. I didn't
want to. His car couldn't be there. What if he was dead inside Shay's
house? Two bodies instead of one.

"He drives a blue Escape, right?" Shouting now.

"I don't know. I haven't been in a car with him for years." Then an
image from last year popped into my head. I left Muldoon's one morning after meeting with a client and saw Turk pull up in front of the
restaurant. A Ford Escape. "Metallic blue."

I didn't need to hear her response. I already knew what it would be.

"There's a metallic blue Escape parked inside the crime scene tape
in front of Shay's."

Something struck my arm. Hard. Moira's fist. Again. "You told me
he wouldn't go to her house! He killed her!"

He couldn't have. The Turk I used to know couldn't hurt a woman.
He'd spent his whole life defending them. There had to be another
explanation.

"We don't know that." But right now, everything pointed that way. And if Turk's car was there, he was, too. Murder-suicide? My heart sank into my stomach. Sweat pebbled my forehead. "I have to find out if Turk's in there."

I opened the car door.

"Stay in the car." A hand around my forearm. "You can't just walk onto a crime scene. The police aren't going to tell you anything. Let's just go. I don't want to be here."

"I have to find out if Turk's alive." I pulled her hand off my arm.

I got out of the car with my cane, but my foot caught something hard, and I stumbled forward. Moira's door opened and closed. A helicopter overhead, an unintelligible voice squawked on a police radio somewhere, a woman crying, footsteps to my left, then a hand on my arm.

"If you're going to do this, I'll lead." Moira.

I grasped her bicep and held my cane perpendicular above the ground. We took twenty-nine steps before a voice stopped Moira.

"I'm sorry, ma'am, you can't come any closer. This is a crime scene." Male. His voice read early twenties. A barrier to finding out if Turk was alive, but probably a rookie. His voice lacked the command presence of a seasoned cop. A possible weak link to exploit in the phalanx LJPD would keep cinched down around the perimeter of the crime scene and on any information about the body or bodies the coroner was examining inside.

"Who's dead inside that apartment, Officer?" Needing to hear, but dreading the answer.

"Please step back from the crime scene tape."

Moira grabbed my arm, but I held firm.

"I need to know if Thomas Muldoon is inside that apartment and if he's alive or dead. He saved my life." I yanked off my sunglasses to show my scar as an exclamation point to my statement, which was true. Turk had saved my life. But it had been years before I was shot in the face.

Any edge I could use.

"Please step back." More plea than command presence and slightly distant like his head was tilted down instead of looking at my mangled face. The beginnings of a crack.

"Just tell us how many bodies are in there. Male or female?" I kept my sunglasses off and pointed my face directly at where I'd heard his voice. The knot in my gut cinched tighter. "Come on, man. This is my best friend I'm asking about. I wouldn't even be alive if it wasn't for him."

"There's one. A—"

"Cahill!" My name cut thought the early morning air like a guillotine. A female voice I recognized and had hoped never to hear again.

La Jolla Police Detective Hailey Denton.

"There's an angry detective walking toward us." Moira grabbed my arm again.

"She's walking towards me, not you." I leaned over and spoke to Moira in a low voice. "I'll deal with this. You can take off. I'll Uber home."

"I'm staying here." She increased the pressure on my arm. "With you."

"What the hell are you doing at my crime scene, Cahill?" Each word louder as Detective Denton got nearer. "Wow! That's some scar."

The scent of rubbing alcohol and cucumber just above it filled the air. The first, hand sanitizer. A cop's best friend. The cucumber? Shampoo, I guess. I didn't remember the scent of Hailey Denton's shampoo or perfume the few unpleasant times I encountered her in the past or if I even noticed one. Smells didn't matter then.

I put my sunglasses back on. I wasn't embarrassed. I just didn't want Denton to be able to stare at a wound that could be seen as a weakness. The show of weakness worked on the young cop. It wouldn't on Denton. My pride wouldn't allow that tactic with her anyway.

"Can I help you, Detective?" Moira snapped off each word. She let go of my arm and took a step forward. My protector.

"No." Dismissive. "But you and Mr. Cahill can get into your car and leave my crime scene."

"We're outside the police tape. We have a right to be on a public sidewalk." Moira hated being told what to do as much as I did. But she usually hid it better than me. Denton had struck a nerve.

"Got yourself a little mini-me, Cahill?" The voice close and directed at me. "I guess that makes sense. Hard to be a lone wolf private dick when you can't see. But why are you here?"

"Detective, why is the coroner van parked outside that apartment?" Moira, barely holding her venom at bay.

"I'm speaking to Mr. Cahill, ma'am."

I expected a retort by Moira, but instead I felt a void next to me and heard footsteps disappearing on my left. She'd walked away. Maybe she saw something that needed a closer look. Maybe she just wanted to get away from Detective Denton. Or me. Whatever the case, I still had Denton in front of me.

"Who's inside that apartment, Detective?"

"Answer my damn question, Cahill. Why are you here?"

I couldn't tell her the truth. Not yet. Whatever P.I./client privilege I had with Turk was gone if Shay was dead. Or if Turk was. But my loyalty to him wasn't. The truth would come out eventually. I just didn't have to be the one telling it.

"We were in the neighborhood and saw police cars and crime scene tape, so we stopped." I didn't have any qualms about lying to the cops, if the cop was Hailey Denton. "Who's dead inside that apartment, Detective?"

"You saw? I thought you were blind." Mocking. "Or is all this a ruse?"

"Figure of speech. My friend saw Thomas Muldoon's car. Is he inside the apartment, Detective?"

"I don't buy your *in the neighborhood* story, Cahill. Even blind, you're still sticking your nose in where it doesn't belong."

"Who is the coroner here for, Detective?" Nothing to do but go at Denton head-on. Subtlties might work on the rookie cop manning the crime scene, but not Denton. Niceties didn't work either. Maybe if I pissed her off, she'd blurt something out. She'd done that before. "Somebody's obviously dead, or LJPD wouldn't have its crack homicide detective here."

"I don't have time for you, Cahill, but you're going to make time for me. I want you and your chauffeur girlfriend to be down at police headquarters at noon today."

"Who's in the apartment?" My last chance for an answer.

"Headquarters at noon." Footsteps going away.

"Please step back, sir." The rookie.

I moved backwards a couple steps until my feet found grass.

Footsteps and coconut shampoo. Moira returned to my side.

"Turk's alive."

"What?" My breath caught in my throat. "How do you know?"

"I saw a detective questioning him. They were behind the coroner's van, so I couldn't see him at first."

"Thank God." I let go a long breath and my shoulders relaxed for the first time since we got to Shay's apartment.

"He just got into the back of a squad car."

CHAPTER FOURTEEN

"WHAT?" MY WHOLE body tightened and my gut swallowed itself. "Was he handcuffed?"

Hum of engines and mesh of tires rolling on asphalt behind Moira.

"No. He got into the squad car and it took off behind a detective car." Moira's voice, worn out. "They must be taking him to the police station for more questioning."

"Shit." Turk was alive, but might be a suspect in Shay Sommers' murder or whoever was dead inside her house. "Was the detective who questioned Turk in his mid-thirties, tall, glasses?"

"Yes."

"Detective Sheets." At least Turk was dealing with the one cop at LJPD I trusted to be fair and without a personal agenda. Unlike his partner, Detective Denton.

"Let's go." Moira grabbed my arm.

"No. We need to stay here. We might learn something. We have to meet Detective Denton at the Brick House at noon, anyway."

Moira pulled me away from the crime scene. I stopped and shook my arm free after a few steps.

"Why does Detective Denton want to talk to us?" Moira.

I told her what I'd told Denton.

"Why didn't you just tell her the truth?"

"Client confidentiality."

"There is no client confidentiality. Shay's dead." Seething. "Turk killed her. Just like I feared he would. You told me he wouldn't hurt her."

"I don't believe he did."

Double thumps to my chest sent me backward two steps, and I almost lost my balance.

"You're blind, Rick. He killed her." Too angry for irony. "We're done. Our job ended when Turk killed Shay."

"We don't even know what happened. She could have committed suicide or been murdered by someone who broke into her house. It might not even be Shay who's dead in there. That's why we should stick around to see what we can find out. Are the police still questioning the woman who was crying in front of the house?"

"No, but it doesn't make any difference. I'm done."

"Is the woman still here?"

"Yes!" A hiss on the end.

"Where is she?"

"Across the street from Shay's apartment outside the tape. But who cares?"

"Let's go talk to her and find out what she knows."

"I'm leaving."

"Okay." I took two steps forward. "But do me a favor first. Lead me over to the woman. You can leave me here and go wherever you want to after that." I reached out my hand. "Please."

"He killed her." The anger throttled down to despair. "If you weren't his friend, you'd see it."

"Help me gather evidence so I can see what you see. Lead me over to the woman. Please."

A hand on my arm. "Two steps to your right and then we step down onto the street and cross it."

Moira let go of my arm and I took hers. We started our walk toward the woman. I didn't count the steps across the street. I was busy trying to find the right words inside my head that I could ask Shay's grieving friend to get her to tell me what she knew.

"Rick?" A woman's voice, choked with grief. Familiar.

"Kris?" Kris Collins, Turk's manager at Muldoon's. The Crying Woman?

Arms wrapped around my neck and a damp face pressed against my cheek. I let go of Moira's arm and hugged Kris back. She sobbed and shuddered in my arms. I held on until she finally let go.

"It's so awful. Shay . . . She's dead." She let go a sob.

A low moan escaped from Moira. Any hope that Shay Sommers somehow wasn't the body being examined by the coroner inside her house was gone. Moira's fear of a repeat of the Doctor Donnelly tragedy had come true. Half of it. The worst half.

"What happened? Why are you here?" I knew Kris lived in Pacific Beach, two or three miles away.

"We were supposed to go running this morning. And then I found her!" More sobs and gasps. I hugged her again. They must have been friends, which made sense because Kris was close to Turk. I waited for her breathing to settle before I spoke again.

"Are the police done talking to you?" I finally asked.

"Yes. I'm waiting for a ride from a friend. My car's inside the police tape and they won't let me have it back yet."

"We can give you a ride." Moira surprised me with the offer. I thought she'd want to distance herself from the whole situation as quickly as possible.

"It's okay. Thanks. I have a friend coming. She's probably already left."

"It's no trouble. We're right here." Moira, calm and soothing. Putting someone else's grief above her own. Or, maybe she had another motive.

Kris was a witness. Moira and I both wanted to hear what she knew.
Each with different expectations.

"Why don't you let us give you a ride home? I'm worried about
Turk." I didn't have to feign real concern. "I need to know what happened today so we can help him if he needs it. This is Moira
MacFarlane. She's a private investigator. If the police think Turk is
responsible, we need to know what they know."

"Do they think he killed Shay?" Panic.

"They may not. It's just the police's standard operating procedure to
look at the people closest to the victim and then work outward."
Moira jumped in before I could do any more damage. Her voice, vel-
vety smooth. "There's nothing to worry about at this point, but it
would be helpful if you could tell us what you know. You sure you
don't want us to give you a ride? It's no trouble."

"Okay. Yeah. I guess." Her voice, still brittle, ready to shatter with the
next crack. "I'd better call my friend and tell her not to pick me up."

A hand tugged my arm. Moira. I took a couple steps backward with
her. She waited until Kris started talking on the phone, then asked
me how I knew her. I filled her in. I'd hired Kris as a hostess when I
was the manager at Muldoon's. One of my best hires. She was capable,
reliable, and friendly. Valuable traits in any business. Kris worked her
way up the Muldoon's ladder after I left and now was the manager.
Moira didn't make any comments and I couldn't read her silence.

"I talked to my friend." Kris, still a wobble in her voice. "I'm ready
to leave whenever you are."

"We're ready." Moira. "I'm parked across the street." She offered her
arm and led me back to her car. Kris' footsteps fell in with ours as we
crossed the street in silence. I got into the back seat and left the front
for Kris so she could be next to Moira when Moira asked her about
what she'd seen at Shay's house this morning. She had a softer touch
than I did, as she'd already demonstrated.

Kris gave Moira directions to her home in Pacific Beach and the car pulled away from the curb but stopped abruptly just as the front wheels started to turn to the left. I figured Moira must be waiting for another car to pass going the other way, but I didn't hear one.

"What are they doing?" Kris.

"Photographing evidence in situ before they bag and catalog it."

"What are you looking at?" I asked. No improved smell or hearing could help me deduce what the women saw.

"Can't see yet." Moira. "A crime scene tech is taking photographs of something in the hedge between Shay and her neighbor's apartment."

"Ma'am." The rookie cop's voice drifted in Moira's window from afar. "You have to move your vehicle."

"Shit." Moira.

"What?" I asked.

"They just put up a couple screens around the hedge. Whatever they found, they think it's important."

CHAPTER FIFTEEN

WE DROVE IN silence for a block, before Moira took charge.

"Can you tell us exactly what happened this morning?" Her tone caught between soothing and her normal clipped. "Why did you go by Shay's house?"

"To go for a run." Kris fought to control her voice. "We run together or go to the gym four times a week."

"What time did you get there?"

"Seven thirty. We always run at seven thirty." Reciting her routine seemed to sturdy Kris' voice and give her momentum. "Shay didn't answer the door, but her car was parked in the front. I called and texted her, but she didn't respond so I called Turk to see if she was with him. She wasn't. I could tell by his voice that he was as worried as I was. He drove over from the restaurant and unlocked the door."

Turk had a key to Shay's apartment. Not unusual, but something the police could use to show he could enter her apartment on his own at any time.

Another loud intake of breath. Then sobs. Kris reliving the discovery of her friend's dead body. I'd lost friends. I'd lost my father. I'd lost my wife. There were no words that could supply the comfort needed. Only an understanding of the pain.

"I'm sorry, Kris." I put my hand on her shoulder. The best I could do. The best anyone could do.

A hand on mine, then movement in the seat like Kris had turned around in the front seat to face me.

"I'm so sorry about what happened to you." Her voice full of tears. "I'm sorry I never called you or came by. I meant to, but the restaurant . . ."

"No need to apologize." My mother didn't even venture out from Arizona when she found out I'd been shot. A phone call and a get-well-soon card were the extent of her efforts. Our relationship soured when she divorced my father and married someone else. It didn't get any better when I chose to become a cop like my dad before me.

Kris and I had only the briefest of interactions over the last few years. Unlike my mother, she wasn't blood. She didn't owe me anything.

"Did you go inside with Turk?" Moira, soft but coaxing. Forcing Kris to relive the worst moment of her life. Lived in real time only an hour ago.

Moira had picked up my quest for the truth. And my bad habits. Necessary for the quest, but their repercussions weren't always justifiable. I understood her need and her pain. She'd taken Turk's case against her better judgment. The murder and suicide of Rachel and John Donnelly forever fresh in her mind. Now she had to live with what she thought were the consequences of that decision.

"Turk opened the door and went inside." The rustle of Kris turning back around in her seat to face Moira. "I followed him and we both called out Shay's name. We went into her bedroom . . ." More sobs.

Neither Moira nor I said anything. We let Kris' pain roll out. I found her shoulder again and gently rubbed it. The sobbing ceased, followed by a few deep breaths. She sat silent. I didn't probe.

"Where was she?" Moira. Soft, compassionate, but the question forced Kris to relive the horror she just saw. I suddenly hoped we were almost at Kris' house so she could grieve without having to answer questions and watch it all over again inside her head. But I didn't intercede. My own need for the truth wouldn't let me.

"She was on her back on her bed. She didn't have any clothes on. One eye was swollen shut. All black and blue. Her other . . . her other eye was open. Bulging . . . like, like." Deep breaths. "And she had a red line around her neck. It was horrible."

"What did Turk do when you found Shay?" Moira.

"He tried to revive her. He gave her mouth-to-mouth resuscitation and pounded on her chest, but she was dead. I knew as soon as I saw her."

"Was her body stiff?" Moira asked. She was trying to pin down a time of death. Rigor mortis usually begins four to six hours after death.

"I don't know." Frustration bubbled up from Kris' sadness. "She was . . . she was just lying there. Dead."

"What a horrible thing to have to see. I'm so sorry, Kris." Moira's voice soft as satin. I waited for the hook hidden in the soft folds of fabric. "How did Turk react when he knew Shay was dead?"

There it was.

"What do you mean how did he react?" An edge to Kris' voice like she suddenly discovered the game. "He was crying just like I was. Because he loved her. How would you feel if you found your boyfriend or husband dead?"

"I didn't mean anything by it." Full retreat now. A rare posture for Moira. She could have mentioned that she found her husband dead from a heart attack eight years ago but didn't. I give her credit for that. "I'm sorry I upset you. We're just trying to learn all we can."

We, not *I*. She dragged me in with her.

"For who? You told me you wanted to help Turk." The edge now sharpened to a stiletto point. "But it sounds like just the opposite. You can drop me off here. I'll walk the rest of the way."

"It's only a couple more blocks." Moira, the satin gone. "I'll take you the rest of the way."

Time to referee. "Kris—"

"No! I want to get out. Now!"

The car pulled over and stopped. I pushed open my door and leapt out, tripped over the curb, and fell onto all fours. An abrasion raspberried along my left palm from the sidewalk and ripped open the one from my fall last night. I hustled up to my feet, my support cane still clutched in my right hand. I unfolded it into a straight line and let its plastic oval tip find the ground.

"What are you doing?" Moira's voice through Kris' open door. "Are you okay?"

The door slammed shut.

"What *are* you doing?" Kris, a steadying hand on my arm, but still angry.

"I'm okay. Thanks."

"But what are you doing?"

"I'm going to walk you home."

"No, you're not." The hand dropped from my arm. Footsteps on the sidewalk going away from me, then stopped. "I don't know what kind of game you and your partner are playing but it's sick and I don't want any part of it."

A car door opened.

"Rick, get back in the car." Moira, staccato.

"I'll catch an Uber and call you later." Over my shoulder to Moira. I turned my head back to Kris. "I'm not playing a game, Kris. Turk's my friend. I want to help him."

"Leave me alone." Footsteps. Quickly moving away. I tapped after them.

"Rick!" Moira.

"Leave!" Over my shoulder again.

Slammed door. Screeching tires. Gassed acceleration.

I tapped ahead, faster than I ever had. Faster than was safe. The footsteps ahead faded. I pronged forward. Kris' house was tacked onto a map in my head, but I didn't know where I was on it. Cars zoomed past me on my left. My cane found air and I stopped just in time to keep from plunging off the curb. Tires skidded to a stop in front of me. The stink of burnt rubber filled my nostrils.

"Rick!" Kris from far ahead. "Wait right there. I'll come get you."

I took a step back and waved for the driver I couldn't see to continue. Tires slowly rolled on asphalt in front of me, then sped off.

"Stay there." Kris, closer now. Then footsteps running toward me. A hand on my arm. "Come this way."

She gently pulled my arm and I lifted my cane off the ground and stepped down into the street.

"It works better like this." I pulled her hand away, then grabbed the the back of her right bicep with my left hand so that she was between me and the street. A lifetime of chivalry reversed in an instant with one gunshot to the face.

We took twenty-three steps, then Kris warned me about a curb. After we stepped up from the intersection onto a sidewalk, our pace slowed to a comfortable speed. The tension in Kris' arm eased slightly. The air still and stale.

"I apologize for Moira's questions." Even though they had to be asked. But maybe not today. "She's just worried that something that happened with another client of hers might have happened with Turk."

"What do you mean?" Concern. Angle change of her arm, like she'd turned slightly to look at me.

"The reason Moira and I were at Shay's this morning is because Turk hired us to spy on her."

I'd broken the private investigator–client privilege, but I didn't care. I wasn't really even a P.I. anymore, anyway. My word still meant something to me, but the object of our surveillance was dead and the police were questioning Turk right now, no doubt, trying to link him to Shay's death. The best way to help Turk was to find out as much as I could, and to do that I had to tell Kris the truth.

"What?" She stopped walking and spun out of my grasp to face me. "Why did he want you to spy on Shay?"

"Because he was afraid she was cheating on him."

"I don't believe you." Hot steam sizzled on her voice. "Turk loved Shay and she loved him. Why would he think she was cheating on him?"

I told her about Turk following Shay to La Valencia a couple times and what Moira saw last night and the Mercedes Benz Maybach.

"It doesn't mean she was cheating on him." No edge left in Kris' voice. Just a dull dismay. She slowly started walking again, leading me along the sidewalk.

"You're right." I tried to sound optimistic on a day devoid of optimism. "Do you know of anything Shay had to celebrate about?"

"What? No. Why?"

I told her about the champagne and cake.

"That's odd. She rarely drank alcohol or ate sweets. She was really into health and fitness."

"Was she planning to have a get-together with friends that you know about?"

"She didn't have that many friends here. She really only hung out with me and Turk." A wistful exhale.

"How long did you know her?"

"About a year and a half. Since she started working at Muldoon's."

"How soon after she started did she and Turk begin dating?" I asked.

"A couple months."

"Did she leave Muldoon's to work at Eddie V's because Turk didn't think he should date an employee?"

"Sort of."

"What do you mean?" I got the impression from Turk that he'd gotten Shay a job at Eddie V's so as not to break the Muldoon's management/employee fraternization rule. But the timing was off. They were dating close to a year before she changed jobs.

Kris stayed silent so long I was about to ask what she meant again, but she finally spoke. "She was rude to one of our customers."

Everyone who's ever worked in the service industry has had a customer complain about them. I had a few when I ran Muldoon's. Even employees with the sunniest of dispositions rub a customer the wrong way on occasion. Often, a complaint is based on a misunderstanding or the customer is just a jerk.

One complaint, unless outrageously egregious, never warranted dismissal. Or in Shay's case, an arranged new job at another restaurant.

"What was the customer's interpretation of rude?" Some people took my resting face as a scowl. Even when it wasn't meant to be.

"The customer said Shay called her husband a fucking coward." Kris made the statement sound like a question. "Her words exactly to me on the phone the next day. I couldn't believe what the woman was telling me. Shay is . . . was one of the sweetest people I've ever known."

After years as a cop and a private eye, I knew all too well that people could surprise you. In the worst ways.

"Did the husband and Shay have some sort of history from another time he came in the restaurant?"

"I don't know." The emotion of the day still clung to Kris' voice.

"A hostess doesn't have that much interaction with guests after she seats them. Did anyone else see Shay talk to the man?"

"No. According to Shay, he left his glasses case behind and she caught the couple in the courtyard right after they left."

"What did Shay say happened?"

"She said that the woman was a little drunk and must have misunderstood what she said to the man."

"What did Shay say she said to the man?" I asked.

"Something like, 'Sir, you forgot your glasses' and handed them to him."

"Did you believe her?"

"I don't see what any of this has to do with Shay being murdered and the police questioning Turk about it." Steam back in her voice.

Kris had a point. The answers to my questions probably had nothing to do with Shay's death. But Shay might not have been the sweet woman everyone thought she was. She'd lied about things. Where she went at night, and, possibly, what she said to a Muldoon's customer. What else had she lied about?

Maybe Shay lied to the wrong person about the wrong thing and it had gotten her killed. The one thing I knew in my heart was that Turk didn't kill her.

"I don't either. Yet." I turned my blacked-out-sunglassed face to Kris. "But you never know what piece of information could help Turk if he needs it. That's all I care about. Finding the truth so I can help Turk."

"I believe you." Tired. Like the weight of the morning had finally won and beaten all resistance out of her. "I remember when you and Turk were like brothers. He still talks about you sometimes."

Kris' comment blew the air out of me. Turk *was* my brother. And he needed my help.

"Did you believe what Shay told you about the woman's complaint?"

A long, sad exhale. "No."

CHAPTER SIXTEEN

THE LA JOLLA Police Department headquarters is located in a two-story brick building that was once a library. Thus, the Brick House, the nickname the rank and file gave it decades ago. My father worked there for twenty-two years until he was fired without a pension for reasons that were never officially made public. I knew the reasons. And I still held a grudge.

But so did LJPD. They held me responsible for the perceived sins of my father and those of my own.

I'd spent too many hours inside the Brick House in a square white room under bright fluorescent lights. At least today I'd have sun-glasses for the lights. I'd bought new ones at a Sunglass Hut on the Uber ride over. Large enough to cover the hole in my face, but with lenses that would let in enough light for me to test my improving vi-sion. Hopefully the test results were positive. So far, I only saw unde-fined shapes against darkness.

I told the desk sergeant that Detective Denton had requested my presence. The sergeant told me to wait on the uncomfortable wooden bench near the front door. LJPD headquarters was fairly quiet. There was a bit of macho banter from the desks on the left side of the room where uniform cops filled out reports.

I once had a disagreeable talk with the former chief of police in the roll-call room just behind the desk area. He was a vindictive little man with a boulder-sized chip on his shoulder who was now a member of the U.S. Congress. He'd finally found his true calling.

Upstairs to the right housed the detective bureau offices and the ambitiously titled Robbery Homicide Division. There were plenty of robberies in La Jolla but only four or five homicides a year. Unfortunately, I'd been questioned about a few of them.

A couple minutes into my wait, a shadow passed in front of me. A distinct coconut scent. Moira's voice to the desk sergeant confirmed my suspicion. He told her to wait on the bench. Another riffle in the darkness. Moira sat at the opposite end of the bench from me. And didn't say a word.

We waited in silence. And waited. I didn't ask my phone for the time, but the discomfort of my ass on the wooden bench told me we were approaching an hour when footsteps came down the staircase from the detective bureau. My guess was male. The footsteps got closer and an unformed mass stopped in front of us.

Male cologne that was vaguely familiar.

"Ms. MacFarlane, I'm Detective Jim Sheets. Hello, Mr. Cahill."

The one LJPD cop I trusted. So far.

"Detective." I heard the rustle of clothes as Moira stood up. I did the same and pushed out a hand.

"Hello, Detective Sheets." He shook my hand.

"Would you mind following me upstairs so we can talk up there?" Sheets' voice still had a youngish tone that matched his looks, which I remembered to be tall, thin, dark hair, and black horn-rimmed glasses. When I first met him, Sheets came across as more grad student than homicide cop. But he was smart, diligent, and fair. That's all I could ask for when dealing with the police. Especially the *fair* part.

"Sure," Moira answered and we followed Sheets upstairs to Robbery Homicide. They sandwiched me as I tapped up the stairs. Sheets in front, Moira behind.

Moira nudged me to the right after a few steps down a hall at the top of the stairs.

Robbery Homicide. I'd been there enough times to remember what it looked like. A large room with low-walled cubicles in the middle that housed the detectives' desks.

Another disturbance in the void.

"This is Detective Dabney Holt," Sheets said. "He's going to talk to Ms. MacFarlane in one of the interview rooms. and I'm going to talk to Rick."

"Miss MacFarlane, you can call me Detective Dabbs. Everybody does." A booming baritone with some south in it that was more Barry White than Dabney Coleman. I didn't recognize the voice. I would have remembered it if I'd heard it before. Even before sounds became so important to me. "Come right this way, ma'am."

"You can call me Moira."

"Yes, Miss Moira." Heavier southern accent than in his introduction.

Two sets of footsteps moved away.

"Mr. Cahill, please follow me." But no sound of Sheets moving, yet. "Oh, do you need me to guide you?"

"I can follow your footsteps, Detective, but thanks." I could have followed his fuzzy outline, but I didn't want to admit to it. Not to anyone yet. Especially a cop from LJPD. "And I almost have the way memorized. Interrogation room one or two?"

"Interview room three. It's about twenty feet down the hall to the right." Sheets' shadow moved in front of me. I tapped along behind it. My cane hit the frame of the door, and I followed Sheets' footsteps to the right. They stopped a couple seconds later. "The doorway is about one step forward and one to your left. There is a table in the left corner with a couple chairs. Please take the one on the left against the wall."

"Roger."

Blind and a witness instead of a suspect and LJPD still wanted to corner me against the wall. I tapped my way into the room and heard the hum of fluorescent lights overhead. They flared above like jagged edges of lightning. I found the chair on the left and sat down. Instinct and memories flashed hot on the inside of my skin, and I could feel sweat already forming under my arms. I didn't have to see the square white room to feel its menace. I'd been on the wrong side of too many of them here in La Jolla, San Diego, and up in Santa Barbara not to have scar tissue.

Squeal of chair feet on linoleum. I could now make out a shape in front of me under the bright fluorescent lights. Detective Sheets sat at eye level. His cologne floated in the air between us. We were alone.

A wave of relief ruffled through me. Sheets was going to interview me without Detective Denton. The relief was short lived and replaced with a gnawing dread. If Detective Sheets was alone with me and Detective Holt was with Moira, that meant Denton was with Turk. No doubt badgering him while he tried to grieve the loss of his girlfriend. I suddenly wished Denton was across from me instead of Sheets. I'd had practice battling Denton and her tricks. Turk needed somebody with a conscience, like Detective Sheets.

"Mr. Cahill, why were you at Shay Louise Sommers, apartment this morning? And just so you're aware, this interview is being audio and video recorded."

"Of course. And you can call me Rick, Detective. We've done this enough to be old friends." A weak attempt at humor, maybe to gain a sense of control. A simple domestic surveillance had turned into a murder and my onetime best friend was in the cops' crosshairs. The lights hummed and lightninged above. I wished I still had on my blackout sunglasses.

I hated the square white room.

"You're right. Sorry about what happened to you, by the way." Sheets sounded sincere.

"Thanks."

"How about you start at the beginning?" Friendly.

"Turk Muldoon hired Moira and me to check up on his girlfriend and—"

"To be clear, you're referring to Thomas Arthur Muldoon and Shay Louise Sommers, correct?"

"Yes."

"And why did Mr. Muldoon hire you to check up on Ms. Sommers?" He made the words *check up* sound nefarious.

"He was concerned that Shay might be seeing someone else." I just gave LJPD a motive. I would have lied if I was working the case alone, but Moira was in the next room telling Detective Holt the truth.

"When did you and Ms. MacFarlane begin this surveillance?"

"Last night around nine. We watched her until about midnight and picked the surveillance up this morning at eight-thirty at her house. But, of course, you guys were already there when we arrived."

"What did you and Ms. MacFarlane observe Ms. Sommers do from nine until midnight last night?"

"Well, I didn't *observe* her do anything." I smiled, but I doubted he did. I told him what Moira told me she saw: Shay walking from Eddie V's to La Valencia, the elevator up to the Sky Suite, the man in the Italian suit, the Mercedes Benz Maybach, the drive along the ocean, the stop at Gelson's, and the lights going out around midnight at her apartment.

"And did you report all of this to Mr. Muldoon?"

"Yes. We went over to the restaurant after we left Shay's apartment last night."

"How did Mr. Muldoon react to this information?"

Delicate territory. I'd lied to the police so often over the years that it was second nature. Something I didn't really even have to think about, like my subconscious now counting steps when I walked from one place to another. The rhythm of an interrogation told me when to lie as much as the words being spoken. The ebb and flow of the conversation. The feel of a trap being set. It was now more reflex than even instinct. I usually told the lies to protect myself or someone I cared about.

I know where the investigative compass pointed at the beginning of a murder investigation. Without an eyewitness, video, or inculpatory evidence, it points directly at the spouse, partner, or family member. And that's where it stays until evidence to the contrary is found. Police departments always deny it, but it's human nature. Occam's Razor. Keep it simple. The boyfriend did it.

Turk hadn't done anything wrong. A little anger leaked out when we told him about Shay and the man in the limo, but that was a normal human reaction. And normal human reactions can be twisted into motives for any homicide cop sitting on the top of Occam's Razor.

"What do you mean, how did he react?" I played dumb.

"Did he become angry, upset, volatile?"

"He didn't become anything. Certainly not volatile. He stayed calm."

"So, you told him that his girlfriend was fooling around and he just sat there stoically?" His voice pitched higher and rose at the end of the question like I'd said something ludicrous.

"We didn't tell Turk that Shay had been cheating on him because we didn't find any proof of that." But it didn't take much of an imagination to see that she could have. "Do you know something I don't, Detective?"

"Did Mr. Muldoon tell you he planned to talk to Ms. Sommers about what you told him last night?"

I was supposed to answer Sheets' questions. Not ask my own.

"No. We told him we'd pick up the surveillance at Shay's house in the morning and asked if he'd be there and he said he wouldn't."

"Have you ever known Mr. Muldoon to become violent?"

There it was. That murder investigation compass was pointing straight at Turk and Detective Sheets wasn't going to move off him until he was nudged.

Or pushed.

"Turk is one of the nicest, gentlest people I know. We played football together for a season at UCLA. He made All Pac-12 as a linebacker. That was the extent of his physicality toward other people."

"So you never had a physical altercation with him?" Sheets' voice told me that he knew the answer to the question.

But how could he? No one else had been around when Turk and I went to fists. We were on the roof of Muldoon's Steak House. Unless Sheets somehow tracked down a seagull in the last hour that flew over the restaurant seven years ago, no one saw or knew about the fight.

"We may have roughhoused like brothers do a few times in our teens, but that's it." My pulse stayed constant, breath even, the sweat under my arms already dried. Lying was the easy part. The hard part was dealing with interrogators' rebuttals.

"You and Turk had a falling-out a few years ago, right? When you left the restaurant?"

He'd gone from Mr. Muldoon to Turk. Less formal. Just shooting the shit between friends. No repercussions over a wrong answer. Or the truth.

Then it clicked on me. Kris talked to the police at the crime scene. Did she know about our fight on the roof of Muldoon's? How could she? Only Turk and I knew about the fight. She mentioned earlier that Turk still talked about me sometimes. Had the fight story floated out of Turk as a true confession during a late night of drinking? Things I'd like to change in my life? Maybe it was the answer to a "what really happened to you and Rick" question. Or maybe he spilled it to someone else under similar circumstances and that person talked to the police.

Whatever it was, and whether it came from Kris or not, Detective Sheets knew about the fight that was the exclamation point to the end of our friendship.

"I changed careers. People do it all the time. Turk and I are still friends." I could have said friends *again* to be more truthful. Even that may have been due to my coming to a family member's defense. Estranged or not, Turk was still family. The big brother I never had. Until I met him.

"So you and Turk never got into a real fistfight?" Slight agitation penetrating the grad student façade.

"I already told you, Detective, Turk and I roughhoused a little as teens. Like all kids do."

"You are aware that this conversation is being taped, aren't you, Mr. Cahill?"

"Well." I tapped the lens of my sunglasses. "I'll have to take your word for that, Detective Sheets."

"Do you think Ms. MacFarlane's story will corroborate yours, Rick?" The grad student had graduated to fully accredited homicide cop.

"Corroborate sounds a lot like a courtroom term for a friendly conversation. I don't know exactly what Moira saw, only what she told me she saw. But I'm pretty sure we heard the same things when we talked to Turk."

"I got to tell you, Rick. You're sounding very evasive." Faux cop friendliness, but holding a get out of jail free card over my head. "Seems like you're hiding something or trying to cover for Mr. Muldoon."

"I think maybe you misinterpreted what I've said." I smiled. "When you lose your eyesight, you become much more reliant upon your other senses. Hearing, in particular. So, it's understandable that you may be more focused on what I look like sitting here all covered up behind sunglasses while I'm purely focused on the sound of the words being spoken."

"Thanks for coming in." The temperature in the room suddenly dropped twenty degrees. Scrape of his chair on the floor. A shadow rose in front of me. "Should I get a uniform up here to help you down the stairs or can you manage on your own?"

"I'll go solo. Thanks." I stayed seated. "But I have a question for you, Detective, if you don't mind."

"As I'm sure you can understand, I'm very busy today. Thanks for coming in."

"Was there an opened champagne bottle and a piece missing from a chocolate cake at Shay Sommers' house?"

"I can't talk about a crime scene of an ongoing investigation. Thanks for coming in today." The shadow moved toward the opening in the gray background. The door.

"Shay bought champagne and chocolate cake after meeting someone at La Valencia." I stood up. "She was a health freak who rarely drank or ate sweets. Sounds like she was celebrating something. You might want to find out who rented the Sky Suite at La Valencia last night and who owns the Mercedes Benz Maybach with the license plate number L576Q44."

But Sheets had already left the room.

CHAPTER SEVENTEEN

I CAUGHT MOIRA'S scent just inside the entrance of the Brick House. My sunglassed eyesight unable to pick up her form under normal lighting. She'd been waiting for me.

"Rick, I'll give you a ride home."

We walked outside and I heard voices and shuffling sounds and saw ripples in the void.

"That's Rick Cahill." A male voice shouted.

I sensed people closing in on us. A hand tugged me to the right. Moira.

Voices jabbed from the darkness.

"Mr. Cahill, did the police question you about Shay Sommers' murder?"

"Did you know the victim?"

"What do you know about Thomas Muldoon's involvement in Ms. Sommers' death?"

"Back off, people," Moira snapped as she led me onto the sidewalk and down Wall Street.

A few voices and footsteps trailed after us, but finally faded into the background. The reporters didn't want to miss the main event which was Turk leaving the police station.

Neither of us spoke until we got into Moira's car.

"What did you tell them?" I asked.

"What do you mean?" Offended. "I told them the truth. What did you tell them?"

"The same."

"It doesn't sound like it if you had to ask me what I told them, like we needed to get our stories straight." A huff. "You can't play your usual game with the police on this, Rick. A woman died on our watch, and we have to help the police in any way we can."

I understood Moira feeling responsible for Shay Sommers' death. Because of the Donnelly case, she'd gotten emotionally involved over the target of the investigation. A woman she'd never met. Dangerous territory. For your livelihood. And your soul. I'd learned the hard way. Or maybe I never learned at all because I continued to make the same mistake over and over again. Like now. But my involvement was attached to Turk, not his dead girlfriend.

"Along those lines, did your cop friend ever get back to you with the registered owner of the Maybach?" I asked.

"Yes. It's a rental." Clipped.

"And?"

"Luxurious Limos in La Jolla."

"Did you call them and try to find out who rented the Maybach?"

"First of all, the company would never give me a client's name." Sibilant S in "first." She was mad and getting madder. "Secondly, why would I even consider doing that?"

"To find out who Shay met last night at La Valencia. What Turk paid us to do." Now the irritation flipped over to me.

"The case is closed, Rick. The police are in charge now. I'm sending Mr. Muldoon a check for twenty-five hundred and then I'm done with the whole thing unless the police need to talk to me again."

She called Turk *Mr. Muldoon* to further distance herself from him. She may have quit on him, but I hadn't. And I wouldn't.

"The police are tunneled in on Turk. The least we could do is finish the job for him. Don't the champagne and chocolate cake ring alarm bells with you?"

"No."

"They did last night."

"Everything changed this morning."

"But they still mean something. Cake and champagne is celebratory food. Especially for someone like Shay. Turk said Shay only drank at parties and Kris told me she was a health nut." I looked over at Moira in my new sunglasses and saw only shadows. "She was celebrating something right after she met with the guy in the Maybach."

"The police will follow the leads where they take them. I'm done, Rick." All the hiss had come out of Moira's words, leaving her spent like a deflated balloon. The worst thing she feared that could happen had when she went against her gut and took the case. Whether or not she thought Turk murdered Shay, she'd already begun her descent into the dark hole of self-recrimination. It was a lonely, 24/7 existence and took a long ladder to climb out of.

My dictated text to Turk warning him about the reporters sieged outside the Brick House were the only words spoken by either of us on the drive to my house.

CHAPTER EIGHTEEN

Turk called me at 3:20 p.m.

"They think I did it." His voice clogged with emotion. "They think I killed Shay."

"Did you just get out of LJPD?"

"Yeah. They took my DNA and Detective Denton kept twisting my words around." Beaten and worn down after six hours of interrogation all while trying to deal with the loss of his girlfriend. The kind of stress that can choke off your will to live.

"Did you have a lawyer with you?"

"No. I don't have anything to hide."

"You may not have anything to hide, but you need to get a lawyer." I sat forward in my chair. "You just told me Denton thinks you killed Shay and that she's twisting your words. I'm really sorry about Shay. I know you're going through hell and there's nothing anyone can do for you. But do me a favor, don't talk to the police again without a lawyer."

I ignored my own advice when my wife was murdered. I knew what trouble that could lead to. Even if Turk hadn't lied like I did.

"If the police arrest me, I'll have to refinance my house to pay for a lawyer. I don't have the money to hire one now on the possibility that they're going to arrest me."

"I'm not saying hire one now, but if you talk to the police again, don't do it without a lawyer."

"I'm telling you I can't afford one." Anxiety in his voice up a notch. "Business has been down at the restaurant. I'm tapped out."

"Did Shay know your financial situation when you paid her rent monthly?"

So much effort and expense by Turk for someone who seemed like a user to me. A manipulator. Was this the same woman Kris called the sweetest person she'd ever met?

"No." A snap. "Leave Shay out of it."

Did that make Shay less a user if she didn't know that Turk was running out of money to pay her rent? Too late to prosecute that case. It didn't matter anymore. Shay was dead and Turk was the number one suspect.

That's all that mattered now.

Another thought about money popped into my head. As much as I didn't want it to, I couldn't avoid it. The catalyst to the end of my friendship with Turk.

"Any other money problems?" I didn't want to say the word out loud and stick a wedge back between us.

"You mean *gambling*?" Not accusatory, even though he figured out that was exactly what I meant.

"Anything. Including gambling."

"Nope. Haven't laid a bet since the night I was shot at the Cross."

The night he took a bullet meant for me and saved my life.

"Sorry. Had to ask."

"No you didn't." He sounded more hurt than angry. "Do you think whoever killed Shay has anything to do with the man she met at La Valencia last night?"

"I think it's a possibility and worth looking into. Hopefully the police will do just that."

"What does Moira think?"

I couldn't tell him what she really thought. Not with what he'd just gone through.

"She's going to send you a check for $2,500 since there's no reason to investigate anymore." Sounded like he needed the money anyway.

"Tell her to keep it. I want you two to find out who Shay met last night at La Valencia."

Easier said than done. For a lot of reasons. The first of which was that Moira already presumed Turk guilty of killing Shay. She'd do anything she could to help Turk get convicted, not the opposite.

"It's not that simple." I told him about the Maybach being rented from a rental agency and that they wouldn't give up the names of their clients, but that the police were probably investigating it.

"You think the police are really going to dig deep when they already think I did it?"

A valid question.

"I might not if anyone but Detective Sheets was the lead investigator on the case. He's thorough and fair. He'll investigate all leads."

"Maybe, but Detective Denton is convinced I'm guilty."

"She's full of bluster and was trying to get you to confess because that's what she tries to do with everyone she interrogates. Confession first, facts later. Don't worry about her. Sheets will do the right thing." I hoped he still had that capability after years working with Denton.

"I'd still like you and Moira to investigate for a couple more days." The wariness returned to his voice. "If not, could you get me the information about the car rental agency and I'll try on my own."

"We'll investigate." Or I would. I didn't need eyesight to use a telephone and ask questions. And, if I had to, impersonate a police officer. I'd done it before. "You work on taking care of yourself. Is anyone with you?"

"What do you mean?"

"Anyone with you at the house? Your sister?"

"She's out of town."

"I'll grab an Uber and head over." I knew there wasn't anything I could do to lessen Turk's pain. I knew the pain. Your stomach is turned inside out and the tears run until there are none left, but the pain doesn't go away. Ever. It lessens a little with each year, but it never goes away.

"You don't have to do that. I'm better alone, but I can't just sit back and hope the police look for the real killer." His voice caught. "Shay was the best person I've ever met. I was going to ask her to marry me."

The cake and champagne. A celebration.

"When were you going to ask her?"

"Right about the time she started lying to me." A long pause. I didn't interrupt. "I was hoping you and Moira would find out I had nothing to worry about. That whatever Shay was lying to me about was insignificant."

That never seemed like a reasonable possibility to me. You don't lie about what you've been doing at night, meet someone in a $1,000-a-night suite in La Valencia, and get in the back of a quarter million-dollar car for innocuous reasons. But no need to point that out now.

Most of the time being quiet is better than being right.

"Was there anything Shay wanted to celebrate recently or in the near future? Did she think you were planning to ask her to marry you last night?"

"Not that I know of." Bewildered. "And no, I don't think she knew that I was close to asking her. Why?"

The why. Maybe I was way off about the champagne and cake. Nonetheless, I told Turk what Moira had seen Shay buy at Gelson's. A minor detail she'd left out in her report to him last night.

"Kris told us that Shay was really into health and fitness and didn't eat sweets very often. Is that true?"

Turk didn't say anything for a while, but I could almost hear him thinking. I wasn't off about the cake and champagne. They signified something, and whatever it was was running through Turk's head.

"The night of the year anniversary of our first date, we had champagne and chocolate cake." Barely audible, his voice hollowed out.

CHAPTER NINETEEN

I TURNED ON the block caller ID function, then opened the
TapeACall app on my phone and called the Luxurious Limousine
rental agency. TapeACall recorded phone calls so I could store infor-
mation on my phone in lieu of taking notes. Theoretically, illegal in
California if you don't alert the caller that you're recording the call,
but I never used the recordings for anything other than note taking.
Easier for me than using a braille reader. I hadn't learned braille, yet.
Same reason I hadn't sold my car. Hope.

A man answered. Early, to mid-twenties. Slight Middle Eastern
accent.

"This is Officer Bud Gardner with the La Jolla Police Department,
badge number 1785." I gave the man the license plate number of the
Maybach and told him I needed to know who rented it.

"I'm sorry, Officer, but I can't give out that information."

"Well, I need to speak to the person who can give me that
information."

"He's not here right now."

Better for me. The person in charge would be less likely to fall for
my ruse.

"What's your name?" Terse. Command presence hearkening back
to my time as a cop in Santa Barbara fifteen years ago.

"Jamal."

"Last name?"

"Amari."

"Please spell your full name for me." I didn't care about his name. I just wanted him to think I did.

He spelled his name.

"Jamal Amari, your company's vehicle was involved in an accident that has caused massive property damage." I was skating a thin line around a misdemeanor by impersonating a police officer, but since I wasn't victimizing someone I probably wouldn't be convicted if I went to trial. "The driver fled the scene before we arrived and there aren't any witnesses. All we have is your Mercedes Benz Maybach sitting in the living room where there used to be a wall in someone's house. Thank God no one in the home was injured."

"That's terrible, but it's not my vehicle. It's owned by the company."

"Of course it is. And as owner of the vehicle involved in the hit-and-run accident, Luxurious Limousines will be held responsible if we can't locate the driver. Somewhere down the line in court, I'm sure everything will be sorted out. Maybe your boss can afford the attorney fees to spend a few weeks in court and absorb the loss of business and damage to your reputation. Maybe not. But I've got a crime I'm trying to solve and time is of the essence."

"Let me call my boss and call you back."

"Jamal, you don't seem to understand. We've got two tow trucks and a construction crew at the residence right now. You know how much the city bills an hour for these kinds of services? A lot more than the private sector. Luxurious Limousines is going to be charged unless you give me that name and I can track that person down right now."

I waited.

A lump of anxiety grew in my belly. Not in anticipation of Jamal refusing to give me the man's name. But regret that I fell so easily back into my P.I. posture of lying for what I deemed the greater good. I might be putting this man's job on the line because I needed information. That was more important to me than a stranger's livelihood. My quest for the truth and another possible collateral victim.

I hadn't changed. And I wasn't even a real P.I. anymore.

"Jamal, you don't—"

"His name is Keenan Powell. There's a corporate address. Blank Slate Capital, 7850 Ivanhoe Ave., La Jolla 92037."

Ivanhoe T-boned right into Prospect Street where La Valencia was located. Why did this Keenan Powell rent a limo to drive around La Valencia and La Jolla if his office was only a couple blocks away? Was he trying to impress Shay?

Another mystery to solve.

I had Keenan Powell's name and Blank Slate Capital's address. My deception with Jamal was complete. I'd now try to mitigate the damage. And assuage my guilt.

"Thanks, Jamal." I took a deep breath and stepped into the confessional. "Your company is not in any trouble. Everything I just told you is a lie. I'm not a cop. There was no accident. As far as I know, the car is fine."

"What?" An octave higher. "Who are you? What's your name, you fucking asshole?"

"Fucking Asshole works." I hung up. Guilt unassuaged. But I could live with that. Part of the bargain I'd made with myself long ago.

I went up to my office on the second floor. Leah had suggested that I move my office downstairs to the dining nook off the kitchen since I spent most of my time on the ground floor. There was more than enough room and we ate most of our meals on the butcher block island in the kitchen or outside on the deck. An office downstairs made a lot of sense and was easier to navigate for someone in my condition.

I think Leah held her breath every time I went up or down the stairs. But I didn't. It was one of my early challenges that had become routine. I still had to be careful going up and down stairs, as evidenced by what happened last night. But I wasn't going to sidestep challenges for safety sake. That would be too easy and further cocoon my existence. I'd spent most of the last three months cloistered in my house. I wasn't about to close off any piece of that tiny universe.

Midnight settled in under my desk. He liked routine, too. I opened my laptop computer, woke up the voice recognition function on Windows, and commanded the computer to open one of the paid people finder websites I used for P.I. work before Santa Barbara. I commanded the name Keenan Powell and San Diego into the website's search engine and waited.

A few seconds later, my computer told me that a Keenan William Powell lived at 10943 Glencreek Circle in Scripps Ranch. Scripps Ranch isn't La Jolla when it comes to prestige and real estate value, but it's a hidden gem with a lot of undeveloped terrain, snug up against Mira Mesa and Marine Base Miramar to its west and sandwiched between Poway and Tierrasanta to its north and south.

Powell's age was listed at forty-three. From Moira's description, that could have fit the man Shay Sommers took a moonlight drive along the beach with last night. Divorced, two teenage children, one each. That fit about half the population of America. Blank Slate Capital, LLC was listed as his most recent employer.

I commanded the computer to look up Blank Slate Capital, LLC. There were only three listings on Google. Rare to find only three of any listing on Google. Blank Slate was a hedge fund management firm. The firm's address was the same one on Ivanhoe that Jamal at Luxurious Limousines gave me. I listened to the computer list the firm's leadership team. There were no doubt photos attached, but they didn't do me any good.

The founder was someone named Charles "Chuck" Baxter. A few names later came Keenan Powell, Partner, Chief Operating Officer, and General Counsel. A long title with a lot of responsibility at a hedge fund management firm. No doubt, Powell made a lot of money. Someone who could afford a couple nights in the Sky Suite at La Valencia and a few days in the back seat of a rented Mercedes Benz Maybach. But why stay at an expensive hotel when he lived only twenty minutes away?

I command copied Blank Slate's URL, pasted it on an email to Moira, and asked her to look up Keenan Powell and tell me if he was the man she saw with Shay last night. I didn't hold my breath waiting for a quick response. Or any response at all. Moira blamed herself for Shay's death. And, down deep or closer to the surface, she blamed me, too. The last time she blamed me for something, something awful, she refused contact for months.

I'd have to go the investigation alone. Something I did all the time before I met Moira and started teaming up with her on a few cases a year. She made me a better investigator when we worked together. And she could see.

But I'd stumbled through a lot of investigations blind before. Even when I had 20/20 vision.

I had a name, a business address, and a phone number after I commanded my computer to read it off. I called Blank Slate Capital and opened TapeACall again.

"Blank Slate Capital, LLC. This is Rory Bryant. May I help you?" A woman's voice. Friendly, professional with just enough sensuality dripping off it to get the blood and money flowing from a qualified male investor.

"Keenan Powell, please." Brusque. Like I had the kind of money that made my time limited.

"Mr. Powell is out of the office. May I take a message?"

"I need a number where I can reach him."

"May I take a message, please?" She'd figured me out. Anyone important enough to get hold of Powell when he was out of the office would already have his cellphone number.

"Yes. Please have him call Rick Cahill as soon as possible." I recited my number.

"May I tell Mr. Powell what this is concerning, Mr. Cahill?" Enough patronizing "I won" in her voice to make it hurt for someone who took those sorts of things personally. I didn't.

"Yes. You can tell him it's about Shay Sommers. The woman who was murdered in La Jolla last night." Maybe I did take those sorts of things just personally enough to score the last point. I hung up.

I called La Valencia and asked to be connected to the Sky Suite.

"I'm sorry, the Sky Suite doesn't take unsolicited calls from outside the hotel." Male nasally voice. Another gatekeeper happy with his power. "I can take a message and relay it to the guest at an appropriate time. Who's calling?"

I only lied because gatekeepers kept getting in my way.

"This is Detective Bud Gardner with the La Jolla Police Department and I need to speak to the occupant of the Sky Suite forthwith." More command presence with a dash of cop lingo.

"Would you like me to take a message for the guest?" Coy, like he was having fun. "Or would you like to talk with one of your own detectives? Detective Denton is in our lobby right now."

I hung up. The La Valencia front desk got the last laugh, and I was left with no new information on Keenan Powell.

CHAPTER TWENTY

I LISTENED TO the local news at 5:00 p.m. for the first time since I'd been back from Santa Barbara. Shay Sommers' murder was the lead story. The reporter went into more detail than I expected. Beaten and strangled to death. No sign of sexual assault. Sounded like someone at LJPD had leaked information to her. The reporter went on to say that LJPD hadn't named any suspects, but had spoken to an unnamed person of interest.

I knew the name of the unnamed. Turk. I hoped he didn't turn on his television. For months.

Next came comments on a grieving friend they must be showing on the screen. Probably Kris. The press hadn't yet arrived while Moira and I were at Shay's house. My guess was that someone had filmed the scene from their smartphone and sold it to the TV station. Or maybe even the network.

It used to be that you only had to worry about the press intruding on your private grief while you suffered the worst moments of your life. Now you had to add your neighbors to the list. And strangers. Every private moment was now in the public domain. Whether you liked it or not. No matter the damage it caused.

I couldn't remember if I still had Kris' phone number but told my phone to call Kris Collins. A couple seconds later I heard ringing.

"Rick?" Kris' voice still weighed down with grief.

"How are you holding up?" A stupid question. I could tell by her voice. Not well at all. Maybe shared grief would help. Could it make things worse? "Have you spoken with Turk since this morning?"

"Yes. About an hour ago. I'm worried about him." So was I, but kept that to myself.

"Do you think you could go over and sit with him for a while? I think he's all alone." I figured she'd be a much better choice than me.

"I can't. I'm at the restaurant."

"What?"

"Someone has to be here. No one else can open and close. Pat is on vacation in Europe." The bar manager. I'd hired him, too.

"Shit." Even all these years later, I still knew Muldoon's like the back of my hand. I still remembered how to close the restaurant. But I'd never done it blind.

"There's something else I have to tell you." An ache in her voice.

"Okay." Could the day get worse?

"I think I messed up when I talked to a detective today."

"What did you say?"

"He asked me if I ever knew Turk to be violent and I said no."

"That's good." However, I knew there was a "but" yet to come.

"Then he asked if I was sure, not even with an unruly customer, like he thought I was lying and trying to cover something up."

I could have told her that I knew what she was going to say, but that would give it greater significance and make her feel worse. I let her go on.

"So I told him about the time you and Turk got into a fight over the restaurant when you quit." She rushed her words like she was trying to spit them out of her mouth as fast as she could and be done with them. "I told the detective that no one got hurt and that you two remained friends."

"You didn't do anything wrong. That has nothing to do with what happened to Shay. "

"I hope you're right."

Me, too. The police and the DA would use whatever a judge would allow, if Turk was ever arrested.

"How did you know about that?" Two things Kris said about the fight weren't true. That I quit Muldoon's and that no one got hurt. Turk fired me, and the fight, and everything surrounding it, caused a tear in our relationship that still hadn't healed.

"He told me one night when I was feeling down about an argument I had with a friend." These words came slower, almost wistful. "He told me it was his fault and that he wished he would have apologized at the time, but his pride wouldn't let him."

"My pride didn't help either." I could have made the first move. But all of that was moot now. Life had moved on. Turk needed me now and I wouldn't let him down.

My phone interrupted my end with the beep of an incoming call.

"I have to get back in the dining room, but please call Turk. Make sure he's okay." Kris, exhausted.

"I will." I hung up and answered the incoming call.

"Up to your old tricks again, Cahill?" A woman's voice, but not Moira's. Unfortunately, I recognized it. "Poking your white cane in where it doesn't belong?"

"Detective Denton," I said and waited for the worst.

"Or should I call you Officer Gardner? Or Detective Gardner. Apparently, you were promoted between calls to Luxurious Limousines and La Valencia."

Shit. But at least I knew LJPD was following all leads on Shay's murder. Even the annoying tangential ones after the fact.

"I don't know what you're talking about." Lying to the police was easy again.

"Well, let me enlighten you." A loud nostril exhale. "Oops, my mistake. I know you're not familiar with that term. You are the most unenlightened human being I've ever met. I'll educate you, then. Someone impersonating a police officer called Luxurious Limousines and La Valencia today in an effort to get information on a murder investigation."

"What does that have to do with me?"

"Good question. At first, I didn't even consider you after I talked to Jamal at the car rental company and he told me someone had gotten information from him by lying about being a cop. Or even after the desk clerk at La Valencia told me that someone had pretended to be a detective on the phone. I thought an overzealous reporter made the calls to get a scoop on what's turning into a big story. I mean, even the desk clerk knew the person was a phony."

She paused. I guess to let the insult sink in. If I was the kind of person to do what she'd alleged, I wouldn't be so easily offended. I waited for Detective Denton to go on. She hadn't gotten to the part where she threatens me with arrest yet.

"Then I remembered who I saw at the crime scene today and thought about what kind of an interfering idiot with a hero complex you were. And that you are a friend of Thomas Muldoon's and knew about the rented Mercedes and La Valencia because you were with Moira MacFarlane when she followed Shay Sommers last night. So, go ahead and play dumb, Cahill. It's not much of a stretch for you. But, take this as a warning, if you further interfere in my murder investigation, I will put you behind bars, right next to your friend."

"You arrested Turk?"

"Who?"

"Thomas Muldoon."

"I didn't say that. Not yet, anyway."

"Sounds like you're zeroed in on him, Detective. I hope you follow up on all the other leads. It wasn't Turk. He loved Shay."

"Maybe that love turned to hate after you made him think Shay Sommers was cheating on him."

"We didn't make him think anything. And he was fine when we left him." Not fine, but more sad than angry. "Why don't you look into who Shay met at La Valencia? If she was having an affair, maybe the man she met wanted to end it and Shay didn't. Expand your horizons. It wasn't Turk."

"If your friend was fine, why did he go over to Shay's apartment last night and get into an argument with her that her neighbors could hear?" A patronizing one-up in her voice.

"What?" My stomach clenched. Turk hadn't mentioned going to Shay's after we left him at Muldoon's.

"Guess your friend didn't tell you that." Acid. "Stay away from my investigation or I'll make your life even more difficult than it already is." Detective Denton hung up.

I called Turk. No answer. I contacted Uber next and put in Turk's address for my destination. If Turk wanted me to investigate Shay's murder, he needed to answer my calls.

And tell me everything.

CHAPTER TWENTY-ONE

TURK LIVED ON East Roseland Drive in La Jolla. Hidden behind Torrey Pines Road before Torrey wishboned with La Jolla Parkway. He lived in a rambling ranch-style house with a lot of red brick and ash wood on a half-acre set back from the street. At least that's what it looked like the last time I was there. Whether it looked the same or not, there was more than enough room for Shay to have lived there instead of alone in an apartment in La Jolla that Turk helped pay for. And if she wasn't ready to share the master with Turk, she could have had her choice of three other bedrooms.

None of my business. Although, now it was.

The Uber driver dropped me off around 6:15 p. m. Winter dark. If there was a moon, none of its light penetrated my sunglasses into my eyes.

I tapped my way along the cement driveway until I found the opening to the brick courtyard that led to the front door off to the left. The brick was uneven, but I made it to the front door without tripping and rang the bell.

Nothing. After a minute, another double ring. Finally, an orb of light shined above me. Porch light. Then the creak of a door and a dark mass appeared.

Turk.

"What are you doing here?" No slur, but the slight hesitation between words that I used to hear in my father's voice when he was at the beginning of a bender.

I caught the scent of whiskey breath mixed with the stink of embedded sweat. Turk had crawled inside a bottle to battle his grief. I couldn't blame him. He'd started the day finding the woman he wanted to marry strangled to death on her bed. That kind of day could last forever unless you sedated it and somehow found sleep. And then it started all over again when you woke up.

"I know your sister is out of town and Kris is stuck at the restaurant so you got me. How are you holding up?" A stupid question but the way friends tried to help the unhelpable.

"I'm okay. Fucking reporters somehow got my phone number and started calling as soon as I got home from Police Headquarters." A cloud of stale whiskey on an empty stomach came out with the words. "It's been a hard day. I really just want to be left alone. But thanks for checking on me. The police still have my car so I can't give you a ride. You want me to call you a cab?"

"I just got out of an Uber. You mind if I wait a few minutes before I start the process again?" If he didn't want my company, he still had to answer my questions.

"Sure. Sure." His voice, less enthusiastic than his words. He moved to the side. "You have to step up a couple inches entering the house."

I went inside and felt the whoosh of the door swing behind me and thump into the frame. Maybe with a little more force than he meant. Or he was mad that I'd insinuated my way into his house. His time. His grief.

One smudge of light in the middle of the living room ceiling. The rest of the house was dark.

"Which way to a chair?" I asked. I could only make out a few fuzzy shapes, but my lack of depth perception made it difficult to tell how close they were to me.

"Oh." He said it like maybe he expected me to stand the entire time of my short stay.

"Don't worry. I won't be here long. Just a quick recharge then back out into the dark."

"Yeah. Yeah. No problem." Movement, like maybe he was waving his hand. "There's a couch straight ahead about fifteen feet. You can sit there."

I tapped across the hardwood floor toward a horizontal shape and sat down on a cloth couch.

I heard Turk's three-legged gait along the wood floor before he came back into view. As out of focus as that view was. He lowered himself into a chair across from me. I had a feeling he was checking the time on his phone or counting off the minutes I stayed in his head.

My clock was ticking. Best to use the time as a friend would and try to console the inconsolable or do the job he'd hired me to do?

"I found out a few things since we talked this afternoon." I told him about Keenan Powell and Blank Slate Capital. "Have you ever heard that name before?"

"No."

I voice commanded my iPhone to my photos. The last one I'd taken was a screen shot of Keenan Powell's bio page on the Blank Slate Capital website.

"Have you ever seen this guy before?" I stuck my phone out toward Turk and he took it.

"No. Is that the guy Shay met at La Valencia?" An edge cut through the alcohol like a spinning chainsaw. No nuance. No attempt to hide his anger.

"I don't know. I didn't see him." I put out my hand.

"I know *you* didn't see him." Turk put the phone back in my hand. "But what about Moira? She's the one who saw him. What did she say?"

"Nothing. I sent her the photo, but haven't heard back yet."

"What do you mean you sent *her* the photo?" Rising agitation. "She's the one who should be searching the internet for this guy. I hired her, not you. No offense, but she can see and you can't. I don't care if you help out, that's her choice, but she's the one who should be working the case."

"Moira's done. She doesn't think there's anything for her to investigate anymore. It's in police hands now. Like I told you before, she's sending you a check for the unused time."

"I don't care about the fucking money!" Turk moved forward in the chair. "I want to know who Shay was seeing."

My stomach flipped over. Turk said, "I want to know who Shay was seeing" not "I want to know who killed Shay." Had I misjudged everything? I thought I could pick right up and measure the Turk I used to know. Maybe the Turk I used to know didn't exist anymore. Images whirled through my mind until they stopped on the roof of Muldoon's the day our friendship ended. A moment of sudden violence. Maybe that was the real Turk and the one I thought I knew never existed.

"You can take the check from Moira and use it to hire a new private investigator or you can live with me for now. But if you want my help, you have to tell me everything."

"I told you everything." Desperate.

"When was the last time you saw Shay?"

"What?" Hackles lifted off the word. "Why are you asking me that?"

"Why aren't you answering it?"

"Fuck off, Rick." More disappointed than anger. "You sound just like the police."

"Someone saw you at Shay's late last night and heard you two arguing."

Silence.

I probed again.

"Why didn't you tell me you went to Shay's when we talked this afternoon?" I waited. I was either sitting in front of a man who was flailing through the grief of losing his girlfriend to murder or the man who murdered her. A thought that would have never occurred to me seven years ago. Or even last night.

"I went over to Shay's after you and Moira came by the restaurant." Defeated. The same way he sounded last night in his office.

"What happened?" I braced myself for the answer.

"We got into an argument." He left it there like that said it all. It didn't say enough. I didn't want to hear more, but knew I had to.

"Give me all of it, Turk." My irritation slipped out. At Turk for holding out and at myself for asking the question of my grieving friend.

"I didn't kill her, Rick." A wounded bellow. "You know that, right?"

"I'll tell you what I know. Detective Denton thinks you killed Shay and she never changes her mind. I don't know what Detective Sheets thinks, but at least he looks at all the facts before he decides. They both know more than I do. If you want me to help you, I need to know everything."

Another gap of silence filled only by the stench of whiskey breath and body odor. Turk's grief added layer upon layer of stink, filling up the large living room.

The one thing I truly believed at that moment was Turk was not a bad man and he was grieving Shay's death. Dark, desperate grief. But good people sometimes snap and do things in a moment of rage they never thought they were capable of. Things that can't be fixed. Things they'll regret after it's too late.

"I got to Shay's around one. All the lights were off. I knocked, but she didn't come to the door, so I used my key to get inside."

I braced for the worst.

"What happened while you were there?"

"I went into her bedroom." Oh, God. "But she looked like she was asleep so I decided to leave and talk to her in the morning. She called my name as I was leaving the bedroom. There was something about the way she said my name. It went straight to my heart. Right from the first time I met her. I wished I'd never followed her to La Valencia."

He stopped talking but I could hear jagged breaths, like he was crying or fighting hard not to.

"What happened after she called your name? Did you argue in her bedroom or somewhere else?"

"We didn't argue at all. At first." His breathing settled. "She got out of bed and asked me if everything was all right. I think we went into the living room then and—"

"You don't remember where you were?" Didn't remember, didn't want to remember, or didn't want to tell me? Or knew he had to remove himself from the bedroom where the body was found?

"I remember." Snapped off. "We talked in the living room. I just don't remember exactly when we went out there. Anyway, I asked her what she did after she got off work. She lied. Right to my face. Told me she went straight home. She lied so easily. Looking in my eyes, in that sweet voice . . ."

That would make anyone angry. How angry?

"Did she ever admit that she went to La Valencia last night?"

"No."

"Did you tell her that you hired a private detective who followed her there?"

"No."

"Why not?" Now I was frustrated. "She might have told you what she was doing if you confronted her with the truth."

"Because I didn't want her to know someone was following her. If she wouldn't tell me the truth, I wanted definitive proof one way or the other, before I decided what to do."

"How animated did the conversation get?"

"What do you mean?" A slight upturn of his voice at the end. He knew what I meant, but didn't want to tell me.

"The police said a neighbor could hear you arguing, Turk." My frustration bubbled out. "That means one or both of you were shouting. How loud did it get?"

"I got upset. I raised my voice. I asked her if she was cheating on me, but she denied it." His voice picked up speed and volume with each new word. "The only woman I'd ever wanted to marry. I felt like such an idiot. I'd been paying her rent, for Christ sakes."

"How did the argument end?" Why the hell did I have to put us in the situation where Moira was forced to tell Turk what she'd seen last night while tailing Shay? He never would have gone over to Shay's apartment if I hadn't gone to Muldoon's looking for Moira. Why didn't I just stay in the damn car?

"I . . . I . . ." Tears choked his voice. "I . . . I did something awful."

Oh, God. Lord have mercy on his soul.

And on mine.

CHAPTER TWENTY-TWO

NAUSEA WASHED OVER me. Clammy sweat beaded my forehead. My quest for the truth had brought me to this point. I'd gotten the confession I didn't want to hear from a man who'd once been like a brother to me. The only person from San Diego who drove up to Santa Barbara to visit me in jail when I was arrested for my wife's murder. The only friend who still believed I was innocent after the police and press declared me guilty.

But the confession wasn't enough.

My quest for the truth was empty if it wasn't anchored to justice. If Turk was a murderer, he had to pay. Even if I had to betray our friendship to make that happen. The murder of an innocent could never be justified. I had to go to the police. I needed to know the details. I needed to hear the words.

"What did you do?" My own words came out strangled.

"I grabbed her and shook her. I'd never even yelled at her before." Resignation. Ready for his justice. "I kept asking her why she was lying to me."

"Then what happened?" I wiped sweat off my forehead and took a deep breath.

"I let go of her and apologized. She was crying and screamed at me to leave."

"What did you do?" Was he going to lie to me now after everything he'd already told me so far?

"I left."

"Was she alive when you left?" Even if he lied now, I knew the truth.

"What?" The walls shook and Turk's shadow shot up from his chair and loomed above me. "Is that what you think? That I killed Shay?"

I stood up and met Turk's presence.

"You said you grabbed her, Turk." The lid came off. "Where did you grab her? Around the neck? Did your anger take over like it did the day we were on the roof of Muldoon's? Did you kill her before you realized what you'd done?"

"No!" A howl. "I could never do that. How could you even think I'd do that? I thought you knew me."

"I thought I did, too. You just told me you did something awful." I thumped my index finger off his chest. "What the hell did you mean?"

"I told you. I grabbed her and shook her and screamed at her to stop lying to me." His voice now hoarse with guilt. "The police told me she had bruises on her arms. I hurt her. I physically hurt the only woman I've ever loved. The woman I was going to marry. The woman . . . I don't care what she did. She didn't deserve to be treated that way. I've never done anything like that in my whole life. What kind of a man am I?"

I took a step back, caught the edge of the sofa, and sat down hard. Turk was telling the truth. He'd put his hands on a woman. Something antithetical to who he was, how he was raised. That's the guilt I saw. He'd done something awful and his guilt was mixed with his grief. But he didn't kill Shay Sommers.

Which meant someone else did. Keenan Powell? The Invisible Man? No. He had to be from Moira's past, not Shay's. But it didn't matter. Neither were even on LJPD's radar. Turk was their only target.

"Did you tell the police everything you just told me?" They'd twist Turk's grabbing Shay by the arms into him grabbing her around the neck and strangling her to death. The truth could get you indicted, even when you were innocent.

"No, but I'm going to tomorrow." Turk's mass descended back down into the chair.

"What?"

"Detective Sheets called me before you came over and asked if I'd come down to the station tomorrow morning for a few more questions."

It was never just a few more questions and nothing ever good came from answering them. The police had their gunsights targeted on Turk. Anything he told them would be more bullets in the gun.

"You can't do that. Let them get a warrant the next time they want to talk to you."

"I have to go. If I don't, they'll think I'm guilty."

"They already think you're guilty." My voice rose on its own. "If you tell them what you just told me, they'll be convinced."

Movement by Turk, like he'd put his head in his hands. His words came out muffled.

"If I would have just kept calm and not pressed her, I would have stayed the night with her and she'd still be alive. Whoever killed her would have had to go through me. My anger cost Shay her life."

I knew the burden of losing your soul mate to murder when you could have, should have, been with her when she was attacked. And I knew what it was like to have the last words you had with her be in anger. I'd carried both burdens for fifteen years. They could grind your life down to dust. I finally let them go and started to live again in Santa Barbara. In the hospital. Blind. A bullet hole in my face.

"You don't know that." But he'd always believe it.

"Shay died thinking I wasn't the man she thought she knew before last night." His head rose. "I have to do the stand-up thing. I have to be the person Shay thought I was. I'm going down to the police station tomorrow and tell them everything. Maybe they'll believe me and start looking for the real killer."

"That's a bad idea."

"I'm going." Resolute. I'd heard that tone before. Continuing to argue was pointless.

"If you're going to go, at least take a lawyer with you."

He went quiet again, then let out a loud breath.

"Okay. But where am I going to find a criminal defense lawyer on such short notice at night?"

"I know where to find one. A good one."

CHAPTER TWENTY-THREE

WE ARRIVED AT Ellis "Elk" Fenton's townhome around 7:30 p.m. Fenton lived in La Jolla Alta, one of the town's early planned communities up the hill from Kate Sessions Park and the dividing line between La Jolla and Pacific Beach.

"Gentlemen, welcome!" Elk's voice still had a tinge of the goofy adolescent I met in middle school. Slightly over the top, hanging onto the outer edges of the jock clique. We let him hang around when we were young, arrogant, and stupid because he'd do anything for a laugh. That was his in. He didn't need one now but still seemed to be looking for it.

"Turk Muldoon," Turk said by way of greeting. The usual twinkle in his voice at meeting someone new replaced with emptiness. "Thanks for meeting us at your home, Mr. Fenton."

A pause like they shook hands, then Turk's mass moved inside the house and I followed.

"No trouble at all. And please, call me Ellis." Fenton sounded like a too-happy-to-please dinner party host instead of the cutthroat attorney I knew him to be inside a courtroom. But even his courtroom persona had velvet gloves. Wrapped around razor-sharp talons.

When I first bumped into Fenton as an adult, I was working at Muldoon's, having not seen him for sixteen or seventeen years; he was practicing estate planning law after getting out of the criminal side. He gave me some inside information that kept me from going to jail. He went back to the dark side shortly thereafter and hired me a few times to investigate for the defense on court trials. The cases I investigated for Elk ranged from misdemeanors to violent felonies. Our agreement was that I could walk if I thought his client was guilty of a felony. I quit two of the eleven cases I worked for him. The two walk-aways were a burglary defendant and the instigator of a brawl in the parking lot of a Charger game back when San Diegans still cared about the NFL.

"Rick, great to see you out and about." A hand patted my shoulder.

"Hello, Elk, I mean Ellis." I made the same mistake of calling him his childhood nickname every time I met with Fenton when he hired me to investigate a case. To me, he'd always be the goofy kid trying to fit in. I didn't know what I'd always be to him. Arrogant jock with a decent heart, relentless investigator, or, now, the man with sunglasses and a white cane?

"As always, Rick, Elk is fine if you're more comfortable with it. Gentlemen, let's sit down and talk." Fenton led us into the well-lit living room where he and I had discussed cases after hours a few times. Now just a gray mass to me, cut up by fuzzy-edged geometric forms. He used more care than was necessary to steer me over to the sofa where Turk and I sat down. Fenton's less substantial outline sat down across from us.

I'd given Elk a broad overview of Turk's situation on the phone. Now we had to fill in the ugly details. Elk, like anyone in San Diego who paid even the lightest attention to the news, had already heard about Shay Sommers' murder. Turk told him everything the news didn't know. Everything he'd told me in the last thirty minutes.

I kept my mouth shut for a change, waiting to jump in if Turk left something out or shaded the truth as I knew it. I didn't have to say a word. Turk held nothing back. The raw, ugly truth. I only spoke after he was done, to tell Fenton what I'd learned about Keenan Powell online and over the phone.

"First of all, Turk, you have my heartfelt condolences for your terrible loss." Sincerity replaced the goofiness in Elk's voice. "Having to deal with the police badgering you during this time of grief is more than anyone should have to bear."

"Thanks."

"I think you should continue to work through your grief without further interruption by the police. I'll handle any more dealings with them going forward." Elk's voice calm. Parental. "Therefore, I'll contact Detective Sheets and inform him that you are in a state of shock and you're still grieving and won't be coming in tomorrow."

"I'm talking to the police tomorrow and telling them the truth." Turk stood up. "Thanks for your time."

"Okay. Okay. If you're set on that, then I'll be there to advise you." Elk's voice a placating soothe. "Please sit back down and let's talk about how to get the media on our side."

"What?" Turk and I chimed in unison as the couch groaned under Turk's weight. The media, enemy of the guilty and the innocent, alike. Although they do like a good redemption story. After they tear you down in the first place, setting the scene for your Phoenix rise, which they'll report on and enable.

Turk had already torn himself down low enough. I didn't want the media to act as the wrecking ball. Even if they planned to rebuild later.

"That's a bad idea. The media won't let Turk grieve in peace as it is. Why do you want to involve them?"

"Because reporters will be in front of police headquarters tomorrow reporting on who comes and goes. Just like they did today." Professorial. "This is a high-profile case and it's not going to fade quietly into the background. The press is already forming a narrative. We need to get out in front and help them shape it. If they report that Turk was questioned by the police two days in a row, they're going to start calling him a suspect or a person of interest if the police don't beat them to it. We have to present our version of the story."

"Don't you mean *the truth*." Turk, irritated. He wasn't used to lawyer speak.

"Precisely." Elk, nonplussed by Turk's irritation. "We have to remind La Jolla and the city of San Diego what an asset you are to the community. How long has Muldoon's Steak House been a La Jolla landmark?"

"Forty-six years. I've been running it since my father died twenty years ago."

"A great family-owned restaurant for half a century, shepherded by the son of the founder. A man who is beloved by the community."

"You're spreading it on a little thick, Counselor." Turk, not amused. It would be a long time until he ever was again.

"Look, hopefully the detectives down at the Brick House will follow all the clues and find the real killer of poor Ms. Sommers, but we have to be prepared to go to battle."

Elk, in his exaggerated way, was right about two things. Turk was beloved by his employees and customers, and LJPD was locked onto him and, until someone found a key to open that lock, nothing would change their theory of the case.

"He's also the man who saved my life, in case the press has already forgotten." I believed Turk was innocent. And Elk Fenton knew how to navigate the legal/media minefield better than I did. I had to trust him and go all in. "And the community does love you, Turk. You're just too humble to realize it."

A grunt from Turk's direction.

"And that cane you have to use is a reminder of the damage that your heroic actions to save Rick caused." Fenton was rolling now and

I'd piggybacked for the ride. "And let's not forget your heroism, Rick. Your own cane and those sunglasses are a constant reminder of the sacrifice you made to solve the cold case murder of your beloved wife."

Shit. The ride just came off the rails.

Fenton continued, "When I address the press after we talk to the police tomorrow morning, I want each of you on either side of me as a reminder of the kind of person Turk is and the kind of people who support him."

"I don't think you want me next to either of you," I jumped in. "I have a mixed relationship, at best, with the press and a horrible one with LJPD."

"After what happened up in Santa Barbara, you're a full-fledged hero, Rick. And you have the scars to prove it. You're now a sympathetic character. That's what we need."

A character. Playing a part in someone else's movie.

"This is ridiculous!" Turk's voice caromed around the living room. "Did you listen to what I just told you I did to Shay last night? I'm not a fucking hero. I assaulted the woman I love. I hurt her. I bruised her. I'm not going to stand up there while you lie to the press and tell them what a great man I am. I'm going down to police headquarters tomorrow morning to tell them the whole story. You can come along if you want, but I'm not going stand around and listen to you make me out to be an angel to the press. Or anyone else."

The sofa moaned a release as Turk got up and moved quickly into the gray background. The sound of a door opened and slammed hard enough to send vibrations along the wood floor under my feet.

"His car is still in police custody," I said. "We had to Uber over here. He's either contacting them or walking five miles home."

"I'll be right back." Elk's shadow shot up and hurried out of the house.

I understood why Turk didn't want Fenton to make him out to be a hero. He had to deal with the worst day of his life battling the feeling that the last thought Shay had about him was that he was a monster.

Fenton came back inside a few minutes later. "I convinced Turk I'd handle everything with class tomorrow. He's onboard, but he'd like you to be by his side when I talk to the media."

"The police aren't going to let me be in the interview room with you and Turk."

"No, but it would be nice if you were by his side when and if I talk to the press."

"Okay, but how am I going to know when you're done with the police? I'm not going to hang around the Brick House for three or four hours while the police interrogate Turk." Every time I set foot in that building, I had flop sweat fear that I'd never leave.

"I'm not going to give the police three or four hours to question Turk. They'll be working off my timeline." The outline of talons started to show inside his velvet gloves. "I'll give them an hour. They'll have to charge him to have him stay longer."

"That's always a possibility. Detective Sheets may be the lead on this case, but Denton is the senior detective and she has a short attention span." I told him about her threat to me over the phone. "She's liable to slip the bracelets on Turk and charge him with illegal trespass into Shay's house just to hold him while they wait for the DNA tests to come back."

"We'll cross that bridge when, and if, we have to."

I hoped that bridge wasn't over a moat.

CHAPTER TWENTY-FOUR

AN UBER DRIVER dropped me in the parking lot behind the Brick House at 12:10 p. m. the next day. Elk texted twenty minutes earlier to tell me they were done and to come down to the station, almost two hours later than I expected him to. That told me things didn't go according to plan. Which meant things didn't go well.

We agreed to meet behind the Brick House and sneak up on the press who, he informed me, were camped outside the front entrance. I tapped my way up the middle of the parking lot toward the back entrance. It was really only an exit unless you were a cop and had a name tag key card to enter. I avoided the parked black-and-white squad cars, which hovered like blurry baby killer whales through my sunglasses.

My chest filled up and the back of my neck tingled. Usually, this meant I sensed danger. Today it meant something else. Excitement. Not because I was at the Brick House. Because I could differentiate the light and the dark of the cop cars. My natural skepticism tempered my excitement with caution, but the proof was right in front of me.

My vision was improving.

Door hinges squeaked above me. A dark hole opened in the gray background of the Brick House and a blurry form emerged, followed by a larger one.

"Rick." Elk Fenton. "We'll come down to you."

The forms descended from what I remembered was a platform off the back door of the police station.

"How did it go?" I asked.

"Challenging, but nothing we couldn't handle." Elk.

"A shit show." Turk.

"It wasn't that bad. Detective Denton is now the lead detective and she's a bit belligerent. But, we're still in control of the facts."

"That's bullshit." A higher-pitched tenor than Turk's normal baritone. "Denton kept telling me that I needed to confess before the DNA came back. That I'd have a better chance at a plea bargain."

"That's a standard tactic from an old-school cop like Denton," I said. She'd badgered me and played psychological games when she had me cornered in a square white room a few years ago. I was still a free man. "Of course your DNA is going to be in Shay's house. And you told them about grabbing her, right?"

"I told them everything, but they have something we don't know about. I'm sure of it." Turk, still on the high wire. "Denton smirked at me the whole time I was in there."

Elk's silence didn't reassure me, or probably Turk, that everything was under control.

"What could they possibly have if you told them everything?" I spoke when Elk didn't.

"I don't know. I didn't kill Shay, but I think they have something they think can prove that I did."

That wasn't a confidence-building denial.

This time Elk spoke up before I could.

"If this proceeds further, we'll learn whatever surprises they think they have and we'll be able to counter them. Rest assured." Elk, calm, in control. The lawyer I'd seen get acquittals in six of the seven cases I investigated for him that he didn't plea down to lesser offenses. But none of them had been murder cases.

"I just want to get the hell out of here and go home." Turk.

"We have one last task. It will only take a few minutes." Elk, cajoling like he was talking to a recalcitrant youth.

"I don't want to talk to the press. That will just make things worse."

"Turk, we discussed this. You're not going to talk to the press. I am and you're going to stand next to me with your head up and shoulders back with a concerned, but not anxious look on your face. Exactly like we practiced this morning."

"Fuck that." Turk moved toward the sidewalk. "I'm going home."

"Turk!" Elk's voice a sharp whisper. "Come back here. This is important. Even more important than before we met with the detectives."

There it was. Seasoned criminal defense attorney Ellis Fenton was worried right alongside Turk. And me. He must have also feared they had something they were holding back. A bombshell. The evidence in the hedge at Shay's apartment that the crime scene techs examined behind the screen yesterday morning?

Whatever it was, Elk Fenton was already playing the long game. He expected Turk to be arrested for Shay Sommers' murder, but Turk wasn't ready to deal with that, yet. Still, Elk knew he needed to get in front of the press to try to influence them and, more importantly, the potential jury pool watching from their homes.

The kind of maneuver that disgusted me when I was a cop. Before I got on the wrong side of the table in an interrogation room. Even now, the tactic bothered me when I thought a defendant was guilty. Presumed innocent was a nice theory, but it flew in the face of human nature. The police had the advantage of authority and a jail. Snap judgments by the press only added weight to the guilty side of the scale. We humans are only human. But Turk was a friend and I'd presumed him innocent.

So far.

"He's right, Turk. Let's go stand in front of the press and get a jump start on the police." I put my hand on the other side of the scale. "If it turns out we didn't need to, no harm done. Let's do it and move on."

The large blurred-edged square mass rejoined Elk and me.

"Okay." Elk back in command. "Heads up, shoulders back. Once we get to the landing in front of the building, I want to make a statement. You two stand on either side of me, but a step behind. Remember, engaged but resolute. Rick—"

"I know, engaged, resolute, and blind. I'll keep the shades on and make sure my cane is visible in front of me during your statement."

"Well . . ." He seemed to be thinking. Then, "Perfect. Do you need guidance walking up to the entrance of the building?"

I didn't need help, but I still needed the cane. I still had a long way to go before I wouldn't. If I ever made it that far.

"I'll manage. Thanks." I tapped the cane and took a step toward the sidewalk. "Besides, tapping along with the cane helps sell my virtuousness."

"You get it," Elk said.

"What bullshit." Turk.

Sure enough, once we turned the corner from the parking lot onto the sidewalk, shouts and dashing footsteps assaulted us. Blurred forms pressed in on us. A hand on my inside shoulder, helping to guide me. Large and strong. Turk. He was either concerned about the crush of people around me, or he'd come over to Elk's way of thinking. Show the world what a good guy you were and help the blind man.

I didn't know which. Didn't matter. Either way, he'd made the right call.

"Are you a suspect in Shay Sommers' murder, Mr. Muldoon?" A familiar voice. Cathy Cade from Channel Six News. She'd shouted a few questions at me in the past.

"Is an arrest imminent?" Another woman whose voice I didn't recognize.

"Did you kill your girlfriend?" a male voice shouted above the rest.

None of us responded. Finally, we made it to the entrance of the Brick House and Turk guided me up the two stairs behind Elk. We squared up behind him, just outside his shoulders. I stood, stoic, with my cane in front of me. Playing my part in this melodramatic, yet necessary, skit for the press.

"Folks, my name is Ellis Fenton. I'm an attorney and I'm going to speak to you on behalf of Thomas Muldoon." In command, but friendly. "Mr. Muldoon is grieving the loss of his girlfriend, Shay Louise Sommers. Despite this paralyzing grief, he voluntarily came down to police headquarters this morning because he wants to give the police any information he can that will help them apprehend Shay's killer. To the people watching this in their homes, if you have any information that can help solve this heinous crime please contact the La Jolla Police Department."

Elk gave out the LJPD tip line. Brilliant. Turk and his lawyer wanted to find the truth as much, if not more than, LJPD did. He beat them to the punch with this mini press conference.

"Where were you when Miss Sommers was murdered, Mr. Muldoon?" The same loudmouth, at the same volume, who asked Turk if he murdered Shay.

"Is Rick Cahill here in support of Mr. Muldoon?" Cathy Cade.

"Mr. Muldoon is not going to answer any questions or give any interviews at this time. He's in a state of shock and in tremendous grief." Slight annoyance in Elk's voice to reinforce his statement. Jackals feeding at the trough of an innocent citizen's pain. "In the meantime, we're going to let the police do their job and hope you will, too. Mr. Cahill is a lifelong friend of Thomas Muldoon, or Turk, as he's known to his friends and hundreds of San Diegans who regularly dine at his restaurant. Many of you already know Rick, whose heroic actions in tracking down his wife's killer cost him his own eyesight in Santa Barbara last year. The same Rick Cahill whose life was saved by Turk seven years ago, costing Turk his mobility. These two heroic men share a bond that can never be broken."

Laying it on as thick as hot tar.

"Is it true that Mr. Muldoon hired a private investigator to find out if his girlfriend was cheating on him?" Loudmouth again.

The press was unimpressed by our "heroics." That was old news. Their headlines and ratings were now tied to the death of a beautiful young woman and the local restaurateur the police questioned about her murder.

"Any further questions can be directed to my office. I trust you'll honor Mr. Muldoon's privacy and let him grieve in peace during this very sad time. Thank you for your attention." Elk's form stepped down the stairs and Turk guided me after him.

"Is Rick a part of the defense team?" Cathy Cade.

"There is no defense team. Rick is here to support his friend." Elk waited for Turk and me to catch up, then led us down the sidewalk. The mob of reporters encircled us. A buzzing swarm of wasps.

"Is it true that the District Attorney's Office is considering impaneling a grand jury to indict Mr. Muldoon?" Loudmouth.

Turk's guiding hand squeezed my shoulder so hard that I twisted out of his grasp. I hoped the cameramen or women didn't get a shot of that.

The wasps kept buzzing until we got into Elk's car in the Brick House parking lot and drove away. A BMW Series 3 as Elk informed me last night. Not a Mercedes Benz Maybach but plenty of room in the front passenger seat for me and my cane.

Nobody said anything as we cleared downtown La Jolla and got halfway down Torrey Pines Road.

"Do you believe what that reporter said about a grand jury?" Turk, from the back seat. His voice unsteady. "He seemed to have inside information."

"I doubt it. Way too premature." Elk in a calm cadence. "That reporter is just trying to boost his image. No way the DA has the DNA test results back yet, and even if they did, your DNA at the scene is easily explained. If they impanel a grand jury, it would be with a weak case and they would be very unlikely to get an indictment. And even if they somehow did get an indictment and charged you, they'd have very little compelling evidence. We would prevail."

"Easy for you to say. You won't be the one in jail."

"I've seen Elk in a courtroom, Turk." I tried to match Fenton's tone even though I was worried, too. "He's an excellent lawyer. That's why I wanted you to talk to him. But we're getting way out in front of ourselves because of one loudmouth reporter looking to raise his profile. Trust Elk, he knows what he's doing."

Turk didn't say anything for the rest of the drive. Elk pulled to a stop in front of his house.

"Don't answer your phone for the next few days unless you know who it is," Elk said as Turk opened his door. "Today went exactly according to plan. You did very well."

"Thanks for your help. Both of you." His voice, dead, devoid of emotion like he was completely spent. And this was only day two. The door closed and the car pulled forward.

I turned toward Elk and saw a dark outline against a changing gray background as he drove. "If today went according to plan, we must have had the wrong plan."

"No. Today didn't go well."

CHAPTER TWENTY-FIVE

I SPENT THE next couple hours voice commanding my computer and listening to it talk back to me. I learned all I could online about Keenan Powell and Blank Slate Capital, LLC. Which was surprisingly little for an investment firm that supposedly handled hundreds of millions in investments. Blank Slate Capital had only been around since 2010, so it came after the market crash and derivatives mess of 2008. Founder Chuck Baxter's bio described him as a self-made millionaire who was a financial advisor before he started day trading in the stock market and eventually starting his own hedge fund.

Keenan Powell's Blank Slate Capital bio said he got his law degree from the University of Idaho and was an avid outdoorsman who worked on a cattle ranch when he was a teenager. Powell had been with Blank Slate Capital since its inception. The only other information I could find on him was that he went to the College of Southern Idaho for a year before earning a degree in finance from Boise State, and records of his marriage license, divorce, home ownership, and his Idaho, Nevada, California, and New York Bar licenses. No mention of membership in any attorney associations or organizations. That seemed unusual to me. All of the lawyers I knew were in some sort of association. The American Bar Association being the most prominent.

The best thing that came from my search was that I could make out the dark outline of my laptop and the blur of light that made up its screen. I squinted my eyes down into slits. The outline of the computer sharpened, but I could still only see fuzzy light in the middle. No images. No words. No individual colors. Just gray light.

I still had a long way to go. Hopefully. But I stopped betting on hope a long time ago.

I walked Midnight on our horseshoe trek around the block ten times, then took him into the backyard and threw the tennis ball with him. Something my neighbor's daughter, Micalah, did with Midnight four times a week after I'd pay her to clean up his poop. Now I threw the ball and could see a blur of black streak across the gray. Huffing wolf breaths as he sprinted back and forth. He dropped the saliva-soaked ball into my outstretched hand again and again. This was one day the glop on my hand didn't bother me at all.

I hit my garage gym next. Arms, legs, core. Then the heavy punching bag hanging from the rafters that I still had from my teenage Golden Gloves boxing days. Its outline bent out away from me at forty-five degrees by my rapid left-right combinations. I could have made solid contact with my eyes closed or completely blind. One final digging left hook and right cross and I bent over and dropped my hands to my knees. Sweat rolled off me and my breath huffed in and out. The physical expenditure felt good. Necessary.

I hit the bag most days for a workout and to keep my reflexes fresh. Today was different. More power and ferocity, unmatched since my boxing days. I was working something else out. Something internal. Visceral. But unknown.

I trained like I was going into battle, but I didn't have an enemy. Not one that I could see. But I sensed one out there. The Invisible Man wearing the Dove deodorant? Was he even real or just a figment of my vision-starved imagination? A combination of three or four innocent men who crossed my path and my own fear? Maybe. But something deep inside me that I couldn't fully comprehend or describe told me to get ready.

For war.

CHAPTER TWENTY-SIX

MOIRA CALLED AFTER I got out of a post-workout shower.

"I saw you on the news." Disappointment in her voice. I'd been on the news a lot in my life. Too much. So, I didn't expect to hear elation from her for the novelty of it. But I didn't expect to hear displeasure, either.

"I told you I was going to continue to investigate for Turk."

"I didn't know that that included being one of the dogs in the dog and pony show Ellis Fenton put on today."

"Not my idea, but I was happy to do it." Emphatic, bordering on belligerent. "I know better than anyone how the press can try someone on the airways who hasn't even been arrested. Turk deserves to be seen for who he is before the press tears him down."

"Yet."

"Yet what?" A low boil in my voice. I wished I'd let the call go to voicemail. Moira on my side was welcome, but always a challenge. On the other side, she was a problem.

"Turk hasn't been arrested, yet." She hit the T hard in "yet."

"You know something I don't?"

"I know enough to tell you that you should take an unvarnished look at your friend and then walk away."

"I don't walk away from my friends."

"But you also don't turn your back on the truth." Big sister anger trying to educate her little brother about how life worked. "And seeking justice is always where your true loyaltys lie."

"Tell me what you're not telling me." Maybe her contact at LJPD told her something he shouldn't have.

"Did Turk tell you he went to Shay's after we talked to him at Muldoon's Wednesday night?"

"As a matter of fact, he did." But only when I asked him about it after Detective Denton blurted it out to me on the phone. "And he told that to LJPD along with everything else he knows or did. Something else I should know?"

"I'm telling you as a friend, quit working for Ellis Fenton right now. I know what you're capable of when you think you have the truth on your side."

What I was capable of. Moira knew me too well. But, in some ways, she only knew the old Rick. My vision, or lack of it, wasn't the only thing that had changed. I was on Turk's team, but I wasn't an avenging angel. Or devil. I wanted to find the person who killed Shay, but not so I could impose my own justice. So I could keep Turk out of jail or help free him if he was ever arrested. I didn't have an allegiance to Shay Sommers. I was sorry she was dead and wanted her killer to be caught, but I didn't have to be the one to bring him in.

Or put him down.

"I appreciate your concern." I kept my voice even because I meant the words. "But I'm not wrong. Turk is innocent."

"But what if he's not? What if he killed her?" Hard.

"No *what ifs*. He's innocent."

"You might change your mind." A pause, then a loud breath. "You have to promise me you won't tell Ellis Fenton what I'm about to tell you. My contact went way out on a limb on this one."

Moira was my best friend. But Turk used to be and he needed me now more than he ever had. More than Moira ever needed me. And Elk Fenton was the one man who might be able to keep Turk out of jail.

Moira had information that I needed. I just had to tell a lie. To her.

"I can't promise that. I'm still working for Turk. Elk Fenton is his lawyer." Maybe I really had changed.

"Why do you always have to make things so damn hard?" More pain than anger. "They found the murder weapon. A necktie. It matches a man's suit found in Shay's closet. Looks like it's one of Turk's."

"You just proved my point." My body unclenched for the first time today. Now I wouldn't even have to tell Elk. Moira's bomb was a dud. Thankfully for both of us. "I've known Turk for twenty-six years and have never seen him in a suit. Much less a tie."

"If you look up photos for this year's Water 4 Life Global's Casino Night for a Cause, you can find Turk in a jacket and tie."

"I can command my computer to pull it up, but I won't be able to see the picture. I'm blind." Too sarcastic for the situation, but the "Turk was guilty because Doctor Donnelly was guilty and I shouldn't have taken the case bit" was wearing thin. "So Turk bought or rented a suit and tie for one charity event. Doesn't make it the same tie. A lot of ties go with a lot of suits."

"Well, the one in the photo has the exact same colors and pattern as the one LJPD found in the hedge outside Shay's home this morning."

The hedge. Where LJPD's crime techs set up the screen this morning to keep the press and civilian eyes away from potential evidence. It couldn't be the same tie. Turk wasn't capable of murder.

He couldn't be.

CHAPTER TWENTY-SEVEN

ELK FENTON SAT across from me at the picnic table on my deck the next morning. The outline of an outstretched limb connected with Midnight's head. Fenton had never been to my house before, but Midnight sensed that he wasn't a threat. To either of us.

I told Elk about the tie over the phone. However, I didn't tell him where the information came from. Only that it came from LJPD. He didn't press me on the source. The source didn't matter right now. The information did.

"Did you tell Turk about the tie?" I asked. I considered telling him myself before I called Fenton, but didn't want to get in the way of the attorney/client relationship.

"Not yet." Grim. None of the optimism that bouyed his voice when he talked to Turk yesterday morning. The same way he sounded on the phone after I told him about the tie. "That's why I came over here. I wanted to confer with you first."

I didn't like the sound of *confer*. It was something government officials dragged before Congress did with their lawyer while they held their hand over the microphone. Secrets. Strategy. Guilt.

"I'm not your client. What is there to confer about?"

"The evidence isn't lining up in Turk's favor." He paused. For effect? If so, it worked. "Shay wasn't raped, which eliminates sexual predators as possible suspects. Turk was at the crime scene within a couple hours of the victim's death. Witnesses heard a fight. He admitted to assaulting Shay. He has no alibi. He probably owns the murder weapon. His DNA will be on it and on the victim. And he has the oldest motive in the world. Jealousy. It's likely that the police will eventually arrest Turk for the murder. Perhaps soon. I just wanted you to be prepared."

That had always seemed like a possibility, but hearing it come from the only lawyer I trusted sucked marrow from my bones. My legs felt wobbly. And I was sitting down.

"How can I help?" My voice, a broken tree limb.

"You can try to keep Turk's spirits up." No easy task with everything that's happened. "And when we go before the press again, I want you there right by my side as a visible embodiment of a hero's sacrifice and an unwavering supporter of Turk Muldoon."

"Of course." Elk wanted me as a prop, an icon. The flag behind the president during a campaign speech. Kept in a box until the next time I'm needed to be seen. "But I meant regarding investigating the case. Talking to witnesses. I can start with Turk's neighbors to find out if any of them saw him arrive home after he left Shay's. Maybe we can nail down a timeline and a legitimate alibi before Turk's even arrested."

"That will all come if he's arrested."

"We have to get ahead of this." I stood up. Adrenaline pumping strength back into my legs. "Let's get started now."

"Turk hasn't even hired me, yet."

"I'll work for free for the time being." Then it hit me. I didn't make the cut. "You don't want me working this case, do you?"

"Of course I do. I just explained your role." Cajoling. "It's an important one. I need you to be the face of Turk's support. We're going to be in front of the press as much as possible, countering the prosecution. If it comes to that."

"Who's your investigator?"

"There hasn't been an arrest, Rick. I haven't even been hired, yet. Yesterday was pro bono."

"I know you, Elk. You're always prepared. Who do you have on call right now if this thing drops tomorrow?"

"If it does, you'll be a part of the team. An important part. I promise. We'll find something that fits . . ." He paused, but not for effect. He was searching for a lifeboat. "Something that fits your unique skills."

"Got it. The sympathy blind card. I got that covered." I really couldn't blame him. He would probably soon have a man's life in his hands and he'd made a thoughtful evaluation. He needed an investigator who could see and get out in the field. And he didn't even know about my epic fail on Prospect Street Wednesday night.

"I didn't mean it that way." Resolute, not defensive. "I already agreed to give Turk a discount if he hires me. I'm only going to be able to have the budget for a single investigator. A year ago, that would have been you. Now, it can't be. I'm sorry. I wish things were different."

So did I.

"Who'd you put on call?"

"Dan Coyote."

Coyote and I were friends once. Golfing buddies when he was a cop. Things changed when he found out about my past and I stepped on a case he was investigating. They got worse after he retired and picked up a paper badge like me and I tried to reopen one of his old closed cases from LJPD. We became rivals, enemies, vying for Fenton's business along with a couple other investigators.

I wished Elk would have picked one of the other two P. I.'s.

Salt in the wound.

CHAPTER TWENTY-EIGHT

TURK IGNORED MY phone calls and texts over the next couple days. I stayed cocooned at home throwing the ball with Midnight in the backyard and testing my eyesight. Each day, the outline of objects seemed to tighten by a fraction. I wasn't ready to go back to my ophthalmologist for tests, yet. I needed to build up a callous on my emotions first in case the tests weren't as optimistic as I was becoming.

Kris called me one morning while I sat on my deck conducting one of my own eye tests.

"Do you know how Turk is doing?" Concern in her voice.

"I haven't talked to him in a few days."

"I'm worried about him. I haven't talked to him since . . . since last Thursday." The day she and Turk found Shay's body. "He sent me a text the next day saying he was taking a few days off, but now it's been almost a week. I know that's normal for most people after they lose a loved one, but he won't even return my calls or texts."

"I'd give him more time. Some people need to grieve alone." But the pressure of the police investigating him for Shay's murder would make it difficult to truly grieve.

I didn't really start grieving Colleen until the day of her memorial service two months after her death. The day after the district attorney dropped the murder charges against me and let me out of jail. Even then, it took me almost fifteen years to close the wound of Colleen's death while I remained a suspect in her murder. Now there's a scar. Still tender, but the healing process has finally begun.

"I guess you're right." She paused. I sensed it wasn't a pause for me to jump in, but that she was gathering herself to say something else. "I saw you and Turk on the news last week. I guess Turk thought it was a good idea to hire a lawyer . . ."

More a question than a statement.

"It was only for the day. I talked him into it. We both know Turk's innocent, but it's smart to take precautions. Turk handled himself well when the police questioned him." A white lie. "The lawyer talked to the press to cut off their normal inclination to think the boyfriend did it."

"There are TV cameras and reporters outside the restaurant some nights when we open. It's awful. The reporters shout questions at me when I try to shoo them away. They ask me if Turk's in the restaurant, and when I tell them no, they ask if I think he killed Shay."

This was Kris' second go-round with the press hounding the restaurant. The first one was because of me. I tried to help someone accused of murder while I still worked there and I became a suspect. Kris was getting her fifteen minutes the hard way.

"Things will start to die down soon." More hope than certainty.

"Do you think . . ." Her words caught in her throat. "Do you think there's any way he could have done it?"

"No." Another doubter? The power of the press.

The media had resorted to calling Turk a person of interest in Shay's murder any time they did a story on her. At least they did the times I forced myself to check in. Even though I couldn't see them, I was certain the news ran photos of Shay throughout their stories on her. Standard operating procedure. Nothing lifted ratings like the murder of a beautiful young woman. *Dateline* and *48 Hours* had no doubt already sent producers down to San Diego. We were news for all the wrong reasons, but all the right reasons for the press.

Detective Denton, now the face, or for me, the voice, of the investigation always offered a no comment whenever a reporter asked her if Turk was a suspect. Which meant, not only was he *a* suspect, he was the *only* suspect.

"Good . . . I don't think he could either. Ah, I . . ." The pause again.

"What's bothering you, Kris?"

"I remembered something today that I saw about a month ago." Still needing a prod.

"What did you see?"

"I was having dinner with my boyfriend, Seth, at Nine-Ten and I saw Shay having dinner with a man I didn't recognize."

Nine-Ten is a restaurant just down the street from La Valencia.

"What did the man look like?"

"I'd say he was in his early forties. Pretty good looking. Nicely dressed."

"Black, white? Tall, short? Thin, fat? What color was his hair?" I didn't give her Moira's description of the man in the Italian suit who I believed to be Keenan Powell because I wanted Kris to fill in her own blanks.

"He was white, but he was sitting down, so it was hard to tell exactly how tall he was. I'd say average height and weight. His hair was brown and short. I think he had some gel in it. I was kind of shocked seeing Shay having dinner with another man."

The physical description matched Powell, but it could match two hundred thousand other men in San Diego County, too.

"You mean another man, another man, or just some other man? There's a difference."

"I know what you mean, but I couldn't tell and I didn't want to stare and have Shay see me." Stressed. Kris was probably beginning to question how well she really knew Shay and the same with Turk. "I had Seth look at them and he didn't think there was a physical connection between them, whatever that's worth. Seth thinks he can read people, but I'm not convinced."

An idea struck me that I should have thought of earlier. "Do me a favor. Look up Blank Slate Capital on your cell-phone and pull up the Our Team page. I'll wait."

"Why?"

"Look at the photo of Keenan Powell, the COO, and tell me if he looks familiar."

"Oh, I get it. Hold on." She was silent for twenty or thirty seconds. "I can't say for sure, but that could be the man I saw with Shay. The man at Nine-Ten looked older, but his picture on the website could be a few years old. I think it's him."

Keenan Powell was the man Shay met at La Valencia and Nine-Ten. Now, I was certain of it.

"How was their demeanor toward each other at the restaurant?"

"Well . . . that's what was kind of strange." Another pause waiting for a prod.

"Strange how?"

"I could only see part of Shay's profile, kind of a side angle from behind and to the right. I had a better view of the man."

"So, what was strange?" Kris didn't want to get to the point. Hopefully, there was one.

"Shay seemed fine when I first saw her and the guy." Voice hesitant. "But I glanced over when we got up to leave, and she looked really angry. Her face was red and she was leaning forward and gesturing with her hands. I'd never seen her like that before."

"Could you hear what she was saying?"

"No. We weren't close enough and the restaurant was loud."

"What was the man doing?" I asked.

"He just sat there with a calm expression."

"I take it you didn't ask Shay about her dinner with this guy?"

"Actually, I did." She let out a breath like there was no turning back now. "I saw her the next day and asked her what she did the night before."

"She told me she stayed home, at first. But she must have read something in my face, because then she said, 'I almost forgot, I had dinner with a friend.' I told her that I thought I saw her at Nine-Ten and asked who the friend was. She studied me for a second and then said it was a friend of her father's."

Her *father*? He was supposed to have abandoned Shay and her mother when Shay was three and died three years later. How the hell would she know who her father's friends were twenty-three years later?

"Did she ever talk to you about her father?" I asked.

"Not really. She told me once he abandoned her and her mother when she was a child, but she didn't really want to talk about it so I didn't press her."

"Did you think it was strange that she'd have dinner with a friend of her father's, much less even know who the man was?"

"Yes, I did, but I could tell she didn't want to talk about it."

"Don't take this wrong, but for Shay's best friend, you seemed to let a lot of things go. Most women I know keep pressing until they get to the root problem, especially with their friends." Maybe a stereotyping statement, but also maybe the reason why so many female lawyers work in district attorneys' offices as prosecutors. They could be relentless and tough.

"I guess I'm not like most women, then." Hurt. "Maybe if I'd been a better friend to Shay, she'd still be alive."

Shit.

"That's not what I meant at all. I'm sorry it sounded that way." Idiot. I'd offended someone going through the worst time of her life and who was doing all she could to help me. "I know you were a good friend to Shay and you're a good friend to Turk. He'd be lost without you holding down the restaurant right now. Did you ever tell him about seeing Shay with the man at Nine-Ten?"

If Turk knew that the man Shay met at Nine-Ten was a friend of her father's, would he have hired Moira to find out if Shay was cheating on him? Probably not.

"No. Shay asked me not to." She let go a long wavering breath, trying to hold it together. "In fact, she asked me not to tell anyone about it. She said she'd explain why later, but she never did. I let it drift into the background and eventually forgot about it until Seth took me to breakfast at Nine-Ten this morning before I came to work."

I was about to sign off, now convinced that Keenan Powell was the man Shay met at La Valencia the last night of her life, when something Kris told me last week bubbled up in my memory.

"When did Shay have that misunderstanding with your customers?" I asked. "The one where the woman claimed Shay called her husband a fucking coward?"

"About four months ago. Why?"

"I'm not sure. Thanks."

But something in my gut, the organ that I relied heavily upon as a private investigator, told me that Shay Sommers' two acting-out incidents were connected and that Keenan Powell knew more about her murder than Turk Muldoon did.

But my gut had been wrong before. With tragic consequences.

CHAPTER TWENTY-NINE

I CALLED TURK after I got off the phone with Kris. She was worried about him and so was I. But I also wanted to talk to him about the tie the police found outside Shay's apartment and about Shay having dinner with Keenan Powell at Nine-Ten. Respecting his grief and not saying anything negative about Shay was the decent thing to do. But LJPD was possibly only days away from knocking on his door with a warrant. I couldn't worry about grief and decency. I needed to find the truth. It was the only way to keep Turk out of jail.

He didn't answer so I left him a message to call me, then texted him. Silence. I gave him an hour then contacted Uber through the app on my phone. The driver dropped me in front of Turk's house around 10:45 a.m. The sun had been visible, even to my eyes, while I waited to be picked up in front of my house, but was hidden behind the morning haze when I got down to La Jolla. The smell of jasmine reminded me that it flowed down from the pergola above Turk's front porch.

I knocked on the front door and felt a slight tremor below my feet, then saw a shadow cross by the window in the door. But no answer. I knocked again. This time on one of the windowpanes in the door. Five or six annoying raps. The shadow reemerged and a creak and the whir of air signaled the door whipping open.

"I didn't return your calls or texts for a reason." Turk's baritone voice edged with annoyance. "Just like I ignored everyone else's. I want to be left alone for a while. You of all people should understand that."

"I do and I'm sorry to intrude." I felt as much as saw his hulking presence in front of me blocking entrance to his house. His only remaining sanctuary. His mass was still large and intimidating, but seemed to be less than when I last saw him. Maybe it was just that my improved vision now better defined his outline. Or, maybe he hadn't eaten since he found Shay's dead body last week. "But I might not have time to take your feelings into consideration. Let me inside so we can talk."

"What do you mean you might not have time?" His bulk still blocked entry.

"Let me inside and we can talk about it."

He moved away and the door squeaked all the way open. I tapped inside with my cane to a dark interior. I didn't need perfect vision to know that all the curtains were drawn and the lights were off.

I made it over to the sofa and sat down. The stench of whiskey mixed with sweat I'd smelled last week had distilled down to a desperate stink, hanging in the air like invisible fog. No cooking smells or even rotting food. Just desperation, embedded into every texture in the room.

Turk, backlit from gray light coming through the window in the front door, three-legged over to me. Even in the dim light, I could differentiate his legs from his cane.

My vision was getting clearer almost in real time. With the removal of one fuzzy filter after another.

"What did you mean about not having time to take my feelings into consideration?" Weary. The bluster of his guard dog growl blocking the door already drained away. As if he had to summon it to brace against the outside world and felt it ebb away with each step back inside his dark reality.

"Have you talked to Elk Fenton since last week at police headquarters?"

"He left me a couple messages, but I didn't return them. I'll call him if the police arrest me. Otherwise, what's the point?"

"So, you don't know about the tie?"

"What tie?"

Turk was literally and figuratively living in the dark. Sooner or later a spotlight was going to blast him in the eyes. I chose sooner.

"The one the police found in the hedges outside of Shay's house that was used to strangle her and belongs to you."

"What?" Turk shot straight up. "My tie? I don't even own a tie."

"You sure about that?" I stayed seated and calm. "What about the one you wore to the Water 4 Life Global Casino Night?"

"The what?" He sounded genuinely confused. "You mean that charity event Shay talked me into being a part of?"

"Yes. How you became involved doesn't matter. What does matter is that there are photos of you online at the event wearing a suit and a tie that looks exactly like the one the police found outside of Shay's apartment that they contend is the murder weapon."

Turk collapsed down onto a chair with a thump.

"I wore my old man's blazer. The same one I wear to weddings and funerals. And a pair of slacks I bought just for the charity deal." Soft voice, like he was recounting the wardrobe in his head. "Shay bought me a tie to wear for the thing. I only wore it that one night. I don't even know where it is now."

"I do. In LJPD's evidence room."

"This is why you came over? To tell me about some tie I wore once that the police think is a murder weapon?" He was gaining momentum, life back in his voice. I was happy to hear it even though it was through anger directed at me. "How could they even know that this tie was the murder weapon? How many thousands of other ties are there in San Diego? And why would I put the tie in the hedge if I just used it to kill Shay? This is all bullshit."

I'd thought a lot about that last question on my own. The LJPD theory must have been that Turk ran out of the apartment after strangling Shay and dropped the tie in the hedge without realizing it. But what if the killer put it there on purpose to frame Turk? Maybe he thought leaving it around Shay's neck was too obvious so he put it in the hedge, visible to anyone searching for evidence outside the apartment. He had to be pretty sure Turk's DNA would be on it and he knew Shay's was because he'd just used it to strangle her.

A well thought out plan by someone who'd been watching. The Invisible Man? Was he real or was I grasping at theories to convince myself that the most logical theory wasn't true? That Turk murdered Shay in a fit of rage.

I needed indisputable proof or a Turk confession to believe that.

"It probably is bullshit, but you need to know what you're up against." I let go my own long breath. "And I want you to face the fact that the tie LJPD found is probably the murder weapon and will have Shay's DNA on it. And yours, too. Even if you only wore it once, your DNA will be on it."

"Okay," Turk's form seemed to expand. "So what's your point, Rick? If you came over here to cheer me up, you failed miserably."

"You have to be ready when LJPD knocks on that door." I pointed to the only thing emitting light in the house he'd turned into a dungeon. The frustration of being a bystander in the dark boiled out of me. "Call Elk Fenton back. He's the one guy who can help you. He's defended people on trial for murder and gotten most of them off. Start reengaging in your own fucking life or you're going to lose control of it."

Turk's bulk shifted backwards and the chair creaked. His arms went up to his head like he was running his hands through his hair.

"I've been dealing with Shay's death and pretending the rest of this stuff doesn't matter."

"Everything matters." My voice calm now that I'd made Turk understand the shitstorm coming his way. "But that's not the only reason I came over."

I told him what Kris told me about Shay's dinner with Keenan Powell at Nine-Ten and her story that he'd been a friend of her father's.

"Shit."

"From what you told Moira and me, Shay hadn't seen her father since he abandoned her and her mother when she was a child. Right?"

"Yeah. None of this makes any sense." His head slowly moved from side to side. "I was such a fool."

"No, you weren't. You were in love."

"She lied. Right to my face. That's why I got so mad."

"You had a right to get mad."

Silence. I let it settle into the dark, desperate room.

Finally, "I'm yelling at her and the whole time I can feel the ring box in my pocket pressing against my leg."

"Ring box?"

"Engagement ring. I bought it before I suspected she was cheating on me." He laughed. The saddest laugh I'd ever heard. "The jeweler gave me a month to put it on her finger or return it for a full refund. I'd spent the first couple weeks trying to come up with a romantic idea for the proposal. Then I saw her sneaking down to La Valencia those two nights and I had to rethink everything."

"Why did you take the ring with you to Shay's that night?"

"Because the end of the month deadline with the jeweler was the next day. I went over to her apartment hoping she'd tell me about meeting the guy at La Valencia and have an innocent explanation for it. If she did, I was going to propose to her right then."

I didn't say anything. There wasn't anything I or anyone could say to make everything all right.

"I realize now what a desperate idea it was. I just needed any reasonable explanation that I could believe if I didn't examine it too hard. Anything slightly believable so I could put a ring on her finger and convince myself I'd let my imagination run wild with bad scenarios. If she accepted the ring, I'd know she loved me and everything else would work out. Stupid."

"No. Human."

Pounding rocked the front door and echoed in the living room. Turk's mass bolted forward off the couch. I stood up. More loud knocks.

"Who the hell is that?"

I didn't answer. I didn't want to be right.

CHAPTER THIRTY

I FOLLOWED TURK to the side of the front door and saw shadows through the multi-pane window.

"Shit." Turk's voice. A blast of air.

Two more loud knocks. Turk stayed in front of me but didn't answer the door.

"Thomas Muldoon, this is the La Jolla Police Department and we have a warrant for your arrest!" A command that penetrated the door and filled the room. "Open the door now!"

Turk stepped back and bumped into me. He spun away, and I grabbed his arm. Something hard came down on my hand and knocked it away.

"Police! Open the door!"

Turk bolted, three-legged, toward the kitchen where there was a door to the backyard, then a fence and overgrown open space. Running would only make things worse, and he couldn't outrun the police on three legs. Best-case scenario was a hard takedown. Worst case, a bullet.

Two burst strides and I dove at his outline.

"Battering ram!" From outside.

My arms wrapped around Turk's legs and we both went down hard. Two canes rattled along the wooden floor.

"Get the fuck off!" Turk wrested a leg free from my grasp and kicked me in the nose. A crack. My sunglasses flew off my face. Shooting stars burst inside my head. But I held onto the one leg.

The door exploded open, thwacked the wall, and shook the house. Multiple footsteps thundered across the open living room into the kitchen.

"Police! Stay on the ground! Arms and legs out wide! Now!"

I let go of Turk and slid off his leg flat on the floor. My head twisted toward the shouts. Four or five shapes with triangle tops like they were holding guns in two handed shooting platforms. Hopefully with their trigger fingers on trigger guards.

"On your stomach! Now!" The cop outline nearest me shouting at Turk. I was already belly down. Unmoving, except for the blood flowing from my broken nose.

A splot ahead of me. Must have been Turk rolling onto his stomach.

Shadows flashed across my eyes and someone snapped a cuff around my right wrist and wrenched my arm from my side and yanked it behind me at the same time something hard and round pressed into the small of my back. Probably a knee. Left arm next. Then the snap of the twin cuff on my left wrist. Hands patted me down, removing my wallet, phone, and keys from my pockets.

Scuttling sounds beyond my view.

"Stay down!" A hard thump vibrated along the floor.

"Thomas Muldoon, we have a warrant for your arrest for the murder of Shay Louise Sommers." A different voice than the ones that had shouted.

"This is bullshit!" Turk. A wail.

A rustle and a couple groans. A giant outline loomed above me. Turk bordered by two cops holding his arms.

The mass shuttled from the kitchen into the family room toward the front door. The thump of Turk's damaged leg vibrated along the floor with each step.

"I'll call Fenton and get him down to the police station!" I yelled at the receding shadow.

"Fuck you, Rick." And then the shadow was gone.

"Mr. Cahill, we're going to stand you up. Okay?" The voice that declared Turk under arrest.

He must have looked at my driver's license from my wallet.

"Okay."

Shadows. Two sets of hands grabbed my arms and helped me up to a standing position.

"Whoa!" A voice I hadn't heard yet.

"Officer Horn!" The voice in charge, angry.

Then I realized why the reaction. Turk had broken my sunglasses along with my nose. They'd fallen to the floor. Blood dripped over my lip into my mouth. The coppery tang I'd tasted too often in my life. This time because a friend thought I'd betrayed him.

But the blood and my broken nose weren't what shocked Officer Horn. It was the divot in my face beneath my left eye.

"I'm going to remove your cuffs, Mr. Cahill." The outline in front of me. The man in charge. Probably the sergeant of the takedown team. Detectives Denton and Sheets would be waiting for Turk back at the Brick House. "Are you going to behave yourself?"

"Yes."

The outline stepped behind me and took the cuffs off my wrist, then appeared back in front of me.

"What just happened in here?"

"Who am I speaking with?" I stared at the dark outline and could make out the oval of a head, but not its features. "I can't read your badge, so I'd like to know who you are."

"So, it's true. You really are blind." Surprise more than mock in his voice, which suddenly sounded somewhat familiar, though I didn't know from when. Definitely before my blindness.

"Yep." I let the disgust fill my voice. "I'm still waiting to learn who I'm speaking to."

"We've actually met before. I'm Sergeant Ives, LJPD."

Ives had been promoted since he and his partner harassed me for their old corrupt boss who was now long gone. Nice to know LJPD hadn't changed its stripes with Sergeant Ives and Detective Denton still around. I feared for Turk and the railroad job rolling his way.

I stuck my hand out in front of me, but not for a handshake.

"I'd like my property back."

"A couple questions, first."

"Am I under arrest?" My hand still out, palm up.

"Not presently."

"Then please give me back my property."

Movement from the shadow in front of me, then the weight of my phone rested in my hand and the thump and chink of my wallet and keys on top of it. I stuffed the wallet and keys in pockets then commanded my phone to call Elk Fenton.

"Hang up the phone, Cahill. I have a couple questions to ask you."

I pressed the phone against my ear, wiped blood from my throbbing nose, and smeared it on my jeans.

"Rick?" Elk.

"They arrested Turk. He's on his way to the Brick House." I hung up and commanded my phone to contact Uber.

"Hold on, Cahill." Ives. "I didn't say you could leave."

"Unless you're arresting me, you have seven minutes to ask questions before my ride gets here."

"Cancel Uber. I'll give you a ride home."

I thought back to the last time I was in a car with Sergeant Ives. In the back of a police cruiser going to the Brick House, not my home. Handcuffed on trumped-up charges.

"I'll pass, thanks." I put the phone in my pocket and realized I was missing something much more vital than a phone, wallet, or keys. "Can someone hand me my cane?"

"Your cane?"

"Yeah. It's what I use to see when I walk." The cane had to be visible to Ives. I dropped it in the kitchen right near where we were now standing when I tackled Turk. "Could you hand it to me or would you rather watch me crawl around on the floor looking for it."

Ives didn't say anything or move. Possibly considering if he'd prefer me crawling around in my own blood over an act of human decency. Finally, the mass in front of me twisted one way then the other, then centered back in front of me.

"Horn, retrieve Mr. Cahill's cane."

Movement from another shadow.

"Which one? They're two." Horn.

"The white one," I said. I'd forgotten that I'd knocked Turk's cane out of his hand when I tackled him. The cops took him to jail without his third leg. "The other one's Thomas Muldoon's. Is anyone going to take it to him at the holding cell at the Brick House?"

"It's potential evidence. We have a search warrant for the house." Ives.

Turk would feel vulnerable and more isolated without his cane.

"Here you go, sir." Officer Horn.

I stuck out my hand and the shadow put my cane in it.

"Thanks."

"What happened in here just now?" Ives.

"You busted in the door and arrested an innocent man for murder."

"Still a tough guy. Even when he can't see." Ives chuckled. Not derisively. Admiration hidden under the laugh? "When we entered the house, you and Mr. Muldoon were wrestling on the floor. You appear

to have a broken nose. Did Mr. Muldoon assault you when he attempted to evade arrest? Do you want to press charges?"

"You seem to have the facts wrong, Sergeant. Again." I stared at the
dark outline in front of me. "Mr. Muldoon and I were wrestling, but
it was a self-defense workout routine we put ourselves through. We
have to be ready for the worst as disabled citizens."

"We saw Muldoon through the window in the door. We know he
was trying to flee."

"Turk hasn't fled anywhere since he took a bullet in his back saving
my life."

"Do your workouts usually end with a broken nose?" His outline
shifted, like he put his hands on his hips.

"No. Today was an exception."

"You're sticking to that story?"

"Yep. And I'd better head outside or I'll miss my ride." I tapped my
cane around Sergeant Ives and walked toward the front door.

"Your friend's a violent killer, Cahill. Your broken nose is nothing
compared to what he did to that poor girl."

CHAPTER THIRTY-ONE

I GOT INTO the back seat when my Uber arrived. That way, the hole under my left eye would be at a distance and require the driver to peek in the rearview mirror to look at. I didn't want to frighten the driver. I just wanted to go home.

There wasn't anything more I could do for Turk. Elk Fenton was already on his way to the Brick House where Turk would be deposited into LJPD's holding cell before he was transferred to the San Diego County Jail. He'd be arraigned the next day and, unless he made bail, would have to spend upwards of a year in jail before his case went to trial.

"Are you all right?" A female voice pulled me out of my head. The driver.

"Yes, I'm fine." I graded on a curve.

"Are you sure you don't want me to drive you to the hospital instead of the address on Cadden Drive?"

My nose. The blood had dried but I didn't have anything to use to wipe it off. I was worried about an old scar and forgot about my fresh wound. I couldn't hide either.

"No, I'm fine. Thanks." Once again, even in the violent whirlwind of my life, I was reminded there was still goodness in the world. Strangers willing to help the injured, the helpless, and the innocent. There'd been times in my life when I'd been all three. Even innocent.

The driver dropped me in front of my house. I got out of the car, but something wasn't right. There was a large rectangular form in the driveway. A car. The car I still owned and never used was in the garage collecting dust. Maybe the driver dropped me at the wrong address. I knew I was on the right street because the last three months of being driven in the dark in my hometown had carved the turns and sequences into my memory. But the car in the driveway made me reshuffle. The shapes seemed right for my house. My front yard had a lawn and the house I stood in front of was flat in front. Both my neighbors had succulents in their yards making for greater variety of shapes. No, I was at my house.

I tapped my cane along the driveway and bounced it off the wheels and undercarriage on the vehicle. Some kind of SUV, I guessed. I knocked on the front-seat passenger-side window. No noise inside. Leah drove an SUV, but she wasn't due home for four more days. Plus, I'd talked to her last night and she hadn't said anything about coming home early.

I made my way up the walk and was about to put my key in the lock when the door opened. Citrus and sandalwood scent. A willowy shadow.

Leah.

"Rick! Oh my God! What happened to you?"

Arms around my neck. Lips against mine. Tender, careful of my latest injury. A wet nose snuffled my hand. Midnight. Home. With my family. I melted into Leah's arms. She walked me over to the couch with Midnight prancing at my side and I sat down.

"What happened to your face?"

"I'll tell you in a minute. I want to breathe you in first." I pulled her down into my lap and her lips met mine again. We embraced, tight and warm. Silence. Time stopped. The last week faded away.

Leah finally rose from my lap and time started up again.

"We have to get some ice on your nose. Right away." Her slim outline rushed into the gray background of the kitchen.

Leah. We'd been together for less than two weeks when I was shot. We weren't even really a couple yet. Desperate circumstances forced us together and our relationship didn't have a definition when Leah stopped her life to help me start my new one. I hadn't seen her face in almost a year but I still saw her sunrise ocean blue eyes and warm blanket smile every night I closed my eyes in bed. Honey blond hair and square-chinned beauty. Smart, funny, and loving.

A gift. I believed her when she told me she loved me, but I'd never know if we would have survived this long together if I hadn't almost died.

Midnight's head pressed against my hand. I scratched him and heard the vacuum of the freezer door opening, the clank of ice cubes, then a splash of water from the faucet. Leah's shadow came back to me and sat down on the couch.

"Here." Firm cold cloth placed gently against the bridge of my nose. Pain vibrated along my nose and under my eyes. "Lean your head back and hold the ice. I'm going to clean the blood off your face."

I did as told with the ice and felt a warm damp cloth wipe my face. She had to use some pressure to get the dried blood off.

I used to keep ready-made pain-portioned bags of ice in my freezer when I was a private investigator. They came in handy every few months. After Santa Barbara and the loss of my vision, I thought all that was behind me.

Leah cleaned me up, went back into the kitchen, and returned with a bottle of water.

"Do you want me to take over on the ice?" A sweet upturn in her voice.

"I'm good. Thanks." I reached out my free hand, and she filled it with her own.

Leah was the first woman I'd been able to love completely since Colleen died. A true partner who'd been forced to handle too much of the burden of everyday life over the last nine months, while I rehabilitated, drifted, and avoided making a decision on what to do with my new, different life. How would she react when I told her I'd finally decided the next stage was going to be the same as the last stage? The one that had gotten me shot and stolen my vision.

Leah rested her head against my chest for the next ten or so minutes that I iced my nose. The pain numbed a bit, and I loaded up with 2,000 mg of Tylenol that she grabbed from the medicine cabinet.

"Maybe we should go to the emergency room?" She moved her head close to my face like she was examining me.

"Let's give it a day or two." I tried to inhale through my nose. A sliver of air twisted through my left nostril. Nothing through the right. I'd had my nose broken before. Sometimes all it takes to mend is ice and time. "If it's not better by then, I'll go to a doctor."

"Okay. I guess." She leaned back against the couch; her face still pointed at me. "Now, tell me what happened."

That would be tough to do, but I couldn't lie to her like I did to the police. She already knew about Shay's murder from an earlier phone call. I told her about Turk's kick to my face and his arrest.

"Turk did that to you?" She pulled away from the sofa back and sat erect.

"He was trying to get away from the police. He panicked. I don't blame him. Your freedom taken away is a scary thing. Especially when you're innocent."

"When you're innocent." Her voice flat as a concrete slab.

"What do you mean by that?"

"I talked to Moira yesterday." Another discussion that I didn't know about.

"Okay."

"She thinks Turk could have killed Shay in a fit of rage." Delicately stepping over each word.

Shit. The two most important women in my life, the two most important people in my life, thought Turk was guilty.

"He'd never do that." The throbbing in my nose, a stark counterpoint to my statement.

"Rick, you're a fiercely loyal man. That's one of the reasons I love you." She took my hand in both of hers and held it to her chest. "We both know the police are wrong sometimes, but most of the time they're right. They wouldn't arrest someone without compelling evidence. Let the system take its course." The cop DNA that bled through her father, brother, and sister ran through Leah's veins.

"I know Turk. I know in my gut he'd never kill the woman he loved." I also knew people did it all the time.

"Your gut has been wrong before." Flat and sad at the same time.

I got off the couch and walked into the kitchen. No cane needed, no steps counting off in my head.

"I'm sorry." I heard the release of the couch and footsteps coming toward me.

My gut had been wrong before. But it wasn't now. Not about the man who'd saved my life. It couldn't be.

"Don't apologize for speaking the truth." I walked to the refrigerator and pulled out a beer. I'd cut back on my drinking after I went blind. Getting from one place to another was difficult enough when you couldn't see. Stacking loss of equilibrium and clear thought on top was the kind of stupid I knew to avoid. Today I needed a beer.

"I just don't want you to get hurt." Leah.

"We're not going to agree on this so let's not argue about it and spoil your homecoming."

I took a sip of beer and walked to the butcher block island in the middle of the kitchen and sat down on a wooden stool. The sun glowed in from the kitchen windows and put the island's outline in relief from the golden background. Color I could actually see.

"Why didn't you tell me last night that you were coming home today?" I asked.

We talked every night on the phone while she was in Santa Barbara. My daily dose of tranquility during the turmoil of the last week. When I told her about Shay's murder, I left out the part about Turk being the prime suspect. I didn't want her to worry about my involvement and I needed the respite. A quiet reminder of my calm life with Leah the last nine months.

Apparently, I hadn't been the only one holding back pieces of the truth.

"I wanted to surprise you." Leah sat across from me and put a hand on my arm.

"You did. It's a nice surprise." I took her hand in mine. "How long before you have to go back up?"

Silence that sucked the air in the room into a vacuum. Whatever she said next wasn't going to be good news.

"That's why I came back down today." Hesitant. Uh-oh.

"I say *back up*. You say *back down*. Which is it? I thought San Diego was your home now."

"That's what I wanted to talk to you about." Her voice lifted with joy. "I think I've found a solution for both of us."

"O-kay." Life in the dark void had made me more reliant upon people, but even more protective of the insulated world I had left. I selfishly clamped onto it and didn't want to let it go.

"I discovered this nonprofit called DefenseAble and—"

"Defensible?"

"No. Defense and Able together. DefenseAble. They teach self-defense to people with physical disabilities." Real enthusiasm in her voice. And a hint of desperation. "I talked to them about you and they already knew your story. They'd love to have you come work for them. It would be a great opportunity for you. You'd be able to help people. I know that's why you became a cop and a private investigator. This would give you a chance to make a tremendous impact on people's lives who really need it."

"And I'm guessing this is in Santa Barbara?" My voice was less enthusiastic than Leah's.

"Yes. People up there think you're a hero."

Anti-hero to hero in fifteen short years. But hero or anti-hero didn't really matter to me. San Diego was my home. And where I was needed.

"I'm in the middle of Turk's case right now." Not officially, but I was all in.

"You don't have to make a decision right this minute. But the job is there if you want it. All you have to do is meet with Mike Higginbotham at DefenseAble in Santa Barbara."

"What's the job?"

"You'd be kind of an ambassador for them. Meet with people and help advance DefenseAble's cause."

"You mean I'd be a fundraiser?"

Or a figurehead. The job I was suddenly most capable of doing whether it be for Turk Muldoon's defense or people trying to help the disabled. I was a symbol. An icon. An emoji. A representation of what was supposed to be. Instead of what was.

"Not really." Flustered. "That might be just a part of it. Why don't you talk to Mike and find out? He really wants to meet with you."

"I doubt he'll be willing to wait a year or more, because that's probably how long it will be before Turk goes to trial."

"He might. You should talk to him and find out." Zero inflection. I'd drained the enthusiasm out of her. She took a deep breath. "I just signed a contract to finish a 20,000 square foot home in Montecito."

"That's fantastic!"

"Thanks. This is the job that will change my business. I can't be a one-woman shop anymore. I'm interviewing people for two associate design positions and an assistant." Something was missing from Leah's voice. Joy. "I have to drive back home tomorrow. This job will take all of my time and focus for the next six to eight months, at least. I'll be living full-time in Santa Barbara."

CHAPTER THIRTY-TWO

Santa Barbara. The home for Leah that San Diego now could never be. A hole concaved my chest and sank into my stomach. The discordant, yet happy little life I'd greedily clung to was over. If I wanted to grab hold of what remained of it, I'd have to move to Santa Barbara. Shouldn't be a hard choice. The woman I loved lived there. A ready-made new life was waiting for me.

All I had left in San Diego was responsibility.

I didn't say anything.

"Let's get a fresh start in Santa Barbara. Where we fell in love." Leah's lips pressed against my cheek. "You know I love Midnight and he liked my house and my yard. As long as he's with you, he'll be happy. This is a chance of a lifetime for me and a chance for you to start your new life."

"My life is here." My voice, a hollow echo.

"It doesn't have to be." A wavering thread of optimism clung to her voice. "I understand that you want to be here for Turk. We don't have to decide anything right now. Let's drive up to Santa Barbara tomorrow. You, me, and Midnight. I have to interview potential assistants all day tomorrow and Thursday, but Friday and the weekend, I'm yours. Maybe you could talk to Mike at DefenseAble while I'm interviewing people. I know he's really excited to meet you."

Arms around my neck and another kiss on the cheek.

"Turk's arraignment is tomorrow. I have to be there."

"We can leave after the arraignment." Her grip around my neck loosened. "If you really think you have to be there, I can push my interviews back a few hours."

"I want to be there. I can't go up to Santa Barbara with you tomorrow. I'm sorry."

"I understand your wanting to be at the arraignment to show support for Turk. And I know you have to be here every day for the trial." Her arms released from my neck. "But what are you going to do between now and then?"

"I'm going to help with his defense."

"How?" No derision in her voice. Leah didn't mean it as an insult. She genuinely didn't understand how I could aid the defense investigation. I was blind, not yet DefenseAble.

"Elk Fenton wants me to be by his side at every press conference." I realized as soon as I spoke the words that they didn't give credence to my belief I was vital to Turk's defense. My only contribution was as a figurehead.

"He's not going to give a press conference every day or even every week. You can come down to San Diego when Elk needs you and then stay during the trial. I'm sure you could work something out with Mike Higginbotham if you take the job." Another long exhale. "Why are you making excuses not to come with me to Santa Barbara to at least hear what he has to say?"

"I don't want to be the sun-glassed face for DefenseAble. A symbol they prop up at a podium whenever they're on a fundraising drive. And even if I did, they wouldn't want their figurehead to be seen in court supporting an accused murderer. The kind of person their service was supposed to protect against." I couldn't tell her that I didn't want to live in Santa Barbara. That it would always be the place where Colleen was murdered. "I know you're trying to help, but that kind of job is not for me. I'm not exactly a people person."

"Can't you at least talk to Mike?" Desperate. "I'm sure the job is more than that. Whatever it is, it will be a new challenge. Something you may grow to love."

"I love you, Leah." My throat tightened. "I know the last year hasn't been fair to you. That I've been drifting and not doing my part while you tried to juggle living in two cities. You have to pursue your dreams in Santa Barbara. I want you to be happy. But in all the time I've been drifting, I missed the one thing that gave my life meaning. And I finally found it again."

"What?" Anxious.

"Pursuing the truth."

"What the hell does that mean?" The outline of her arms rose, like her palms were open in front of her chest.

"Helping people who have no other place to go. Working as a private investigator."

"Does Turk have nowhere else to go?" Her voice rising. "Are there no other investigators in San Diego who can help in his defense?"

"This is what I need to do."

"But how much can you really help? You can't drive. You can't see." Hard truth.

"Elk Fenton thinks I can help with Turk's defense."

"Doing what? Standing next to an accused killer while his lawyer lies to the press? The kind of symbol you don't want to be for a non-profit that actually helps people? Innocent people." Grit in Leah's voice. "Moira sent me a link to the press conference in front of police headquarters. Fenton and Turk are using you. You think either one of them cares about your well-being? About what this job has done to you? Turk doesn't. He broke your nose trying to run away from the police when you tried to keep him from getting shot. Is that what an innocent person does? Is that what a friend does?"

"Nobody knows how they'll react to facing the possibility of living the rest of their life behind bars until the police knock on their door. I know. I've been through it. I thought about running when my time came."

"But you didn't run because you were innocent. Only guilty people run."

"That's not true." But I knew it was ninety-nine percent of the time. I'd convinced myself Turk was in that rare one percent.

"I know you, Rick. You can't just be an impartial investigator taking direction from some lawyer or client on a case. You have to follow the facts wherever they take you, even if that puts you in danger." Frantic now. Her voice pleading. "You lost your eyesight because you wouldn't wait for the police to catch up with you on the bastard who killed my sister. You don't have a badge. You can't even see. This job almost killed you when you were completely physically capable. What's it going to do to you now that you're disabled?"

There it was. Disabled.

"I can't live cushioned in a bubble-wrapped world." I looked at the rounded outline of Leah's face. She lifted her arm up to it. To wipe a tear away? I didn't have comfort for her. Only the truth. "And my vision is starting to come back."

"What? You can see?" Joy blanketed in tears.

"I can't see objects, but I can see fuzzy outlines. I can see the yellow light of the sun coming through the outline of the kitchen windows, but I can't make out the color of your clothes. I can't see the beautiful features of your face, but I can see the outline of your head."

Arms around my neck pulled me to Leah's face. Her cheek, wet with tears, pressed against mine. Her body convulsed in gasps.

"I've prayed for this every day since you came out of the ICU." Her face pulled away, then I felt wet lips pressed against the concave scar under my left eye. "At first I prayed for you just to survive. I didn't care whether you could see or talk or even walk. I just wanted you to live. Once you got out of the ICU, I almost felt greedy to ask God to give you back your sight after he answered my prayers for you to live. But I asked him anyway and he's still listening."

"I don't know if I'll ever get my full vision back. I saw my ophthalmologist a few weeks ago when I first noticed a slight change, and she did some tests and didn't discern any change. She put it down to Charles Bonnet Syndrome. But it's real. The outlines of things are becoming clearer every day. I haven't gone back to Doctor Kim because I don't want her to tell me I'm not seeing what I'm seeing and convince my brain to stop registering it. I don't want scientific proof of what I can't see."

We held each other until Midnight wedged himself in between us. Leah laughed and pressed her head against his, probably in a kiss.

"You're the best man I've ever known, Rick. And the most stubborn, the most infuriating, and the most dangerous." Hands held each side of my face and Leah pushed her face close to mine. "But I don't want to lose you. You're my miracle. You should have died on my living room floor, but you didn't. Your will to live and God saved you. He saved you for a reason. We can figure out Santa Barbara and San Diego. We can make this work. Don't you want to try?"

"Yes." A tear ran down the edge of my broken nose.

We made love that night. Silently. Desperately. Like we feared, despite our efforts, that this might be the last night we'd be together under a roof we both considered home.

CHAPTER THIRTY-THREE

I MIGHT AS well have driven to Santa Barbara with Leah the next morning for all the support I managed to show Turk at his arraignment at the Central Division San Diego County Courthouse. I wore my scratched blackout sunglasses inside. They hid my two black eyes, but did nothing to disguise my swollen nose. And they made the use of my cane more of a necessity than in the past week. I'd barely tapped my way down an aisle and into a seat when Turk's case was called.

I could only make out blocky shapes in the front of the courtroom. A voice belonging to the judge read out the charges against Turk. Murder in the first degree and resisting arrest. The D.A. obviously overcharged in hopes of forcing a plea deal at the felony disposition conference. She had to know that no jury would convict on first-degree murder. Turk was innocent, but even if someone thought he was guilty, the only reasonable charge would be second-degree murder. A crime committed in passion, not premeditated.

My tackle of Turk didn't keep the D.A. from tacking on the resisting arrest charge. A bargaining chip that I'd paid for with a broken nose. Still, if I'd let him run, or limp in his case, from the police, some adrenalized cop on the takedown squad might have used a bullet to take the case out of the court's hands.

I did the right thing.

The judge's voice asked, "How do you plead?" after each charge.

"Not guilty, Your Honor," was Turk's answer. His voice strong. Resolute. Twenty-four hours in jail, and he hadn't been beaten down, yet. Good. Even if it was just a façade. A façade was better than nothing. Especially in jail.

The bail schedule for a murder suspect in California is $1,000,000 and can only be lowered if there were unusual circumstances for the defendant.

Elk Fenton rhapsodized eloquently about Turk's commitment to the community, being anchored to his landmark La Jolla restaurant, and even his disability incurred while he saved my life. The judge gaveled a million-dollar bail, scheduled an early disposition conference for the following Tuesday, and remanded Turk to the county jail.

I could faintly hear the footstep, thunk, and drag of Turk's cadence as he was led from the courtroom. At least they'd given him a new cane.

Twenty minutes later, I stood behind Fenton next to Amy Burroughs, Turks, married sister, on top of the steps of the county courthouse as he told the assembled press that Turk was one hundred percent innocent and looked forward to his day in court and the chance to clear his name.

Fenton concluded his comments and the media's shadows and forms faded away. The lack of clarity made me miss my new, broken, sunglasses. I accepted Amy's arm to descend the steps.

"Rick?" A familiar voice. "Cathy Cade with Channel Six News."

Shit.

"We're not taking questions, Cathy." Fenton's voice from the street level below.

"Is it true that Thomas Muldoon assaulted you?"

"That's a lie!" Turk's sister shouted as she maneuvered me down to the sidewalk.

Amy was five years younger than Turk, but shared his cornflower blue eyes and fiery burred red hair. But unlike him, she was happily married. I remembered another time Turk gave someone other than me a black eye. When a drunk trust fund punk groped Amy in the bar at Muldoon's. I wondered if Amy remembered.

Three separate masses emerged from the dark background when I hit the bottom of the steps.

"That's enough." Elk, the blob on the left.

"Is it true Mr. Muldoon attempted to evade arrest?" Cade, the smaller mass in the middle. She definitely had an inside source at the Brick House.

I let go of Amy's arm and snapped open my service cane. The top-heavy shape on the right closed in on me. Cade's cameraman. I kept my mouth shut. This was Fenton's game. I was just a silent cheerleader. A symbol.

"If any of these baseless allegations air on the news, I'll sue your TV station for libel." Elk, at his offended best. "How dare you sully the name of a good and decent man."

It sounded like a convincing show. Although, I knew Elk occasionally gave Cade deep background on celebrity court cases. A lot of back scratching, expensed lunches, and switching sides.

"That's a rap, Stu." Cade, her outline now a couple feet from me. "Put some ice on that nose, Rick. It looks awful. Ellis, see you at the EDC." Early disposition conference.

"You're a horrible woman!" Amy shouted as Cade and her cameraman's footsteps faded away. She'd never seen how the game was played before.

"Cathy's just doing her job." Fenton. His voice had a shrug in it.

"This is my brother's life." Annoyed.

"Yes, ma'am." Fenton, polite. "And I intend to see that he lives the rest of it as a free man."

"I hope so. That's why I'm putting a second mortgage on my house." Amy might not have been a member of Turk's defense team, but she was obviously paying for at least part of it. "Rick, do you need a ride?"

"Rick's going to ride with me," Fenton volunteered without asking me. "I'll call you tomorrow. Everything is going as expected."

"Um-hum." Amy sounded like she didn't think Elk was giving her her money's worth. "Thanks for coming down to support Turk, Rick. I know he really appreciates it."

I doubted he did just yet. Amy's footsteps disappeared into the traffic noise on Union Street.

"I'm parked on State Street. This way." He was on my left. "Would it help you to hold my arm?"

"I'll use the cane. Thanks."

I took off my sunglasses and hooked them on the neck of my dress shirt under the blazer I wore for the arraignment.

"Wow." Elk. "He really did a number on your face."

"The bullet hole was from someone else."

"I know." Reflexive. "For a kid growing up in La Jolla, you sure haven't had an easy life."

"Tract home section."

"I guess that explains everything." He didn't laugh. Maybe if I'd ever invited him over to my house as a kid he would have. Ellison "Elk" Fenton grew up on a hillside overlooking the Pacific Ocean in La Jolla. My family lived in a cul-de-sac at the bottom of a hill overlooked by other homes.

The sun was out and rectangle shapes trudged by on the street. Morning traffic in downtown San Diego. Pedestrian traffic as well as I tapped my cane alongside Elk and avoided individual outlines. Every shape and form, unrecognizable, but clearer than yesterday.

Those coming the other way got an unshielded look at my face. I hoped someday to be able to see their reactions.

CHAPTER THIRTY-FOUR

WE MADE IT to Fenton's car parked on the outdoor pay lot on State Street.

"Why the ride?" I asked after we both got into his BMW.

"I thought we could chat about next steps while I give you a ride home."

"We can chat, but can you give me a ride somewhere else?"

"Of course. Where do you need to go?" A hint of the goofy kid from my childhood leaked out in Elk's voice. I guess it was his default persona. Where he went when the mask slipped and he didn't have to be a ball-busting lawyer or a calm consigliere.

"Sunglass Hut on Prospect Street in La Jolla."

"Okay, but we'll probably pass near four or five of their stores before we hit La Jolla."

"I know. I want to go to this one, if you don't mind." I had a reason other than sunglasses to go to that area.

"Sure."

"What did you want to chat about?"

"I'd like you to accompany me to the EDC on Tuesday. From what Cathy Cade said, it sounds like the press is going to cover every hearing up to and through the trial and it's important to continue to show support for Turk. Especially, since he's been arrested."

"Sure, but you heard her question about Turk assaulting me." A low-slung car sped by on the right. I could see that it was a convertible. More progress. "She's obviously got an in at the Brick House and my presence is more likely to remind her to ask the tough questions no one else knows about yet."

"I'll worry about Cathy. I need you by my side." Confident lawyer.

"You think the D.A. will offer to drop the resisting arrest charge and dangle murder two at the EDC?"

"Yes, the D.A. must want a plea agreement. That's why she over-charged the case. That tells me their case isn't locked down. But I'm sure her prosecutor, Dana Hess, wants to go to trial. This has the potential to be a career-making case. The networks are already covering it. A murdered beautiful young blond woman is catnip to the press. A ratings bonanza."

"What about you?" I asked.

"What do you mean?"

"Is this a career-making case for you?"

Fenton had been nothing but professional in all the cases I'd worked for him, as well as in Turk's so far. But I always sensed a longing in him for a bigger stage. High-profile cases always went to other defense attorneys in town. Ones with higher name recognition. This case might be the one to put Ellis Fenton on the big stage.

Everyone was allowed higher aspirations. Especially someone who only got to see his two daughters every other weekend. But a man who had saved my life and, once, been like a brother to me was about to stand trial for murder. I couldn't take anything for granted.

"Yes, it would be." Sour. I'd hurt his feelings. The tagalong kid from my childhood. "But Mr. Muldoon's future is my primary concern. I thought you understood that."

"I do, but Turk's family to me. Glad we're on the same page." I was done apologizing for being who I was. I apologized to Leah, because she'd deserved it. Everyone else could take or leave me.

Elk was quiet the next few minutes as he maneuvered the Beemer through downtown San Diego. I hoped he wasn't waiting for an apology or a qualifier. The car negotiated a turn and smoothly accelerated. We were on I-5 heading toward La Jolla.

"Do you think Turk would agree to manslaughter if I could get his sentence to be under ten years? He could be out in five or six years."

A sniper shot from a thousand yards.

"No. He'd be admitting to something he didn't do. He's never going to do that. He's innocent. Guilty people plead down to manslaughter. Do you think he's guilty?"

"I don't think in terms of guilty and innocence. My job is to protect Turk's rights and get him the best possible result."

At least he was proving to me that Turk was his top priority. You grab headlines with a four-month pyrotechnic murder trial in court, not a five-minute plea deal.

"I thought you said the D.A. must not have a strong case. Turk pleading now doesn't make sense."

"I said she probably doesn't have a locked-down case, not that it wasn't strong." No-nonsense lawyer. "They've got Turk arguing with Shay at the murder scene near the time of death window. They have him admitting to putting his hands on her. They have the murder weapon, which belongs to him and will have both his and Shay's DNA on it. And they have Turk not being completely truthful in at least one of his interviews with them."

"At least one of his interviews? You're implying that he probably was less than truthful in the other one, too?"

"I'm looking at all possibilities." Calm, in charge. "And one of them is that the evidence will be strong enough for Turk to consider pleading to manslaughter if I can get it for him."

"Is one of those possibilities looking for evidence of other suspects?"

"Of course. And we may even get lucky if the DNA comes back and points to someone else." He didn't sound optimistic for that outcome.

"Why don't we get a jump on the investigation and get a list of convicted sex offenders in the area?"

"Because that's a waste of time and resources." A hint of annoyance. "Shay Sommers was not raped. There hasn't been any evidence that her home was burglarized. There was no sign of a break-in. Someone was probably let into her apartment or had a key and that person killed her. He beat her up and strangled her with a tie and then left. No sign of sexual assault. Shay was discovered naked, but Turk said she slept that way. No staging of the body. This wasn't a serial killer or a rapist. More than likely, the person who murdered Shay knew her."

I didn't say anything. The hum of the luxury car rolling over the cement highway might have soothed my nerves if Turk's lawyer hadn't just laid out the facts pointing to Turk as Shay Sommers' killer.

"He didn't do it," I finally said in a voice that didn't even sound convincing to me.

"That's what I have to somehow find a way to prove."

CHAPTER THIRTY-FIVE

ELK DROPPED ME in front of the Sunglass Hut on the corner of Prospect and Herschel in La Jolla and went to find a place to park. La Jolla's version of winter clamped down on the morning. Chilly enough for a sweater and a marine layer of fog that I could sense even with my limited eyesight. I went into the store and bought the same style sunglasses I'd bought last week and was done in less than five minutes. Frames that still blocked my scar, but with lenses that let in more light than my blackouts. I went outside, gave my phone a series of voice commands, then waited for Elk Fenton to arrive on foot.

I spotted him approaching a couple minutes later. I guessed that it was Elk just by watching his outline approaching me. Something loose and childlike about his gait.

"Hello, Elk." I caught him before he reached me.

"Whoa." His outline halted three feet in front of me. "How did you know it was me?"

"Your cologne." He wore Calvin Klein, but I'd spotted the gait before I smelled the cologne.

"Wow, you're good. Maybe I should scale back on the amount of cologne I wear." He chuckled. "Do you want to wait while I go pick up the car? I had to park all the way over on Silverado."

"No. How about you buy me a late breakfast or an early lunch at La Sala in La Valencia, instead?"

"I think they call that brunch, but I'm afraid I don't have time today. I have to go to the office and start prepping my associates for Turk's defense. I'm taking Sophie and Karissa to Cabo on Friday." His daughters and Cabo San Lucas in Baja, Mexico. "I'll be incommunicado for a few days, but will be back on Monday in time for Turk's EDC on Tuesday, but I want my team up-to-date in case there are travel issues. This will be my only chance to take the girls on a mini vacation until the trial is over."

"This brunch pertains to Turk's defense. I'll pay my own way if that will make it easier."

"No, that's okay." Flustered. "But let's make it as quick as possible. I really have to get to the office."

I was stealing valuable prep time in Elk's defense of my friend. Hopefully, the time would be well spent and give him another avenue to counter the prosecution.

"Roger."

We crossed to the other side of Prospect Street and headed north to La Valencia, the Grand Dame of La Jolla resort hotels. I tapped along with my cane, but might have been able to make the walk without it. Curbs and uneven sidewalks were still a concern. Today, I could even make out the outline of the domed tower on top of the Classic Mediterranean hotel.

We got a table right away in La Sala, the bar in the Grand Lobby. I folded up my cane and set it on the table, then made sure to sit with my back to the bar entrance. Something I never did when I had 20/20 vision. Back then, I wanted to meet all potential threats head-on. But today, I wanted Elk to see what I couldn't.

I pulled out my phone, unlocked it, and slid it across the table to Elk.

"Who's that?" he asked.

"Keenan Powell." I leaned in and kept my voice low. "The man I told you about who Shay Sommers met here at La Valencia the night before she was murdered. Keep an eye out for him. Coming or going from the elevator. He may still be staying in the hotel."

While I waited for Elk at the Sunglass Hut, I'd commanded my phone to pull up Powell's bio page from the Clean Slate Capital's website and took a screen shot, then saved it to my photos. I knew his picture was on the page.

"The man Ms. Sommers was having an affair with?"

A waiter interrupted and dropped menus. We both ordered turkey burgers. Neither of us ordered a drink. This wasn't a lazy mimosa-type meeting. This was Turk's freedom.

"We couldn't confirm he and Shay were having an affair." I continued to lean toward Fenton. "The body language between them on the two occasions they were seen together wasn't romantic. The manager at Muldoon's saw them having dinner at Nine-Ten just down the street a couple weeks before Turk followed Shay to La Valencia the first time. She thought Shay was confrontational with Powell."

I told him about Shay's angry discussion with Powell and her story to Kris that Powell was a friend of her father's even though her father had abandoned her when she was only three years old.

"The page you showed me on your phone says that Keenan Powell is Chief Operating Officer and General Counsel for Blank Slate Capital." Animation in Elk's voice. Not goofy kid animation, but the lawyer kind when he found something he could run with. "What is Blank Slate Capital?"

"They manage a hedge fund and have a very limited electronic paper trail online. Only three listings on Google."

Fenton's arm moved toward me on the table. I could hear the shhh sound of my phone sliding along the tabletop. I picked it up and put it in my coat pocket.

"Okay, I'll have Dan Coyote look into this Keenan Powell character and talk to the manager at Muldoon's and her boyfriend soon. Right now, he's interviewing Shay's and Turk's neighbors, trying to nail down Turk's timeline and alibi for the night of the murder. But this is definitely worth looking into." Slightly upbeat. "Good job, Rick."

A pat on the head for the blind guy who you didn't hire as your investigator.

"Have you received any discovery from the D.A. yet?" I asked.

Discovery is the process where the defense learns about the prosecution's case. They're supposed to get copies of the arresting officers' reports and statements made by prosecution witnesses and examine evidence that the prosecution proposes to introduce at trial. It's an ongoing process and less than scrupulous prosecutors are sometimes slow or forgetful with their evidence.

"Just the arrest report. We won't see any discovery until after the preliminary hearing. Why?"

"Ask for the autopsy. They must have it by now and would have no reason to hold it back. Do your indignant protector of the little guy bit and threaten to go to the press."

"Why? What are you hoping to find out?" His voice had a squint in it.

"I'd like to know Shay's stomach contents."

"Why? She wasn't poisoned. She was strangled."

"Both Turk and Kris told me Shay rarely drank and was an extremely healthy eater." Our food arrived and I waited for the waiter's outline to recede into the gray background. "But she bought a chocolate cake and expensive champagne after she met with, presumably, Keenan Powell at La Valencia the night before she died. That's her celebration food."

"*Presumably* Keenan Powell? I thought you said that's who she met with."

"I'm pretty sure it was, but Moira hasn't confirmed the photo is the same man she saw with Shay yet."

"Why not? That information would be helpful."

"She only surveilled Shay Sommers for Turk because I vouched for him. She had an infidelity case last year where the husband murdered his wife, then committed suicide. Moira vowed never to do an infidelity case again until I convinced her Turk was a good, stable man. She's pretty broken up. And mad. So, she's not talking to me right now."

"Doctor Donnelly?"

"Yeah."

"I remember that. Horrible. And now Moira thinks Turk's guilty." It wasn't a question and he didn't sound disappointed or surprised. Probably because he had come to the same conclusion.

Fenton could self-righteously declare that he didn't think in terms of guilt or innocence, that protecting his client's rights and giving him as vigorous a defense as possible were his only concerns, but he was human. And we humans can pretend we have control over all the thoughts and conclusions that pop into our heads, but we don't. Not even lawyers. But that didn't mean Fenton wouldn't do his best to defend Turk. It just meant he'd be able to sleep at night if his best wasn't good enough.

I wouldn't.

"Yes. Right now, she thinks he's guilty." I still hadn't given up on changing Moira's mind. When she decided to start talking to me again.

"Good to know. She'll undoubtedly be a prosecution witness."

"What about me? I was more or less Moira's partner."

"No. The prosecution won't want anything to do with you. I might, though."

I dug into my turkey burger and Elk did the same. Tasty. I'd skipped breakfast before Turk's arraignment and the first bite reminded me how hungry I was. I didn't say another word until I was finished, which only took a few minutes. Elk was in the same mode.

Bob Marley's "I Shot the Sheriff" suddenly sounded from the middle of Fenton's torso. Movement from his right arm into his chest and the song stopped.

"Shit." I'd never heard him swear before. "It's my ex-wife. I'd better call her back. Could be something about the girls. I have to go hide in the bathroom. I can't talk to her in a public setting."

"No problem." Divorce. With kids.

Elk's outline rose and a squeak came from his chair being pushed back. I watched him disappear into the gray background. His gait not as loose as when I saw him approach me at the Sunglass Hut.

I waited while the chatter of conversations and the aroma of food and scent of the ocean floated around me.

Then I smelled it. Under all the other scents, it was there. Hiding. Dove deodorant. Right behind me. Hovering, like it had when I sat in Moira's car last week.

The Invisible Man.

He was right behind me. Staring at me. Mocking me. He thought he could follow me, enter my space, and peak over my shoulder with impunity because I couldn't see him. A blind mark.

I shoved my chair back against his legs, shot straight up, and spun around to face my invisible tormentor. A short, thin outline stumbled backward and groaned.

"Why the fuck are you following me?" I advanced toward the shaky shadow, fists clenched at my sides. Ready. For anything.

"What's wrong with you?" Older woman's voice coming out of a round shape next to the outline of the Invisible Man. She was taller and wider than him.

"I don't know what you're talking about, son." Scared, shaky, geriatric voice from the skinny shadow.

The outline and voice surprised me. Why was some old guy following me? And with his wife? But I was still in defend and attack mode.

I whipped out my phone and pointed it at the thin outline and commanded it to take a photo. I wanted a picture of this guy to show to Moira. Maybe she'd seen him the day the Invisible Man followed us.

"Why were you hovering over me?" I barked.

"We weren't hovering over you. We were ordering drinks at the bar, minding our own business," the woman's blob said as she moved in front of the old man. "And then you assaulted my husband."

Uh-oh.

"Folks!" Elk's shadow appeared. "Pardon my friend. He lost his eyesight recently and is still figuring out how to move around in public."

"Well, he assaulted my husband." The outline of the woman's arms went to her midsection. Her hands on her hips. Posturing for confrontation. Of course, I'd given her the right. "I don't care if he's blind. He pushed my husband and threatened him."

"I didn't push him. I accidently bumped him with my chair when I stood up." Maybe not so accidently.

"I apologize again." Elk. The good everyman. "Let me pay for your lunch."

"Well, we just ordered some drinks and then we're going to eat. In the Med." The Med was the most expensive restaurant in the hotel. The wife knew a leverage opportunity when she saw one.

"Rick, why don't you wait outside while I pay our bill and take care of these nice folks?" He leaned over the table, then stuck his arm out to me. "Here's your cane."

I took the cane and unfolded it.

"Hey, I know who you are." The woman. I'd heard that phrase spoken to me countless times over the last fifteen years. It was never the precursor to a good outcome. "You're a friend of the man who murdered that beautiful girl." A loud intake of air. "And you're the lawyer who's defending that monster. Have you no shame?"

I felt all the remaining eyes that weren't already on us snap in our direction. I tapped my way to the exit and saw human outlines scatter out of my way.

There were benefits to being the blind best friend of a murderer.

CHAPTER THIRTY-SIX

I CANED ALONG with Elk on our walk to his car. The sun had burned through the marine layer and haloed my vision even through my sunglasses.

"Did you have to buy them lunch?" I asked.

"No. They took their pound of flesh in a cash settlement."

"How much?"

"Two hundred dollars." He chuckled. "I got them to agree on video on my phone that the husband, Phil Humphrey, sustained no injuries when you accidently grazed him with your chair."

"I owe you." I'd have to, considering my financial situation.

"No, you don't. You were in the restaurant on business and you gave me some important information." A pause, then his voice regressed to the teenage kid. "But you could explain to me what happened back there. I came out of the bathroom after listening to my ex harangue me for five minutes and saw you ready to attack an old man."

I hadn't told Elk about the Invisible Man. Yet. I hadn't sensed his presence for a week. Moira had half convinced me that he was a character from my imagination and the confrontation with the man in La Sala gave her judgement even more credence. I just needed one more nudge to abandon the theory myself. But Elk deserved an explanation. Especially since he'd just saved me from possible litigation.

I told him about the footsteps and Dove deodorant scent on Prospect Street the morning Moira and I met with Turk the first time. Then the two encounters that night. The last night of Shay's life. Three encounters with the man on the day before Shay was murdered, then no more. Until today.

"Did Moira see this person?"

"No."

"Dove deodorant *is* a pretty common product. A lot of men use it."

"I know what you're intimating, but it's not just the scent of the deodorant." My cadence quickened. Like Elk wasn't the only person I was trying to convince. "It's that smell mixed with individual human musk. It's a unique smell. The same scent I smelled three times the day before Shay was murdered. There's your alternative suspect."

"That elderly gentleman? He had the same musk smell of the man who tailed you on Prospect Street three times in one day a week ago?" He kept his voice modulated so the question didn't imply that I was out of my mind. But the point was taken. Again.

Did I just smell Dove deodorant today or was the same musky scent I'd smelled multiple times the day before Shay was murdered also mixed in? The scent I *thought* I smelled. It had been a week. Could I really be sure the scent I smelled today was the same one I smelled on Prospect Street?

"I'm pretty sure it was the same." Wishful speaking.

"I really have a hard time believing that the little old man whose wife did all the talking for him had the physical capabilities and stamina to follow someone around all day."

"People can surprise you. Somebody followed us that day. I smelled him." I realized how ridiculous I sounded too late to stop my mouth.

"You didn't see him." Of course, I couldn't. Cruel? Probably not, but an exclamation point on the discussion. Elk won.

I shut up for the rest of the walk to his car. He punched the ignition and the $70,000 car hummed to life.

"Can you go over to Fay Ave. and head toward La Jolla High?" I asked.

"Sure? What's at the high school?"

"Nothing. I want to go by a house on the 7300 block of Fay."

"Do you have the address?"

"I think it's 7330. A green California Craftsman cottage."

"Who lives there?"

"Moira."

Elk didn't ask why I wanted to see Moira. Maybe he was just happy to get rid of me after the mess in La Sala. Neither of us spoke again until he made a couple turns and finally pulled to a stop.

"7330 Fay. Green Craftsman cottage."

I looked out the window and saw a mass of rectangle boxes lined up along the street.

"Is there a white Honda Accord parked somewhere near the house?"

Moira's lot was so small that not only did it not have a garage, it didn't even have a driveway. Like me, her business mailing address was a P.O. box in La Jolla. She had an office in her house for paperwork and computer searches. She used a friendly lawyer's office when she met clients face-to-face. I doubted she'd taken on a new case yet. Shay Sommers' death had shaken her. She'd probably armadilloed and was holed up in her home.

"Yes. A couple cars down."

"Thanks for the ride." I opened the door, but stayed seated in the car. "What's next?"

"The hearing on Tuesday, if you can make it. I'd love to have you backing me up again when I get in front or the press."

The symbol. The role I'd been made for since Santa Barbara.

"But what can I do between now and then? I don't want to just sit on the sidelines."

I stared at the outline of his face, willing myself to see his expression. Did I have a purpose beyond the symbolic? All I saw was gray.

"I already have Dan Coyote working the case, as you know." His head turned toward the windshield. He didn't trust his expression even when he knew I couldn't see it. "I am paying you an hourly for the appearances and the meeting we just had. I value your input."

But not enough to give me any real responsibilities.

"You don't have to pay me for supporting Turk." Although, I did need the money. "I'll dig around in Blank Slate Capital and Keenan Powell and see if there's anything hinky there."

"I insist on paying you for your appearances, but, ah . . ." A pause. "If you look into Blank Slate Capital and this Keenan Powell fel-low, it would be best not to associate yourself with Turk's defense. At this time."

My confrontation with the poor old guy in La Sala hadn't raised Elk's opinion of me as an investigator.

"Roger." I got out of the car and shut the door. Hard. Just shy of a slam.

Elk pulled away and I tapped my cane along the cement walkway that split the front lawn in front of Moira's house. I maneuvered up the two steps onto the porch where Moira and I had gasped for air three years ago after her house was teargassed. On a case she'd helped me with. I missed us working as a team.

I missed Moira, period. I didn't know when I'd see Leah again. Or what would become of us. I'd been a lone wolf most of my adult life. Mostly by choice. Today, I suddenly missed the pack.

It looked like the drapes on the windows were closed. I could feel the winter sun on my back. Moira didn't want any part of it.

I knocked on the front door.

No sound from inside the house. I knocked again and rang the bell.

"Go away." Moira's voice through the door.

"Just give me a minute," I said to the closed door. "I need you to look at something, then I'll leave."

A swish of air and the rectangle of the door changed to a darker gray. With a small human outline in the middle of it.

"It's always just a minute, or an hour, or a day." Each word a jab that landed. "For what *you* need. Pulling me into *your* distorted sense of justice. Tangling me up in *your* illegal schemes. All in the scarred quest of Rick Cahill's truth. Did you know that I still have nightmares about the man I killed to save your life?"

"No." But it made sense. I had nightmares after the first one, too. Not anymore. "I'm sorry."

"You forced me to be a conquering avenger just like you." She hadn't wanted an answer. She was on a six-year roll. "And you made me an accessory after the fact to some of the truly evil things you've done. Rick Cahill, above the law for the greater good. But that's bullshit. You're just a common narcissist. Except you're more dangerous. People die while you're chasing the greater good."

Moira's outline disappeared and the door slammed in my face. The foundation of the porch shook and the boom rang in my ears.

The pack didn't want anything to do with me.

CHAPTER THIRTY-SEVEN

I TURNED TO leave and the door whipped open again.

"I asked you one simple favor." Tears in her voice now. "Something that *I* needed. Finally. Something that you could help *me* with. One simple question and you failed. Did you think Turk was lying about not going to see Shay? That was it. If you had had even the slightest doubt, I would have staked out Shay's apartment and stopped Turk from going inside. I don't think he went over there intending to kill her. He just needed to step back and breathe. Hell, he didn't even have to know about what we saw that night if you would have just stayed in the car like I asked you to. But you had to be the hero. The blind fucking hero had to save the day. Well, you could have. You could have saved both of them, but you were wrong. You failed."

"He didn't kill her."

"Shut up!" A screech. "You don't have the right! You were wrong about everything. You convinced me Turk wouldn't go see Shay that night and now you're convinced he didn't kill her? You've been blind for a long time and it's got nothing to do with your eyesight."

There was a lot of truth in what Moira said. I followed my own sense of justice. I told myself that it was because I'd seen the real justice system fail too many times. Maybe that was just a convenient rationalization. How I justified and lived with what I'd done. I did drag

Moira into some bad situations and made her an accessory after the fact. And I'd do it again to keep evil from ending her life. Or mine.

I had been wrong about Turk. He did go to Shay's house. But he didn't kill her. If I was wrong again, he'd spend the rest of his life in prison. If I was right, he might end up there anyway. I couldn't let that happen or rely on Dan Coyote to find the truth that could save Turk. He just followed orders. I followed the clues wherever they took me. I was just narcissistic enough to believe I could make a difference. And couldn't live with myself if I didn't try.

"I can't bring Shay back. I'm trying to find her killer. If that's Turk, so be it. But, I'm going to keep investigating until I find the truth, one way or another.

"Another quest to fill up that emptiness inside you." She shook her head. "You know what? It's my fault. I had doubts and I should have followed my own instincts instead of letting you convince me to follow yours. That's on me. So, I absolve you of responsibility. You can continue on your hero's journey. Go forth and conquer. You're a guiltless man, Rick."

The door started to swing shut, but I stuck my foot out to stop it. Moira's shadow stood to the side.

"My guilt is the one thing I don't delude myself about." I nudged the door with my knee and it crept open another six inches.

"That is true. The long-suffering Rick Cahill. So much of his fucked-up life is due to his own actions."

"Guilty again." I leveled with the door-jamb. "But at least I take action. I understand you feel badly about Shay Sommers. So do I. But what if you and the police are wrong? What if there's evidence out there waiting to be found that points to the real killer and there's nothing you could have done to stop him? Are you going to stay hidden in here behind the closed curtains for another week or do something about it?"

Movement. Something slammed into my stomach. Air exploded from my lungs. I staggered backwards and doubled over. I gasped for air that wouldn't come. Sucking sounds I couldn't control from my mouth. My face ready to explode.

"Fuck! Fuck! Fuck!" Arm around my waist. "Inside. Walk! Walk!"

I let Moira guide me into her house. Still hunched over. Still gasping for nonexistent air. We stopped and she grabbed my arms and lifted them up. Her tiny frame trying to get them over my head.

"Straighten up. Extend your diaphragm." She pushed my arms higher. "I'm sorry! I'm sorry!"

A wisp of air vacuumed into my diaphragm. Then another. I began to believe I might live. I sucked a few more breaths in like I'd done it before and finally regained my breath. Somehow, I kept from vomiting ground turkey all over Moira's hardwood floor. Would have served her right, though. My stomach was a sore knot, like a heavyweight boxer had just sucker punched it. Not a forty-something five-foot tall woman.

"Mind if I sit down for a second or do you want to punch me again?"

"Shit." An arm around my waist led me to a couch. Moira helped ease me down.

"I appreciate you're not punching me in the nose." I humphed a laugh. "Was that because you could see someone already had done that or because you couldn't reach it?"

"I'm sorry." Real pain. "I hope I didn't hurt you badly. There's no excuse for that. I'm sorry."

"I'm fine. A female MMA fighter once kicked me in the face without warning and knocked me unconscious. Of course, I wasn't blind then."

"You make it hard for anyone to feel sorry for you." She sat down next to me on the couch.

"Good, because that's not one of my everyday goals." Unless it could get me closer to the truth.

"What happened to your nose? It looks awful."

If I told her about Turk, she'd never believe he could be innocent.

"Sometimes you bump into things you can't see when you're blind." Like the foot of someone who didn't want to go to jail.

"I don't believe you."

"It's not the first time."

"I'm sorry about the things I said to you." Moira's head faced the floor. "Well, most of them. But Shay Sommers is not your fault."

"She's not yours either." I found the back of her neck with my hand. "You were paid to do a job and you did it as best you could, but you didn't get a chance to finish it."

"Stop." She twisted away from me. "I didn't punch you in the stomach so you could cheer me up. Cheering people up is not one of your strengths. You have just enough empathy to keep you from being a sociopath. The bare minimum. So, stop. Even if you mean it. Stop."

She was wrong about my empathy. I just expressed it differently than she did. Or most people. But now wasn't the time to argue. And I still needed her help.

My needs.

"Do you believe Turk thinks you're a good private investigator?"

"What? What the hell does that have to do with anything?"

"Just play along for now."

"I don't want to play along with anything. You seem to be breathing fine now." She stood up. "I don't want to keep you any longer."

"Give the narcissist one single minute." I stayed seated on the couch. "Does Turk think you're a good P.I.?"

"I guess." A hiss.

"Then why did he want to keep you on to investigate who killed Shay? Pretty stupid if he killed her. Another pair of eyes searching for the truth."

"To make himself look innocent."

"Pretty big risk."

"You're down to thirty seconds."

"Okay." I grabbed my phone out of my pants pocket and commanded it to pull up the most recent photo. The one of the old man in La Sala. "Have you seen this man before? Specifically, last Wednesday when we were on Prospect Street, day or night?"

"Hmph." She took the phone from my outstretched hand. "The frightened old man?"

"Yeah."

"Nope. Never seen him." She didn't hand the phone back right away. "This is in La Valencia, isn't it? La Sala."

"Yep."

"Why does the old man look so scared? What did you do to him?"

"He was wearing Dove deodorant. I thought he was peeking over my shoulder." No further explanation needed.

"Oh, that again. The Dove Stalker." She chuckled. "And you thought is was this poor old guy? Everyone in the bar is staring at you. Way to stay undercover."

"You're sure about the old guy in the photo?"

"One hundred percent."

What I expected to hear, but neither good nor bad news. It didn't confirm or deny that we'd been followed. Just that it hadn't been the old man.

I reached out my hand for my phone.

"Hold on a second."

"What?"

"I don't know who the old man is, but I do recognize someone else. Our friend from the ride in the Maybach. The man you fingered as Keenan Powell."

"What?"

"He's sitting in the back of the room by the window. I enlarged the shot to make sure. That's him. Looks like he's with someone else, but they're blocked by another table of diners. Can't tell if he's with a man or a woman."

"What's Powell doing?"

"Looking at you. Most people in the photo are. You must have made quite a scene."

"Not quite a scene, just a normal scene. Here."

I stuck out my hand and Moira put the phone in it. I took off my sunglasses and stuck the phone up to my face, almost against my nose. All I could see was light with a dark human outline in the upper edge. I'd acted on instinct and then willed myself to see the features of Keenan Powell. Folly, of course.

"You can see?" Her voice broke high.

"Not really." I pulled the phone away from my face. "But I am getting some vision back."

"That's great!" Elation in her voice. "How long has this been going on?"

"For a couple weeks. It gets better every day, but I still only see outlines and shapes. I don't know if I'll ever get enough back to be able to walk without a cane or recognize people I know."

"I thought something was going on when we were in the car waiting for Shay to get off work that night." She sat back down next to me on the couch. "I watched you looking out the window without your sunglasses."

"I'm trying not to get too optimistic about it until I can actually really see things. Let's keep it between us."

"Must be hard for you to tamp down all your natural optimism."

"It is, but I've been taking my cues from you."

"I'm really happy about your eyesight, but I can't get involved in one of your crusades right now. I'm beat up. I have to recover and re-evaluate. The one thing I feared came true. I couldn't save that girl."

"You're right. There was nothing you could do to save her."

"You know that's not what I meant."

"But it's the truth and I'm going to prove it."

"Are you still working for Ellis Fenton? I saw you on TV with him again after the arraignment."

"I am a symbol of heroic sacrifice who stands up for another heroic sacrificer. That's my gig. I'm even making hourly doing it."

"But that's not all you're doing." Gotcha voice. "You're working something on your own."

"Fenton has a plan and a timeline on how to handle things."

"But you have one of your own, don't you?"

"My timeline's just shorter." I turned toward Moira. Even her blurred outline was petite. "Kris Collins and her boyfriend saw Shay with Keenan Powell having dinner at Nine-Ten a month ago. A couple weeks before Turk followed her to La Valencia and got suspicious."

"That doesn't change anything. Actually, it makes it even more likely that Shay and Powell were having an affair."

"Kris and her boyfriend didn't get a romantic vibe between Shay and Powell and you didn't either the night we followed them by the beach."

"That doesn't matter. It's what Turk thought that matters, and he thought Shay was cheating on him."

"It only matters what Turk thought if he killed her. If he didn't, then everything else matters." I told her about Shay's angry discussion with Powell at dinner and about her first lying to Kris about where she was and then telling her that she met a friend of her father's.

"Like I already told you. None of this changes anything." She stood up. "I'm not going out on that limb with you. Not on this one. Just promise me you'll be careful."

"Heroic symbols don't have to be careful." I got up and used my white cane to find my way outside, back into the world.

CHAPTER THIRTY-EIGHT

I LET MIDNIGHT out to the backyard and went up to my office after I Ubered home. The only thing I learned from my trip to La Sala with Elk Fenton and at Moira's afterward was that the Dove-smelling old man I scared the crap out of wasn't the person who'd followed Moira and me last week. And I was down to fifty-fifty that someone had really followed us at all.

My increasing doubt about being followed hadn't eroded my confidence that Turk was innocent. Even if the "facts" pointing to his guilt were as strong as the ones pointing to my not being followed. There was work to do. A single thread to pull.

I commanded my laptop to search Keenan Powell, San Diego. Google didn't have anything different from the pay investigative websites I checked last week. The mechanical voice read me info I already knew. Keenan Powell, lawyer, partner, COO and General Counsel for Blank Slate Capital, licensed to practice law in New York, California, Nevada, and Idaho; University of Idaho Law School grad-uate; Boise State undergrad.

Idaho. Something clicked in my mind. The information Moira gave me about Shay Sommers the day we met Turk. She'd been born in Bellevue. My mind registered the state of Washington at the time, but now it was trying to convince me I'd heard Bellevue, Idaho. I didn't even know if there was a Bellevue in Idaho. According to my Google search, there was. Barely. Less than 3,000 people lived there. The nearest "big city" was Twin Falls, sixty-five miles away.

Was Shay from Idaho and not Washington? The same state where Keenan Powell had gone to college and law school? Kris said Shay told her she'd met with a friend of her father's when she was with Keenan Powell at Nine-Ten. An Idaho connection?

I searched the University of Idaho where Powell went to law school and found out it was in Moscow. Idaho, not Russia. Over 400 miles from tiny Bellevue. A long haul. Next, I found that Boise, where he was an undergrad, was 135 miles from Bellevue. Closer, but still a hike.

I dug deeper on Keenan Powell and found something that I'd glossed over on the first go-around. That he went to the College of Southern Idaho in Twin Falls for a year before he went to Boise State. Twin Falls. Just 65 miles from Bellevue, Idaho.

I called Moira. I needed her intellect and abilities on Turk's side. My side. My needs.

"I hope you're calling to tell me you've quit Muldoon's defense team and are going to write that autobiography Leah told me about. "

Just like old times.

"Not yet. Did you tell me that Shay Sommers was born in Bellevue, Idaho, not Bellevue, Washington?"

"Another Rick Cahill *It Will Only Take a Minute* request." I could hear the head shake in her voice. "That's what I remember, but let me check the file to be sure."

"Thanks."

"Shut up."

The clunk of the phone set down on a table. Somewhere in between a set and a slam. I hoped it had a protective case.

"June Elizabeth Sommers of Bellevue, Idaho, gave birth to Shay on April 16, 1991, at the St. Lakes Wood River Medical Center. Father listed as Colton Riley Benson."

"Thanks. That puts a different spin on things."

"Okay. Well, good luck. Good—"

"Kris Collins said Shay told her she met a friend of her father's at Nine-Ten the night Kris saw her there with Keenan Powell."

"I know. You already told me that. I have to go."

"Wait. Hear me out. Keenan Powell—

"You already used up your Rick Cahill *It Will Only Take a Minute* request."

"Well, give me another one." Now I was irritated. "Powell is from Idaho. He went to the College of Southern Idaho for a year, then to Boise State as an undergrad, and got his law degree at the University of Idaho."

"Idaho is a large state."

"The College of Southern Idaho is in Twin Falls, which is only sixty-five miles from Bellevue. You can look it up."

"I already told you, I'm not joining you on this ride."

"Keenan Powell and Idaho are the keys to Shay's death."

"You're way out on a limb again, and I'm not climbing out there with you." A release of air and then a shift of the phone like she stood up. "Sixty-five miles is not just around the corner. That's about the same distance from San Diego to Dana Point. Do you have friends you hang out with in Dana Point?"

"I don't have many friends anywhere."

"Don't be a jerk. You get my point."

"Idaho is largely rural. Twin Falls is probably the nearest place to Bellevue that has a mall or a Walmart. People from Bellevue probably drive there a couple times a month to stock up on supplies."

"Shay would have been four or five when Powell went to the college in Twin Falls. Are you saying she met him hanging out at the mall after she rode her tricycle sixty-five miles from Bellevue? This is a coincidence, not a clue. You're starting to get all spun up like you do before you do something stupid." Her own voice was spun up. "Tell Ellis Fenton about your theory and let him run with it. Stay on the sidelines. At least until you can see for real. And I pray that when that day comes, your vision will be coupled with wisdom. Please don't do anything stupid. Goodbye, Rick."

She hung up. Moira may have been right about talking to Elk, but she was wrong about the rest. Keenan Powell and Idaho were the keys to finding the truth about Shay Sommers' death.

Unless I was wrong and everyone else was right.

And Turk really killed her.

CHAPTER THIRTY-NINE

I CALLED ELK Fenton and told him about Keenan Powell and the Idaho connection.

"That's an interesting theory." The tone of his voice put a lie to his words. "But right now we're working on Turk's alibi timeline. Once we get that nailed down, we'll start working on alternative murder suspects."

"Since I'm not a part of the timeline investigation, I'll continue digging into Keenan Powell and Idaho."

"Hmm." A disconcerting pause. "That could be helpful. However, I'd prefer that you didn't contact anyone directly. I want my investigator to be the first person to talk to any potential witnesses. We don't want to come across as a split team."

Or, I was suddenly a liability who couldn't be trusted to talk to potential witnesses.

"I think I'd be coming across as a member of a single team." I cinched down the lid on my temper. "I could save Coyote some time by getting preliminary information that he could prioritize however he wanted to."

"Rick." Solemn voice. "You haven't worked a case in almost a year. Of course, that's not your fault. However, it does make you out of practice for a murder defense. I'm sure, given the time, if you decide you want to continue as a private investigator that you can be an effective one once again."

Effective. Hardly a ringing endorsement.

"This is about my misunderstanding with the old guy at La Sala, isn't it?"

"We really need everyone doing what they do best to keep Turk from going to prison. And, right now, you being a visible supporter of Turk is how you can best help him."

"A symbol." I snapped off the words.

"That's not how I see you." Talking to a child again. "But I really have to return to getting my associates back up to speed on the case before I fly out of town. I'll call you when I get back home on Monday night and we can discuss how to handle the press at the early disposition conference on Tuesday. Okay?"

"Roger." I hung up.

Whatever confidence Elk had in me as an investigator, and rational human being, evaporated when he came out of the bathroom at La Sala and saw me about to pounce on an old man whose only sin was rolling on Dove deodorant that morning.

That didn't mean I was going to sit still and wait for my next iconic appearance as a sidekick in front of the press.

I got online and made an appointment to visit Turk at the Central County Jail downtown tomorrow at 1:00 p.m. I didn't bother to get Fenton's consent. Firstly, because Turk wasn't yet a potential witness in his own defense. And more firstly, because I didn't want Fenton to tell me not to and have to defy him.

I just hoped Turk had forgiven me for stopping him from fleeing the police and would agree to see me. Or, agree to see me even if he was still mad. I needed to find out how much Turk knew about Shay's childhood in Idaho.

* * *

I walked Midnight later that evening, sans my sunglasses. Streetlights gave off enough illumination that I could follow Midnight's head at my side, slightly ahead of my left knee. After twenty-five steps, I folded up my cane and stuck it in the back pocket of my jeans. Above the auras of the streetlights, I could make out the blurred three-quarter moon. I felt freer than I had since my painkiller-induced altered reality dreams in Santa Barbara Cottage Hospital nine months ago.

The rectangle forms of houses and parked cars slid shadows across the sidewalk, but I kept following Midnight's head and listened to the happy tinkle of his license tapping against his metal name tag with each stride. He stopped when we got to the end of the block where it T-boned into Moraga Ave. Our normal routine was to go back the way we came and walk around the horseshoe cul-de-sac. Tonight, I wanted to push the boundaries.

"Let's go." I gave Midnight's leash a gentle tug to the right, and we turned and descended the sloping sidewalk on Moraga. I kept a running step count in my head. Our walk downhill on Moraga left us no longer protected from the wind by the sets of parallel tiered streets above my house. A chilled breeze rolled over my face. A welcome reminder that I'd left my cocoon.

The sounds of Midnight's sniffs grew louder and more frequent. Unknown territory. Back when I could see, I took Midnight to the massive dog park at Fiesta Island where he could chase balls, run with other dogs, and swim in Mission Bay. Or I'd take him to Marion Bear Memorial Park off Genesee just south of the 52 Freeway and let him roam off leash as we hiked to San Clemente Park and all the way down the Rose Canyon Hiking Trail. Now, his routine was relegated to my much narrower parameters.

Tonight, we were expanding those parameters by a few hundred yards. We continued to descend the hill. The night was still except for the breeze, which rattled the leaves of the occasional tree we passed. Midnight halted and shifted and I smelled the urine at the exact same time as I heard it spraying down on leafy-sounding ground cover.

A car approached from below on Moraga as we started walking again. Probably coming from Balboa Avenue, the main artery that connected Clairemont to Pacific Beach. The sound of the engine told me it was a sedan before I could make out the boxy form approaching. Sounded a lot like Moira's car. An Accord or similar sedan. Had Moira decided to drop by unannounced? The car slowed as it approached. I stopped walking, tightened the grip on Midnight's leash, and kept my left ear angled at it instead of my eyes. One ear was better than two eyes. At least for now.

The car picked up speed when it evened with us and continued up the hill. The engine sound dissipated, then silenced somewhere behind us. It wasn't Moira.

We walked down another block and turned around before we hit the Balboa intersection. I kept my eyes trained on Midnight's head as he led along the sidewalk. My left foot stepped on something that gave and my ankle rolled. Sharp pain. I hopped a couple steps yanking on Midnight's leash and managed to stay upright. But I'd tweaked my ankle. A sprain. Not too bad. I could still walk, but the pain was building and my left stride was more of a drag than a step.

I removed my cane from my back pocket and unfolded it. Not for support, but to tap what I couldn't see. Apparently, I wasn't ready yet to break through the next barrier.

Midnight angled left at step number four-hundred-seven. I looked up from Midnight's head and my cane and could tell by the open space to the left that we'd reached my street.

We walked toward my house. Two houses in, Midnight growled and snapped tension in the leash. This wasn't a growl ending with a bark, noting another dog or a cat. This was low and guttural. Danger. Defend by attacking the danger head-on. I stopped and strained my eyes to try to see what Midnight saw. All I could make out were rectangle shapes and shadows.

My home was only three houses away. I sniffed the air and caught a whiff of a neighbor's pine tree. No Dove deodorant. I held tight to Midnight's leash and we edged forward. Midnight's growls intensified. He wasn't a trained attack dog, but I trusted his instincts more than my own. He risked his life to save mine once. I didn't want him to have to do it again.

Two houses from my own, Midnight jerked toward the street, almost knock me over.

"Wait," I commanded. He settled but continued his attack growls.

I still couldn't even make out the outline of what he saw, but I followed the angle of his head to the middle of the street. Someone or something was out there. And Midnight sensed danger. I led him along the sidewalk toward my house, but he strained against me. I could hear saliva in his constant growl.

"My dog is usually friendly, but for some reason he doesn't like you," I said to whoever or whatever was there in the street.

No response. We continued forward, but Midnight's attention and menace stayed directed to the right, somewhere in the street or on the other side of it.

My fifty-seventh step in from the corner of the block put me at the edge of my front yard. A car door clicked open and then shut directly across from my house on the other side of the street. I snapped my head in that direction and saw a blurry rectangle. The car's ignition started and the sound of the engine moved slowly away. But I lived on a cul-de-sac. The car would have to circle back by my house to exit the street.

Midnight quieted once the car moved away. Danger contained. For him. I followed the car with my eyes but lost it in a couple seconds. I waited. The sound of the car grew louder as it rounded the cul-de-sac and started back toward us. I aimed my face at the sound. An outline emerged and moved slowly along the street toward me. It paused for half a second directly across from me. All I could see was a rectangle outline. The car accelerated and drove away.

My head followed its path. I lost sight of it, but listened until the sound of the engine faded into the night.

Someone had parked across the street from my house. The driver had gotten out of the car and approached my home. At the least. At the most, he'd gone onto my property, then watched me as I approached. If he had an innocent reason for coming to my house, he would have answered when I called out to him. Who was he? What did he want? Did he wear Dove deodorant?

The Invisible Man?

I walked up the path to the front door and ran my hand along the jamb feeling for a business card. Nothing. I sniffed around the porch, which was slightly enclosed by the eaves hanging overhead. No Dove. Just the gluey smell from the rubber plants that bracketed the front door.

Maybe he'd gone to my neighbor's house. Or was just leaving there after visiting. I hadn't noticed his car when I left my house earlier, but my limited vision had been pointed at the Midnight's head.

Or, maybe he was afraid of dogs. Especially those that growled at him.

CHAPTER FORTY

MY PHONE RANG on the Uber ride to the county jail the next day.

"Rick, it's Ellis." Concern in his voice. "I got a look at the autopsy report. It was brutal. She fought for her life. She had a fractured eye socket . . . It was awful."

"What about her stomach contents?" I wished Shay Sommers had died in her sleep, but, right now, I had to figure out how to free the man she loved from jail.

"You were right about the cake and champagne. There were remnants of both in Shay's stomach when she died. But only a tiny amount of champagne."

I was right. Shay had celebrated something the night she was murdered. But I still didn't know *what* she was celebrating.

"And she was pregnant," Elk added.

"Whoa." That was the concern I'd heard in his voice.

"Yes. Another motive, as if the prosecution doesn't already have enough."

"Maybe not. Turk told me he wanted to have kids with Shay. This was before she was murdered. So, he'd be happy about her pregnancy. Maybe that was what Shay was celebrating."

"Except that she'd been pregnant for eleven weeks. She had to have known well before the night she bought the cake and champagne."

"I'm guessing no DNA on the child, yet?"

"None that the state would show me if they already had it, but the test probably isn't back from the lab yet. If it comes back with any DNA other than Turk's, we've got a real problem."

"We don't even know if Turk knew she was pregnant." If he did know, why didn't he tell me when he told me he wanted to have a child with Shay? What else hadn't Turk told me?

"I'll find out when I see him today at 3:00 p.m."

I had a two hour jump on Fenton. He'd be able to talk to Turk in a private, non-monitored room. I didn't have that option. I wasn't an official member of the defense team. Fenton had a job to do. I needed to find the truth.

"Roger." I kept my visit to myself.

"There is one bit of decent news in the autopsy. The medical examiner described the bruising on Shay's arms as mild. Detective Denton made them sound like Shay had been squeezed in a steel vice when she questioned Turk the day after the murder."

Decent, at best. But at this point, anything that wasn't negative was positive.

"That's something. Is Coyote going to look into Keenan Powell?" I knew in my gut that Powell was an important puzzle piece in solving Shay Sommers' murder. I just didn't know where he fit in the puzzle yet, but I didn't want to sit on the sidelines while someone else figured it out.

"Yes, of course."

"When?"

"We already discussed this, Rick." A frustrated tone edging toward anger that I'd never heard Fenton use outside of a courtroom. And never directed at me. "This will be my eleventh murder trial. I've gotten four acquittals and two hung juries that didn't result in retrials in the previous ten. I'll put that record up against anyone. I know what I'm doing. I have a process. I'd appreciate if you'd start trusting it."

"What time do I have to be at the courthouse Tuesday?"

"I'll pick you up at 8:00 a.m."

"I'll be waiting." But not behind Fenton in line at the jail to talk to Turk. I may have been a cardboard cutout of support on Turk's defense team, but I was a flesh and blood friend. One who needed to know the truth to see where that friendship stood.

Now.

CHAPTER FORTY-ONE

THE SAN DIEGO Central Jail is on Front Street downtown. It's a cement building with a squat foundation and a twenty-three-story tower shooting up from it. Even at that, it can barely hold all who have been charged and await trial and those convicted of misdemeanors and serving sentences of less than a year there.

The visitation room was really a long, narrow concrete bunker. Smells of sweat, fear, and desperation closed in from all sides. And I was on the freedom side of the reinforced glass. The stench from the other side permeated any pores in the windows, walls, and seals it encountered. The room was a fetid bog of despair.

I sat on a metal stool riveted to the cement floor. A guard handed me a phone handset from the hook on the wall dividing me from the next visitor over.

A hulking presence appeared in front of me on the other side of the glass. The outline I'd learned to recognize as Turk. His hand went up to the partition on his side.

"Everything in here is being filmed and audio recorded." His voice slightly tinny in the old-school phone receiver.

"I'm not worried about that. Neither one of us has anything to hide." But I was worried. About his end. I peered through the glass,

trying to see features on his face. Just a blur. "Fenton doesn't know
I'm here."

I guess I did have something to hide.

"Why not?"

"He's got another investigator. I'm here as a friend."

"Got it. Sorry about your nose." Flat. "It looks broken."

"It's fine. How are you?"

"I'm in jail. Cooped up in a cell with a lowlife for half the day and
among the scumbag general population the rest of the time." An
edge in his voice that I'd never heard before. I'd heard him angry, but
this was different. Visceral. He'd only been inside two days, but you
don't go into jail and come out the same. No matter how short your
stay inside.

"Any progress on bail?"

"I don't have a spare hundred grand laying around to pay a bail
bondsman." Still the edge. "Nor do I have another nine hundred in
collateral."

"Your house has to be worth well over a million."

"To the bank. I took out a home equity loan earlier this week just
in case I got arrested. Prophetic." He hit the "P" hard. "I'm using it to
pay Fenton. It was either bail and rely on a public defender or stay in
jail and pay Fenton."

"What about your sister? I thought she was contributing to your
defense."

"She is, but Fenton is sucking it all up. Murder trials are expensive.
Even when you're innocent."

"Shit."

"Yeah, shit."

"Fenton got a hold of the autopsy report." I pressed the phone
hard against my ear and shifted forward toward the glass between

us. Freedom on my side. Bars on his. The truth in between. "Shay was pregnant."

I squinted and moved even closer to the glass, but only saw a blur on the other side. I couldn't read Turk, not even if I took off my sunglasses and pressed my face against the glass. Surprise or confirmation? I didn't know. Truths or lies, I couldn't see. I had to hear or feel them.

"I know." An ache. For what he'd lost or what Shay had done behind his back.

"Was the baby yours?"

"Fuck you, Rick!" A blast of anger vibrated my ear.

"Muldoon." Movement on Turk's side out of the corner of my eye. A large squarish outline approached Turk. "Knock it off or you're going back to your cell."

"I'm cool." The square outline receded out of my vision.

"Were you the father?" My voice just above a whisper.

"Yes, of course I'm the father. Was the father." Anger and sadness on the wrong side of a glass wall.

"Why didn't you mention Shay was pregnant when you told me you wanted to have a child with her?"

"I didn't expect Moira to bring you with her when we met at the restaurant. Do you know how hard it was for me that you knew I had to hire a private detective to find out if the woman who was pregnant with my child was cheating on me?" The walls came down. No glass between us. Seven years evaporated. "You were like a brother to me. You used to look up to me. I haven't laid a bet since I was shot, but I'll always have that hole in my life. The thing that drove us apart. I know you saved the restaurant for me. I don't know what you did, but I know you saved it. And you never said a thing to me about it. You never held it over my head. But I knew we couldn't be friends

TT COYLE

anymore. I couldn't bear to see you and wonder what you saw when you looked at me."

"I saw my brother." A swell of emotion tightened my throat. "Ever since you took me under your wing at the restaurant. I still do. That's why I'm here. But I can't help you without knowing the truth. All of it."

"I lost my whole family the night Shay died." The words came out on whips of heavy air. Laden with despair. "I was upset that Shay was cheating on me. But I didn't kill her. I'd be killing myself."

"We don't know if she was cheating on you. There's too much I don't know about Shay and I need you to fill in the blanks."

"Like what?"

"How much do you know about Shay's childhood back in Idaho?"

"Not that much. Why?"

"Remember the guy I told you about who Shay met at La Valencia the night before she died and a few weeks before that at Nine-Ten? Keenan Powell, the guy Kris saw with her?"

"Yeah?" Wary.

"I dug up his background and found out he's from Idaho. Undergrad degree at Boise State and law degree at University of Idaho. Here's the kicker, though. He went to a community college in Twin Falls for a year. Sixty-five miles south of Bellevue, Shay's childhood home."

"All I know about Idaho is that Shay lived on a ranch when she was young and that her father stole the proceeds from its sale from her mother and abandoned them both."

"What? How much did he get away with?" Shay's father was a real gem. Not only abandons his family but leaves them destitute. Another hook into Idaho. Something about a ranch itched along my scalp, but I didn't know why.

"I'm not sure, but I think it was a lot. Shay didn't like to talk about it, so I didn't press her." A huffed laugh with no mirth. "You know me. I don't sweat the details."

"What else do you know about her father?"

"Nothing really. I don't even know his name."

"According to the research Moira did, his name was Colton Riley Benson," I said.

"She never told me his name. Just that he ran away with the money."

"According to what Shay told Kris, some friend who knew Benson when he was still alive twenty-plus years ago somehow tracked Shay down in La Jolla or vice versa. I'm positive that friend was Keenan Powell. He's forty-three; Benson died in 1997 when he was forty-six. That would make Powell twenty at the time. How many forty-six-year-olds do you know who hang out with college kids?"

"None, but what's your point? What does all this have to do with Shay's murder?"

"I'm not sure, yet. But I'm going to find out." I leaned on the waist-high metal shelf that was attached to the glass. "The other thing the autopsy showed was that Shay had remnants of chocolate cake and champagne in her system when she died. Neither you nor Kris knew of any parties or birthdays coming up. Shay was planning to celebrate something ten minutes after she left her last meeting with Keenan Powell. What if she'd just won some concession from him worth celebrating and he wasn't happy about it?"

"You think this Powell dude killed Shay?"

"I don't know, but I need to find out if he had an alibi for the time of the murder." I stood up to leave, but still had the phone in my hand. "One other thing about the autopsy. The marks on Shay's arms were classified as only mild bruises."

"Yeah, but they were still bruises."

We said our goodbyes and I went outside to wait for an Uber pickup. Two minutes in, the tingle I'd felt along my scalp when Turk said Shay grew up on a ranch hit my spine. A ranch. Keenan Powell's bio on the Blank Slate Capital website stated that he worked on a cattle ranch when he was a teenager. Is that how he and Shay knew each other? Her mother's ranch in Bellevue, Idaho?

Keenan Powell was the key to solving Shay Sommers' murder, and Bellevue, Idaho, might be the lock.

CHAPTER FORTY-TWO

MOIRA ANSWERED ON the third ring.

"I need your help."

An irritated laugh.

"This is a joke, right?"

"No."

"You couldn't even make it twenty-four hours without asking for my help again."

"I wouldn't ask if I could see."

"Maybe not about whatever it is you're going to ask me now, but there'd be something else you'd need even if you could see."

"You're right." I leaned my elbow onto the kitchen table and pressed the phone harder to my ear. "You get the short end of our friendship nine times out of ten."

"Ten out of ten."

"Why do you put up with it?"

"If this is a reverse psychology ploy to get me to help you, it's not working the way you planned."

"Only partially." Six years later, I still wasn't sure why Moira befriended me. "You'd probably be better off never having met me, but I don't know where I'd be without you. Most likely dead."

"You're laying it on pretty thick." Her voice was soft and didn't match her words.

"A rare moment of truth from the man who claims to always be pursuing it," I said.

"I'm stuck with you, Cahill. Somewhere along the line of helping you with cases and keeping you out of jail, you became my responsibility. And I take my responsibilities seriously. But that doesn't mean I have to help you with every bonehead scheme you come up with."

"How about I tell you what the bonehead scheme is first and then you can tell me what you think?"

A sigh. "Go ahead."

I told her about Shay growing up on a ranch and Keenan Powell's teenage years as a ranch hand in the same state.

And that Shay was pregnant with Turk's child.

"Oh, God." The pain of Shay's murder and the Donnelly murder-suicide thick in her voice. "A baby."

"You couldn't have done anything to stop it."

"Only if Turk is innocent. The pregnancy gives him another motive. If the baby was someone else's."

"It wasn't."

"Is there DNA yet?"

"No. But I believe Turk. I know Turk. He's still the man I used to know. Flawed, but decent. I know he's innocent."

"Well, I'm not convinced. Where does the favor come in?"

"I need you to fly with me to Boise, Idaho."

"What?"

"At seven thirty tomorrow morning. And then drive me two hours from Boise to Bellevue. The good news is there's a direct flight back the next day."

"What do you expect to find in Bellevue?"

"I can't be sure until I get there, but Bellevue is the key."

"How so?" Irritated.

"When Kris asked Shay what she did the night she and her boy-friend saw her with Keenan Powell in Nine-Ten, she said she met a friend of her father's. Her father's been dead for twenty-three years. Any friends he had who would know about Shay have to go all the way back to Bellevue and the ranch. And like I told you, Powell worked on a ranch as a teenager."

"You think there's only one ranch in Idaho? And who's to say Shay wasn't lying about who Powell was? We know she lied. A lot." Emphasis on the last two words.

"But why a friend of her father's? Why not a friend of her moth-er's, which would make much more sense since she only died three years ago."

"Who knows why liars lie?"

"The answers are in Bellevue. I feel it in my gut."

"How many times has your gut been wrong?" Like she was count-ing the misses in her head.

"A few, but it's right about this one."

"Why do you need me? Why not just hire a driver out there?"

"Secondly, because I did the math and it probably costs about the same to buy your plane tickets and rent a car as it does to go alone and rent a driver."

"*Secondly?*" An arched eyebrow I couldn't see now, but had many times before. "What's firstly?"

"I need your eyes, your brain, and your instincts."

"My instincts tell me that this is a fool's errand."

"I only need them when we get there. Not before."

"Why isn't Ellis Fenton going with you?"

"I didn't tell him I'm going."

"Why not?" Agitated.

"He hasn't caught up to me yet. He's preparing to go to trial. I'm trying to find the real killer and avoid a trial. You know how this works. The trial date probably won't be for a year. I don't want Turk to spend another day in jail for something he didn't do."

"Something he didn't do." She made it sound like something that shouldn't be spoken out loud. "But what if he did do it? What if you find evidence that proves Turk killed Shay Sommers? Would you continue to defend him and be used by Fenton as Turk's personal Statue of Liberty in front of the press?"

"No, not if I was certain."

"And you're willing to look at the existing evidence and any new evidence with an open mind? Guilt or innocence depending upon the facts?"

"Yep. Are you?"

"Buy the tickets. I'll pick you up at five thirty tomorrow morning." The natural rapid cadence that I hadn't heard in a while.

"Roger. We're flying Southwest, so no first class, but flying with a blind guy will get you bumped up to pre-boarding. I'll be sure to stumble at the gate for the sympathy vote."

"Asshole."

*   *   *

I bought the tickets through the voice function on my computer, the first time I'd ever done that. I was pretty sure I got everything right and we were flying to Boise. Thank God the closest airport to Bellevue wasn't in Moscow, Idaho.

Two hours later, I packed a backpack with a pair of socks, underwear, and a collared shirt. It didn't matter what color the shirt was. All my collared shirts were dark and went well with the pair of jeans I'd wear.

Midnight growled and scuttled out of the bedroom and downstairs after I rolled up the shirt and put it in my backpack. A couple seconds later, someone knocked on the door. Hard. I grabbed my cane and went downstairs. Another couple hard knocks and Midnight growl by the time I hit the foyer.

"Quiet." To Midnight.

Someone outside was agitated and wanted to talk to me. The police? Maybe Detective Denton had decided to arrest me for impersonating a police officer on the phone. Doubted it. She had her man behind bars. That would be petty even for her.

Someone mad over a case? No. I hadn't officially worked one in almost a year.

If it was someone who wanted to hurt me for some other reason, they weren't being very stealthy about it hammering on my door at five thirty in the afternoon.

I put on my sunglasses and opened the door.

"Who the hell said you could visit Turk and talk about the case in the public visitors area in jail?" Elk Fenton angrier than I'd ever heard him.

"Who told you I did that?" Had Turk ratted me out when I asked him not to?

"A sheriff's deputy, but that's not the point." I thought I could actually see a red tinge to the outline of his face. "You could have jeopardized the whole case! You know those conversations are recorded."

"Do you want to come inside so we can calmly discuss this?"

"No, I don't."

"Did Turk tell you what we talked about?"

"Only after I convinced him the deputy told me you'd been there." He shook his head and blew out a loud breath. "He's as loyal to you as you are to him. Two stubborn idiots."

"If anyone listens to our conversation, they'll hear a man who is grieving the death of his girlfriend and his unborn child. Nothing he said made him sound guilty. Just the opposite."

"You don't know that. You're not a lawyer. And even if you're right, it's the principle. You should have checked with me first."

"You would have told me not to go." Defiant, even though I knew he was right. In principle. "Plus, Turk told me something about Shay I didn't know about her. Did you know that she grew up on a ranch in Idaho?"

"Of course. Turk is my client."

"Idaho is where Keenan Powell grew up and worked on a ranch as a teenager." My face heated up. "Idaho's the key. Why aren't you sending Coyote out there?"

"I'm not going to have this argument with you again. In fact, I'm not going to have any more arguments with you."

"What does that mean?"

"You're a loose cannon, Rick. That's dangerous in a murder trial." Calm now. Almost remorseful. "I don't trust your judgment and, quite frankly, I don't trust you. I can't risk having you a part of the team anymore. I'm going to pay you for the time you would have spent at the EDC, but you won't be there. Or at any other court dates."

"How did Turk look to you today?" Calm, myself.

"You're not going to change my mind."

"I'm not trying to. I don't care about being on the team. I was a cardboard cutout, anyway. But you know, as well as I do, that jail is a lot harder on the innocent than it is on the guilty. How do you think Turk is going to look a year from now when the trial starts?"

"You think I want my clients languishing in jail while I try to get them bail and prepare for their trials?"

I wasn't going to get Turk out of jail if I worked through the system. That was the problem with me agreeing to help in the first place.

"There might be exculpatory evidence in Idaho and you should be there looking for it."

"You'll get a check next week." Elk turned sideways, then stopped. "You can't play by your own rules anymore, Rick. It's too dangerous."

He walked away and disappeared.

My own rules were the only ones I had.

CHAPTER FORTY-THREE

THE FLIGHT TO Boise the next morning took four hours with a layover in Las Vegas. Being first in and first off the plane made flying a little less painful. Anything that can lessen the tedium of air travel nowadays had to be cherished. Along with the tiny pretzels. And, if you're lucky, tiny Lorna Doones.

I didn't tell Moira about Fenton booting me from the team. It didn't change anything. The Boise trip wasn't sanctioned by him even before he fired me. If we found anything exculpatory, I'd give it to Fenton. That hadn't changed. I was here for Turk, not a paycheck or a pat on the back.

The Boise air had a snap to it that we might get a couple days every few years in San Diego. Probably low- to mid-thirties. What we call freezing in Southern California. I wore my bomber jacket, jeans, and boots. Not cowboy boots, Galls cop duty boots. No gloves. Real cowboys don't wear gloves unless their breath freezes and falls to the ground when they exhale. Or if they don't own a pair.

Moira rented a Nissan Pathfinder on my credit card because she wanted something with four-wheel drive in case we hit snow or ice. I gave her the address to Smokey Mountain Ranch, just south of Bellevue. It had taken me over an hour of searching real estate and people finder websites last night to locate the ranch that June Sommers sold to the owners of the adjacent property twenty-five years ago before Colton Benson ran off with the money. The best I could tell, Smokey Mountain Ranch was still owned by the original buyers, Jake and Jim Hunter.

We got onto Interstate 84 going southeast. My limited vision told me that the terrain was mostly flat. After about an hour, I sensed some dark breaking landscape to the left side of the windshield. Mountains.

"What's your plan?" Moira broke the silence that had settled between us since we got on the road. "Do the owners of the ranch even know we're coming?"

"Yes. I left them a message on their voicemail last night and Jake Hunter left me one this morning while we were in the air. He'd be happy to meet us."

"Why did you tell him we were coming by?"

"I told him the truth. Mostly." My usual practice as a private investigator. It didn't take long to backslide into my bad habits. "That we were detectives from San Diego investigating a homicide and have a few questions regarding some people from Bellevue."

"Detectives?"

"Yes." Feigning obliviousness to her concern.

"Not private detectives?"

"I might have left that part out, but I didn't say police."

"When was the last time you referred to yourself as a detective instead of a private investigator?"

"Last night on Smokey Mountain Ranch's voicemail."

"You may have just wasted a lot of money and my time to come all the way out here for nothing." The heavy rumble of a big rig filled the inside of the car then receded into the background. "I'm not going to impersonate a police officer. And what if the Hunters don't want to talk to a private detective?"

"I'm not asking you to impersonate a cop and I'm not going to either. Let me handle it. We'll be fine."

Neither of us spoke again for over an hour. Finally, Moira broke the silence.

"GPS says we're eight miles out. We're in a valley between some mountains. It's beautiful out here."

"I'll take your word for it." Although I did get the sense of rolling terrain on each side of the highway.

After a few more minutes, Moira spoke again. "The entrance to the ranch is just up ahead."

The Pathfinder slowed, then turned left, and the road went from asphalt to gravel crunching under the tires. The sound and the texture signaled real country living. We crept along for almost a minute until Moira pulled to a stop.

"Large wood and stone modern ranch house with a peaked roof and a huge covered wooden porch. Gorgeous." Awe in Moira's voice. "There's even a whipping post out front."

"A whipping post?"

"You know, where they tie up horses after they ride them."

"That's called a hitching post."

"Whatever." Dismissive, like a millennial. "There's a pickup truck parked in front of it instead of a horse. There's also a guest house back to the left next to a massive barn."

"Bunkhouse for the hands."

"Aren't you the cowboy?"

"I used to watch Westerns back when I was a kid."

"Let's go."

I got out of the heated SUV and an icy wind slapped me in the face. The smell of pine trees and dry grass swirled around me.

The gravel crunched under my duty boots as I put my hand on the Pathfinder and walked around the front of it to meet Moira. I could see the dark form of the ranch house. Even the area in front of the porch that was a small staircase. I just couldn't tell how many stairs there were. I took the cane out of my pocket and snapped it to its full length.

"You okay with the stairs?" Moira, a few feet ahead of me.

"Yeah. Thanks." My ankle was still a bit sore from twisting it the other night. But, workable.

Moira waited while I caught up to her and tapped up the three wooden steps first. I knocked on the wooden front door.

"I didn't see any cows when we drove up along their property." Moira.

"Cattle. I think you call them cows when you milk them and cattle when you slaughter them."

"Blind or sighted, you're still an asshole."

The door opened after a few seconds, replaced by the outline of a human. A woman.

"May I help you?" Fifties or sixties by the tenor of her voice.

"Yes." I tried my friendly smile under my sunglasses and broken nose. "I'm Rick Cahill and this is Moira MacFarlane and we're here to see Jake Hunter."

"The detectives from San Diego?"

"Yes." I answered before Moira could give a more specific answer.

"I'm Claire Hunter, Jake's wife. Please follow me." Her body moved away from the door, then stopped. "Oh, I'm sorry. Would you like me to lead you?"

"Thanks, but I can see just enough to be able to follow you."

We followed her down a hall. The click of what must have been her cowboy boots on a hardwood floor led us into a large open space on the left. The living room. Light came in from the back of the room through two huge windows.

"What a beautiful view," Moira said.

"Thank you. Those are the Smokey Mountains, and most of the land you see in front of them is part of the ranch."

"But where are all your cows?"

"Cattle," I said.

"Shut up, Rick."

"They're grazing down near Mountain Home. We get too much snow in the winter for them to feed here. We've had mild weather the last couple weeks, but there's a storm on the way," Claire Hunter explained. "Have a seat, but watch out for the coffee table right in front of the couch."

"Thanks," I said.

Moira and I found a large dark sofa behind a knee-high flat platform object. The coffee table. By the sound it made when we sat down, the sofa was leather.

"I wouldn't mind waking up to that view every day." Moira, ready to trade in her flip-flops for a pair of cowboy boots.

"I've been waking up to it for thirty-three years and it never gets old. I'll go get Jake." A rustle and footsteps on hardwood echoing away.

Deference in her voice. Jake was the boss. Moira sat quietly on the couch, so I did too.

A minute or so later, two sets of footsteps approached. One heavier than Claire Hunter's. Two figures entered the room. Claire and a considerably larger male. Square torso and head. Maybe a flat-top haircut.

Moira stood up and I followed.

"I'm Jake Hunter." A baritone that filled the large room. He stopped in front of Moira and it looked like they shook hands.

"Moira MacFarlane and this is Rick Cahill."

The figure moved in front of me and an arm came out. I found his hand and shook it.

"Thanks for seeing us on short notice," I said.

"Please sit down." He waited until we sat, then descended into a large object that sounded a crinkle of leather.

"Can I get you something to drink?" Claire. "Some iced tea? Fresh-squeezed strawberry lemonade? We grow the strawberries right here on the ranch."

I usually forgo perfunctory hospitality offerings, but Claire Hunter was so genuine that I took her up on the lemonade. So did Moira. Claire left, presumably to the kitchen.

"Now what can I do for you folks?" Jake Hunter.

"Moira and I are here investigating the murder of Shay Sommers."

"You mean June's daughter? The little towhead?" His voice pitched higher. He was shaken. I figured with the national attention the murder received, everyone in the Bellevue area who knew the Sommers family would have already heard about it.

"Yes. I'm sorry to have to break it to you. I thought you would have already heard about it."

"No. We haven't heard a thing. I haven't thought about the Sommers family since June died in Portland two or three years ago. That's a real shame. Shay was the sweetest little girl you'd ever want to meet. Murdered, you say?"

"I'm afraid so."

"Did you catch the person who did it?"

Here's where things could get tricky. I hadn't said we were with the police, but I didn't mind Jake Hunter thinking we were. Law-abiding citizens would be more willing to open up to the police working on behalf of the prosecution than they would be to investigators working for the defense, even though, technically, we weren't. Americans believed in the principle of innocent until proven guilty, but the power of the badge conveyed guilt to most people who were busy living their own lives.

"There is someone in custody," I said.

"What do you need from me? I always do what I can to support law enforcement. I'm truly sorry Shay Sommers is dead, but I haven't seen her in twenty, twenty-five years."

"We're not law enforcement." Moira saved me a decision. "We're private investigators."

A figure appeared in the living room with arms outstretched in front of it. Claire Hunter with a tray of strawberry lemonade.

"Little Shay is dead?" Claire Hunter, a quaver in her voice.

"Yes, ma'am. Did you know her?" I tried to sprint past the detective versus investigator issue.

"You're not the police?" No such luck. Jake Hunter, his head tilted to the side.

Claire set the tray down with a clack on the table in front of us, then hovered in front of me.

"No." Moira.

"I put your lemonade right in front of you, Mr. Cahill." Claire, her voice still caught in the news of Shay Sommers' murder. She moved over to where Jake was sitting and stood behind him.

"Thanks."

"Then why did you say you were on the phone?" Hunter, directed at me.

"I think I said I was a detective."

"But not a private detective." Sharp. "When people hear the word detective all by itself, they think police."

"My mistake. I apologize."

"If you're not police detectives, then why are you here?"

"We're investigating Shay's death, and a man from Idaho named Keenan Powell keeps popping up." I pulled out my wallet and flipped open the clear holder on the flip side of my driver's license that held my private investigator's license issued by the California Bureau of

Security and Investigative Services. "We're trying to gather any information we can about Shay Sommers and people she might have known, like Keenan Powell. He's from this part of Idaho and his bio says he worked on a ranch when he was a teenager. You folks own the biggest ranch around here. Have you ever heard of him?"

"Nope." Jake Hunter. "And it's time for you to leave. You should have been up front when you left a message on the phone. We like to deal direct with people here. I guess this kind of deception is commonplace out in California, but we don't appreciate it here in Idaho."

"You're right." I nodded my head and wished, not for the first time, that I was more like Moira. "I should have been more direct. I'm just trying to make sure the police have the right man in jail. Moira came out here to help me because she's my friend. She's got nothing to do with my detective/investigator game of semantics."

"Are you investigating for the defense?" Jake Hunter.

"Not officially." I leaned in Hunter's direction and spread my hands. "Here's the whole truth. The police arrested a friend of mine for the murder. I don't think he did it. Moira's not sure, but she's willing to track down any clues that lead to the truth, whatever it is. This Keenan Powell person could lead to the truth, one way or the other." I took out my phone and unlocked the screen, bringing up the picture that I'd saved there of Keenan Powell's Blank Slate Capital's bio page with his photo. "Please look at this picture and tell me if you've ever seen this man."

I stuck my phone out in Jake Hunter's direction. The ripping sound of movement on leather, then an arm reached over and grabbed my phone.

"Nope. Never seen him." The phone was placed back in my hand.

"Ma'am?" I held the phone up in Claire Hunter's direction.

"I've never seen him, either." Quick, backing her husband.

A gust of wind blew in from the hallway and a door slammed.

"The wind's coming up." Loud male voice. Boots on hardwood floor. "Colder than a you know what out there."

A figure entered the living room with a triangle-shaped head. A cowboy hat. I would have known it was a male even if I hadn't heard his voice. The cocksure walk even translated to a blind man. The figure strolled toward Moira. Cigarettes, leather, and horse smells roiled together to form a cloud of Cowboys' brew.

"Jimmy Hunter." An arm down to Moira. "Nice to meet you."

"This is Moira MacFarlane and Rick Cahill." Jake Hunter jumped in. "They came here from California impersonating police officers and they are about to leave."

"Whoa." A laugh from Jimmy.

"Sorry you folks had to come all the way out here misrepresenting yourselves and come up empty, but it's time to go." Jake Hunter.

I saw Moira stand up out of the corner of my eye.

"Big Jake has spoken." Jimmy Hunter. "Time to go. I'll walk you out."

Moira took a step and her outline turned toward me. "Rick."

I carefully found the lemonade glass and took a sip. The taste made me wish I would have been more straightforward. I stood up.

"Thanks for allowing us into your home. Mrs. Hunter, that's the best lemonade I've ever tasted."

"Thank you." Reserved, like she wasn't sure how much credence to give me.

A grunt came from her husband's direction.

I should have listened to Moira and been honest from the jump. Starting with the phone message I left on Jake Hunter's voicemail.

Old habits die hard. So does stupidity.

CHAPTER FORTY-FOUR

MOIRA AND JIMMY Hunter were waiting on the porch. An artic wind froze my cheeks.

"You pissed off Lord Jake." He chuckled. "Never a good idea. What kind of a con were you trying to run on him?"

"We weren't running a con." Moira, full-auto delivery. "We're private detectives investigating the murder of Shay Sommers and—"

"Murder?" His voice broke high like his brother's had. "That cute little girl? Son of a bitch. What happened?"

"That's what we're trying to find out," I said. "And we think this guy is somehow connected." I pulled out my phone, unlocked it, and thrust it toward Hunter. The photo of Keenan Powell should have still been on the screen.

A hand grabbed the phone.

"How old is this picture?"

"Maybe three or four years." Moira. The one person between the two of us who'd recently seen Powell in person. "He doesn't look too much older now."

"The name Powell rings a bell and his face looks kind of familiar, but the Powell I'm thinking of was a nephew of the foreman who used to run the ranch hands before we incorporated the old Lazy S ranch into Smokey Mountain. The kid worked on the ranch a couple weeks each summer. He was a teenager back then. I think he went by Bill or Billy."

The hair on the back of my neck spiked and it had nothing to do with the icy wind.

I turned toward Moira. "Keenan Powell's middle name is William."

"Mr. Hunter." Moira. "Can we buy you a cup of coffee?"

"Follow me." Hunter hopped off the porch. "Coffee shop's five miles north in Bellevue."

*   *   *

We drove for nine or ten minutes, then pulled into a parking lot next to a one-story structure with an overhang jutting out sideways from the roof area. We got out of the car into the cold and followed Jimmy Hunter under the awning into the building. Hunter had a confident strut that was so bowlegged that even my limited eyesight could discern the gap between his legs.

The bitter aroma of coffee smacked me in the nose when we entered the building. I'm not a coffee drinker but the smell was homey and comforting and the room was warm.

"Welcome to Coffee Corner," a female voice greeted us before the door closed behind me.

We settled at a small table in the corner of Coffee Corner. I ordered a hot chocolate, Moira a latte, Jimmy Hunter, coffee. Black, of course.

"How many summers did this Billy work on the ranch?" I asked.

"Well, let's see." Hunter's cowboy-hatted head went back like he was thinking. "Maybe two or three. I think he stopped around the time we bought the Lazy S."

"Was the Lazy S the Sommers' ranch?" I asked.

"Yep. Sure was."

Was the ranch the connection between Shay and Keenan Powell? But Shay would have only been two or three years old, and Hunter said Powell stopped working at Smokey Mountain Ranch *before* Shay's mother sold the ranch and Colt Benson ran off with the money.

"How old do you think Powell was his last summer on the ranch?" Moira. She'd taken the bit.

"Sixteen, seventeen. It was a long time ago and I probably talked to the kid maybe ten times. Quiet. Seemed like he worked hard. I might have run cattle with him once his last summer on the ranch. Competent. But I could be confusing him with any of the other twenty or thirty kids who worked on the ranch part-time in the summer over the years."

Sixteen or seventeen years old could have been Keenan Powell's junior or senior year in high school. After that he would have been onto the community college in Twin Falls.

"What's Billy Powell's uncle's name? Is he still your foreman?" Maybe he was still in the area and could give us more information on Keenan Powell.

"Oh, hell no." A chuckle. "He's long gone. Probably been dead twenty, twenty-five years."

The back of my neck prickled.

"What was his name?"

"Colt Benson."

Moira's head snapped toward me. I couldn't make out her expression, but I didn't have to. Colt Benson. Shay Sommers' father.

"The man who was Shay's father?" Moira, wanting to be sure.

A shadow popped up next to me. The girl from behind the counter with our hot beverages. Table-side service. That beats someone mispronouncing your name and shouting it across the coffee shop.

"Well," Hunter picked back up after a sip of coffee and a loud "ah." "Ole Colt claimed to me and Jake once that he wasn't really the father, but was standing in as him because the real one wouldn't step up and left town."

"Did you believe him?" I asked?

"Maybe half of it." Another chuckle.

"What do you mean?" Moira

"Colt was not a stand-in or stand-up kind of guy." Hunter's hand went up to his head. When it came down, his head had a normal rounded outline. He'd taken his hat off and set it on a chair at the next table over. "He was just the opposite of one. Maybe that makes him a sit-down kind of guy. Anyway, whether he was or wasn't Shay's actual father, he took on the responsibility so he could stay close to June Sommers, Shay's mom."

"Why would he do that?" I asked, but I was pretty sure I already knew the answer.

"In my opinion, he started formulating the plan the first day he saw June when he, Jake, and I met with her to discuss her interest in selling the Lazy S. She was a city girl who didn't know the first thing about ranching. Her parents died in a small engine plane crash and left her the Lazy S."

"Wait a second," I jumped in. "I thought June Sommers was from Bellevue. All due respect, even blind I can tell this isn't a city."

"She grew up in Portland, Oregon. Her parents moved out here and bought the ranch after June went to college." Another sip of coffee and another "ah." "They didn't know anything about ranching either, but they dabbled in livestock. Cattle for a few years, then pigs, then back to cattle. Nice folks, but still greenhorns by the time they died."

"So June Sommers showed up, and you and your brother offered to buy the ranch from her." I took my first sip of the hot chocolate. Hot and chocolate. Perfect for an Idaho winter's day.

"Yeah. Jake saw the opportunity to expand and pick up another six hundred fifty acres of grazing land. At first, June wanted to keep the ranch in the family because her parents loved it so much. Didn't take her very long to figure out she was in way over her head. By then, she was dating Colt, and he quit Smokey Mountain to work at the Lazy S as June's foreman. Now, they only had fifty, sixty head of cattle at the time and didn't really need a foreman. June already had three or four ranch hands—one of them, Eddie Sands from McCall, was kind of the de facto foreman. But Courteous Colt convinced her that she needed someone to lord over the hands. Waste of money."

"How long did he work at your ranch?" I asked.

"Nine or ten years."

"Did Billy Powell go work for his uncle after he took over the Lazy S?" I asked

"Hell, no. Colt couldn't afford to pay the kid what we did."

"You clearly had a low opinion of Colt Benson. Why did he work at your ranch for so long?" Moira asked.

"He was a friend of my brother's from college." A sniffed laugh. "And as you can tell from your talk with Jake, he runs the show. Colt grew up in Bozeman and he did know his way around a horse, but his best asset was his mouth." Hunter shifted in his chair to face Moira. "He could charm the rattle off a rattlesnake."

"And that charm worked on your brother?" Moira shifted slightly forward in her chair.

"Mostly. It was wearing off by the time Colt jumped ship. But it started a couple years before that after Colt convinced Jake to invest in some stock market gimmick that turned to shit. Pardon my language." A nod in Moira's direction. "Jake lost about twenty grand. A lot of money to him back then. Hell, a lot of money to me right now."

The skin on the back of my neck prickled for the second time in the last hour. The stock market. Keenan Powell, CFO and general counsel at Blank Slate Capital, which managed a hedge fund. Had he picked up where his uncle left off?

"Your brother took stock advice from his ranch foreman?" I asked.

"A ranch foreman with a degree in finance who worked on Wall Street right out of college, but supposedly wanted to return to the more simple life of his childhood."

Colt Benson, uncle to Keenan Powell, had worked on Wall Street. The tumblers were clicking into place, but the last number wouldn't fit. It couldn't.

"You don't believe Colt Benson left Wall Street on his own terms?"

"The guy was too slick to me from the jump." Hunter now shifted toward me, hunched over the table. "What everyone else thought was charm, I read as smarm. So, when I found out Big Jake was investing with him, I did a little research on Colt's Wall Street past. I didn't find any kind of smoking gun that the guy was crooked or that he was fired from Merrill Lynch and Lehman Brothers. But no one had anything nice to say about him. Nothing derogatory, but none of the four people I was able to talk to on the phone endorsed him. What they didn't say said a whole lot more than what they did."

"You know that Benson stole the proceeds from the sale of the ranch and disappeared, right?" Moira.

"Yep. We let June and Shay stay on the Lazy S rent free for as long as they wanted, but June found a job down in Twin Falls within a year. The whole Colt thing left a bad taste in her mouth, and she wanted to get out of here as soon as she could."

Twin Falls. Where Keenan Powell went to community college for a year. I wondered if his year overlapped when Shay and her mother lived there.

"Did your brother ever hear from Benson after he disappeared?" Moira.

"No. He was on the lam. According to June, any large withdrawals from their joint account required both of their signatures and he forged hers." Another nasal laugh. "Actually, June found out he went to the bank's branch in Boise to make the withdrawal. Had a woman with a fake ID who forged June's signature. The police in Twin Falls and Boise lost interest pretty quickly and June hired a private investigator, like you folks. I don't know what became of that. She moved down to Twin Falls around that time and I only saw her once or twice after that."

"Do you know the name of the investigator she hired?" I asked. Maybe the P.I. found out something useful about Colt Benson and, more importantly, Keenan Powell.

"I don't, but Jake does. He started using a private investigator to run background checks on prospective employees after the Colt Benson mess." The laugh. "He figured if he didn't know what kind of a person a friend of his really was, he'd better start checking up on strangers he wanted to hire. I'll call him and find out the guy's name."

Screech of a chair pushed back along the floor and Jimmy Hunter's body stood up.

"If you'll excuse me, ma'am." Hunter's form turned toward Moira. "Big Jake may not be in the best of moods, so I'll call him outside."

Boots on wooden floor, then out the door.

"Well." I slid toward Moira. "We don't know why Shay and Powell were meeting, but at least we know they weren't having an affair."

"Maybe. It's still a possibility. But all this Idaho intrigue doesn't mean that Turk didn't kill Shay. He clearly thought Shay *was* having an affair. That's all that matters." Moira cut me off before I could even get to the pass. "The police arrested him for a reason. They must think whatever forensic evidence they have is a slam dunk."

I hit my hot chocolate. Still hot, rich, and creamy and had crept into my top five all time hot chocolate list.

"Is that for my benefit or your own?" I smiled. "I think you're starting to come over to my side. Something's not right about Keenan

Powell. Why did Keenan 'Billy' Powell from Smokey Mountain Ranch and nephew to ole Colt Benson, making him and Shay cousins, meet with Shay multiple times in La Jolla after not seeing her for twenty-five years? A long way—in many ways—from Bellevue, Idaho."

"We don't know if their meetings in La Jolla were the first in twenty-five years. They could have been talking all along. Maybe they were close."

"Between the two of us, you're the only one who saw them together. Did they look like they were close to you?"

"Not particularly. I'll concede that and I agree there are some things that need to be checked out." Moira's head seemed to be angled between me and the door of the coffee shop. I couldn't see her eyes, but I bet they were on the door. "This is where you need to rein in your gut and follow the facts that we know and not your hunches. I know you too well. You're about to jump blindly into this Idaho conspiracy and close your eyes to all other facts. Pun intended."

"Maybe, but my gut is telling me something else, too." I said.

"Oh, no. Another conspiracy?"

"Nope, just something I can see with my own two eyes. That ole cowboy outside has taken a shining to you."

"Wrong again." Light tone to her voice. "And he's not that old."

A cold breeze sliced through the coffee shop and the clank of a shut door came behind it. Return of the not-so-old cowboy. Jimmy Hunter sat back down at the table.

"Took a little back-and-forth, but I got a name, phone number, and address for you. Sonny Hester. His office is in Twin Falls, about an hour down the road." Arm movement and something clanked down on the table in front of Moira. "Jake texted me his number. It's on the screen with his address."

Movement from Moira and she pulled something out of her purse and pointed it at the table. Her phone to take a photo of the information.

"Got it. Thanks, Jimmy." A slight lilt in her voice.

"My pleasure, ma'am." I had the feeling he would have tipped his hat if he hadn't already taken it off. "When are you folks flying back to San Diego?"

"Tomorrow." Moira. Couldn't tell if she batted her eyelashes. "We fly out of Boise."

"Anybody in California still eat meat? There's a steakhouse down the road that serves Smokey Mountain Ranch beef. The best you'll ever eat. They treat me like a big shot when I go in for dinner. It would be my honor to host you two."

He meant *one*.

"We prefer faux meat." I jumped in before Moira could answer. "Any tofu burger joints around here?"

"Shut up, Rick." A little giggle in her voice. "We'd love to take you up on that, but we're driving back to Boise tonight. We fly out early tomorrow morning. Rain check?"

"Of course."

"And if you ever make it to San Diego, dinner's on me."

"Us," I said.

"Shut up, Rick."

CHAPTER FORTY-FIVE

WE GOT TO Sonny Hester's office in Twin Falls by 5:30 p.m. I called ahead and he agreed to keep his office open until we arrived. Normal closing time, 4:30 p.m. By the sound of his voice, that might be the exact time he took advantage of nearby restaurants' senior citizens early bird specials.

We lost the ranch and pine smells from Bellevue when we got out of the car in Twin Falls. From the look of the horseshoe of rectangle shapes attached to each other, I guessed we landed in a strip mall. I tapped alongside Moira until we reached what looked like a glass door. Moira opened it and we went inside. To a cigar shop. At least that's what it smelled like. With a fresh one lit.

"Mr. Hester?" Moira asked.

The room was dark and I could only make out a desk-like structure in the back with a dark human shape slumped behind it.

"You sound surprised." The gravelly voice I heard on the phone. "Is that because you didn't expect to see a black man in Idaho or a private dick so old?"

"The second one," Moira said. "And smoking a cigar."

"Well, your friend here, the blind one, told me on the phone that you two are private detectives from California." A barbed cough with a lot of phlegm. "Maybe out there, you're all private dicks to the stars, but the rest of us don't get rich running skip traces, and spying on adulterers and workers comp fraudsters. I'm seventy-four years old and I don't have a comfy retirement waiting for me, so I still work five days a week and smoke in my own damn office. Is that a problem for your Hollywood sensibilities?"

I told Hester on the phone who we were and that we wanted to talk to him about June Sommers. I was surprised when he invited us down immediately. He didn't have to try to remember who June Sommers was or ask what we wanted to know. It had already been a long day for both Moira and me after getting up at 4:30 a.m. for the flight with a layover in Vegas and then the two-hour drive from Boise to Bellevue. We both would have preferred to talk to Hester over the phone, but agreed we couldn't afford not to take advantage of a face-to-face.

Now I was concerned that we'd just wasted another hour on the road. Hester seemed prickly enough to prefer to argue rather than be forthcoming with information.

"Not a problem," I said and took a step closer to the desk. "And we're from San Diego, not Hollywood."

"Same difference." Hester put a hand to his face. A drag off the cigar.

"Not to San Diegans." I found the back of a chair in front of the desk and tapped with my cane to the left to make sure there were two. Moira pulled the second chair away from the desk and sat down right after my cane clanked off it. I followed her lead. The chair was wooden and uncomfortable. Perfect.

"You all comfy now? Can I get you an espresso or a Perrier?" A snort from behind the desk.

"We're here to talk about June Sommers." I leaned forward and set my forearms on the desk. "You still have her file?"

There were a couple upright rectangles against the wall to the left of Hester's desk. File cabinets. Hester may have had a personal computer way back in the early '90s, but I guessed his file on June Sommers, if he still had it, was in one of those file cabinets.

"I got it right here on my desk, Longstreet." Hester raised something over his head.

"Longstreet?" I said.

"Forget it." He brought his hand back down to his desk. "You're too damn young. No sense of history."

"We understand that Ms. Sommers hired you back in 1994 or '95 to find Colt Benson who'd stolen a lot of money from her, the proceeds from the sale of her family ranch." Moira.

"By Ms. Sommers, if you mean June, then yes, that is correct. And the actual amount was eight hundred sixty-one thousand dollars. He didn't just steal the ranch from June, he stole almost her entire life savings." Cigar back to his face. "But you're really here on account of the murder of Shay, aren't you?"

"Yes." I answered for both of us. "I didn't know that you'd heard about her death."

"Why? You don't think we have cable TV out here? Satellite? The internet?"

Prickly.

"The Hunters hadn't heard about it." Time to give in. "Faulty assumption on my part."

"Faulty assumption is right. Making an ass out of you and not me."

"Is there a good steakhouse near here?" Moira, a step ahead of me as always. "We haven't eaten anything since an Egg McMuffin in the Las Vegas airport this morning. Why don't you grab that file and we can discuss it over dinner?"

"You're buying?"

"Of course." Moira.

Sonny Hester's mass shot up from behind the desk and he was past us in three long strides.

"Idaho Joes is just down the street." He tucked something against the broad frame of his body. The file. "They have fine steaks, but I go there for the chicken pot pie."

*　*　*

I went with the chicken pot pie. Brought back memories of Friday nights as a kid when my parents went out to dinner and left frozen pot pies in the oven for my sister and me. Idaho Joe's were better. Moira went with a ten-ounce ribeye.

Hester got down to business halfway through dinner.

"I know you're not here on behalf of the police." He blew on a fork-ful of pot pie, shoved it in his mouth and continued. "So, you must be working for the defense."

"Neither." Moira. "I'm here to tie up a few loose ends."

"What about you, Longstreet?"

"My friend was arrested for the murder. I don't think he did it. I think a man named Keenan William Powell had something to do with it or knows something about it."

"The nephew."

"You know Powell?" Moira and me in unison.

"Not personally, but I know a little bit about him and his uncle." More pot pie.

"And?" I said.

"I've been waiting for this day for twenty-five years."

"What do you mean?" I leaned forward. "For Shay to be murdered?"

"Lord, no. That sweet little girl." His head went back and forth. "So sorry it came to that. I mean someone contacting me about Colton Riley Benson. A snake of a man. And I mean that in the biblical sense. Evil."

"We're here about Keenan Powell, not Colt Benson."

"One leads to the other."

"Please explain." I pushed aside the remnants of my pot pie. Eating didn't sit well with discussing evil.

"I consulted this file after you called." Hester patted the folder on the table. "But I didn't really have to. I remember the case like it was yesterday. I kept it open and investigated on the side when I had time over the years for free. I finally stopped when June died."

I appreciated Hester's feelings for June Sommers, but we didn't have time for nostalgia and he wasn't making much sense.

"I'm confused. Do you mean you stopped working the case after Benson died?"

"Did I say that?" He turned toward Moira. "Did I say that, young lady?"

"No."

"Correct. I am not a doddering old fool or a dummy." More pot pie. He continued with the sound of food in his mouth. "It took me almost three years. Thirty-four months to be exact, but I finally found Benson. I tracked him to a little town in Northern California called Laytonville living under an assumed name. The town's about three hours north of Sacramento." He appeared to take something out of his pocket and the smell of burnt stogie filled our booth.

"I don't think you can smoke that in here." Moira.

"Who says I'm going to smoke it?" He put his hand up to his face and his profile had a long thin beak. "Anyway, I used a fax machine and a telephone to track that sonofabitch. He liked to gamble and I got close in Reno, but I finally tracked him to Red Fox Casino in Laytonville. Named after the Indian tribe, not the comedian. The director of security showed the photo I faxed over to all the employees. Dealers, pit bosses, chambermaids, cocktail waitresses, mainte-nance crew and he got a hit on Colt. He was going by the alias Clint Banks by this time. I contacted the Bellevue Marshall's Office and the Mendocino Sheriff's Department, which handles Laytonville, and gave them the rundown. Well, you guessed it—by the time a sheriff's deputy rolled up to the casino, Benson was in the wind."

I was ready to pack it up and drive to Boise so we could get some rest before our flight tomorrow. Smokey Mountain Ranch and Jimmy Hunter had been a hit. Sonny Hester was a miss. A cranky old fart who, despite being antisocial, was lonely and took the opportunity to tell us the story about the one that got away.

"All due respect, Mr. Hester, I don't see how that changes the narrative. Is there anything else you can tell us about Colt Benson and Keenan Powell?"

"*Change the narrative?* Is that how they talk in California? Some stupid phrase instead of being direct?"

"The story you just told us doesn't explain why you kept the Colt Benson file open long after he was dead." The frustrations of the last two weeks leaked out into my voice. "Is that direct enough for you, Sonny?"

"Rick!" Moira.

"That's okay, young lady." Hester's arm went up. "I'm not some frail old man who needs protecting. Let's see what kind of private dick Mr. Longstreet here is. Now, may I continue with my *narrative?*"

"Sure." I couldn't wait until we were done with Hester so I could look up *Longstreet* online.

"I didn't hear anything about Benson for another year." Hester grabbed his stogie and rasped out a cough, then put the cigar back in the hangar. "I kept sending out faxes and talking to law enforcement from all over the West, Mexico, and Canada, seeking information on Benson or Clint Banks, the alias he used in Laytonville. Nothing. Radio silence for another year. Then I get a hit in Mexico, under his own name, Colt Benson. I alerted the Bellevue marshall and they contacted the Federales and two days later Benson died in a car crash in Tijuana. Anything strike a nerve for you there, Sherlock?"

His cigar was pointed at me. *Sherlock*. That one I knew.

"Yeah. Presumably he'd been using aliases while he was on the run, then all of a sudden you find him under his own name, and he dies shortly thereafter. Pretty convenient. But it's not like he went missing on a sailboat out at sea. This was a car accident. There had to be a body. Right?"

"Yup. But don't lose the thread, Columbo."

"Who identified the body?"

"You're not as dumb as you look." A cigar-bobbing chuckle. "All due respect, of course."

"Of course. Are you going to tell us who identified the body?"

"Yup and now you'll understand why I kept the case open." His hand went to his mouth and his beak disappeared. "Keenan 'Billy' Powell."

CHAPTER FORTY-SIX

"You think Colt Benson faked his death and Keenan Powell was in on it?" Moira asked.

Our waitress showed up at that moment to clear our plates and tempt us with dessert. Hester ordered a piece of apple pie and a coffee. Chocolate cream pie for me. Coffee for Moira.

"That's certainly a possibility, young lady, but's there's more to it, isn't there?"

I doubted Moira liked being called *young lady*, but she held her tongue. Gathering information came first and Sonny Hester suddenly proved to be a fount of it.

"If Colt Benson faked his death, that meant someone else's body was in his place." Moira.

"Bingo, Jessica Fletcher."

I'd heard of her and Columbo. Longstreet was still a blank.

"Wouldn't they at least check dental records?" I asked.

"This was Mexico twenty-five years ago." Sonny. "All things were possible. After stealing eight hundred sixty-one thousand dollars from June Sommers, Benson had enough money to make it happen."

"Even get away with murder?" Moira.

"May not have been murder. Maybe he paid someone at the morgue or a mortuary. Pull a body out of the cremation chamber before they light the fuse and give the grieving family the leftover remains of somebody else. No one's the wiser. Could have done it any number of ways, but, you're right, murder is a possibility. Wouldn't put anything past Colt Benson."

"What about Keenan Billy Powell? Is he a chip off his uncle's old block?" I asked.

"Decide for yourself." Hester shifted backwards and the booth back groaned like he'd settled in. "June told me Billy visited her every couple of weeks after Benson ran off with her money. Said she'd only met him a couple times before Benson left and all of a sudden, he's June's best friend and constantly apologizing for what his uncle did. June moved down here to Twin Falls the summer before the kid was supposed to go off to Boise State for his freshman year of college. He went to the College of Southern Idaho instead. A JC right here in Twin Falls. June and Shay Sommers' new home."

"And all of this started after June hired you to find Benson?" Moira.

"Yup."

"Powell befriended June Sommers to check up on her. Find out if you were making progress in finding him."

"I can tell she's the smart one in your partnership." Hester pointed his cigar at me again. "I guess that makes you the muscle? Although, judging by that swollen nose of yours, maybe you better try something else."

"I'm the pretty one." I could take his insults for a while longer. Besides, the cigar-smelling old guy was starting to grow on me. My grandfather smoked a cigar. "Did June figure out Powell was a spy on her own?"

"No. Once she told me Powell started showing up, I did some snooping around. That's how I found out he had been accepted to Boise State as a freshman. His family could afford the tuition. I knew he was up to no good when he opted out of Boise State and went to the JC here."

"Did you tell June about your concerns?" Moira.

"Yes. She didn't believe me at first. So I had her tell Billy that she couldn't afford me anymore and that I stopped working for her. Part of which was true. She'd stopped paying me months before, but I continued to investigate pro bono. Anyway, sure enough, Billy transferred to Boise State the next year."

"And you kept looking for Benson for the next two decades pro bono?" Moira.

"On and off. When I could." The hacking cough. "I'm not about charity cases. Life is hard and I had seven children to feed. But my daddy ran out on my momma and her five kids when I was four. About the same age it happened to little Shay. He didn't rob my momma dry like Benson did to June Sommers because she didn't have anything worth stealing, but he stole her youth and the life she deserved. And he left a hole where a father should have been. No child and no woman deserve that. Not my momma and me and not June and Shay Sommers."

Yeah, Sonny Hester was definitely growing on me.

"Did you ever get another bead on Benson after his purported death?" I asked.

"Radio silence for twenty-five years."

"What about Keenan Powell? Anything hinky about him over the years?"

"By all accounts an upstanding citizen. Graduated Boise State with honors. Law degree at University of Idaho. Been an attorney in the financial sector for a number of years. I stopped paying attention to him well before June Sommers died. Maybe he got scared straight."

* * *

Moira didn't start the car right away when we got in it. She put her
hand up to the side of her head. Her phone. She kept it there a full
minute or so before she brought it back down.

"Don't get your hopes too high about everything we learned today."

"Did we both hear the same things? Keenan Powell helped Colt
Benson perpetuate a fraud and possibly a murder. Twenty-five years
later he shows up in Shay Sommers' life and she's murdered within a
month."

"I just checked my messages." Deflated. "My inside man at LJPD
told me Keenan Powell has a rock-solid alibi for the night Shay was
murdered."

The knot I hadn't felt in a week returned to my stomach.

"How rock-solid? How does anyone have a rock-solid alibi from
two to five in the morning?"

"He was at Scripps Hospital from approximately one a.m. until late
that morning. Chuck Baxter, the CEO of Blank Slate Capital, had
heart attack symptoms. Powell rushed him to the hospital and stayed
with him the whole time he was there."

My head snapped back like I'd inhaled smelling salts. "Chuck
Baxter? I never noticed it before."

"Noticed what?"

"CB. Colt Benson. Clint Banks, the alias Benson was using in
Northern California—"

"Chuck Baxter is Colt Benson!" Moira spat out the name before
I could.

"Benson's not only alive, but he was in La Jolla the night Shay was
murdered."

"But both Benson or Baxter and Keenan Powell had rock-solid ali-
bis." Her head pointed toward her lap, like she was doing something
on her phone.

"Pretty convenient. They could have easily hired someone to kill Shay and then Baxter complains about chest pains for a few hours so they both have an alibi." I paused, knowing Moira wouldn't like what I had to say next. "Maybe that's where the Invisible Man comes in."

"Not him again."

"Him or somebody else."

"It's possible, but I'm not sold yet."

"What if it's Colt Benson who was staying up in the Sky Suite the night Shay went up there? Powell lives twenty minutes away in Scripps Ranch. It doesn't make sense for him to stay at La Valencia. That's where a rich out-of-town CEO would stay. Maybe Benson-Baxter came into town and Shay tracked him down through Powell."

"Maybe." Moira's head was still down.

"What are you doing?"

"I just took a screenshot of Chuck Baxter's picture from the Blank Slate Capital website and texted it to Jimmy Hunter to see if he thought Baxter could be Colt Benson." Her head rose and turned toward me.

"You two exchanged phone numbers?" My voice rose with my eyebrows.

"He gave me his card." Dismissive. "Back to Shay. She'd been meeting Powell for at least a month. That much *we* know about. They could have been talking to each other for the last twenty years. If he had her killed, why now?"

Moira's phone rang.

"Jimmy? I put you on speaker so Rick can hear. What do you think, could Chuck Baxter be Colt Benson?"

"Maybe. It's been twenty-five years since I last saw him." A pause. "I think it's him. It's the eyes. Wolf's eyes. His nose is different like he had some work done and his hair was brown back then, not gray, but, yeah, I think that's him."

"Thanks, Jimmy." Moira, cheery. "Thanks for everything."

"My pleasure, ma'am. Call any time." Cowboy charm.

Moira hung up and turned toward me.

"All this is interesting, but it still doesn't prove anything." Her voice measured, trying to preemptively tamp down my enthusiasm.

"It's another brick in the wall." Moira could stand outside and reason everything out, but my gut told me I was right. The answers were in Idaho and we just found them. "One other thing I forgot to tell you—Fenton got a copy of Shay's autopsy report and champagne and chocolate cake were in her stomach. She was celebrating something. Maybe she was blackmailing Benson, and he agreed to pay her off that night and then had her killed."

"This is all speculation. It's going to come down to the forensics. I don't want Turk to be guilty either, but the facts will tell. Fenton would be lucky to get any of what Sonny Hester told us admitted in court. It's mostly hearsay and speculation."

"Then we need to get one or both of them to admit the truth."

"How are you going to do that?"

"I haven't figured that out, yet."

CHAPTER FORTY-SEVEN

MOIRA DROPPED ME home after we landed in San Diego the next day. She still wasn't completely onboard with my Keenan Powell/ Chuck Baxter theory. I'd have to make my next move alone.

I took Midnight for a walk after I picked him up from my neighbor's house. We took the same route as the other night. Venturing beyond the bounds of the cul-de-sac. The limp from my twisted ankle was now just a slight hitch. The sun was uncluttered by clouds and throwing shadows I could actually see. Midnight's body, doglike. His movements familiar. I could follow his head from side to side and down sniffing the sidewalk, then back up. Both our shadows angled to the right. I avoided a rock on the sidewalk and managed curbs.

We got back home and I sat in the living room with Midnight facing me. I pressed my face toward his snout. I looked at his eyes. Close. Millimeters away. I could see the curve of his eye socket. Blurred, but visible. Closer still, his eyeball, his pupil. He licked me in the face and I hugged his neck.

I allowed myself hope.

I went upstairs, got on my computer, and voice-searched Charles Baxter, Blank Slate Capital as a starting point on a paid investigative search site. There are a lot of Charles Baxters in the United States and the one who founded Blank Slate left very few breadcrumbs out in cyberspace. But, after a half hour or so, I tracked him down. Charles Lawrence Baxter was sixty-three years old and lived on a five-thousand-acre ranch outside of Casper, Wyoming. If he really was Colt Benson, he'd shaved six years off his age. I guess the nose job and whatever plastic surgery he may have had made him feel younger.

Maybe it worked because his wife, Lyndsay Katherine Baxter, nee Shutler, was twenty-five years his junior. No children. The earliest history I could find about Chuck Baxter was that he earned a degree in Business at the University of Montana Western in 1979. Nothing before that. The only job history I found was financial consultant until he started Blank Slate Capital in 2010.

The three consulting agencies he'd worked for were no longer in business. Convenient for someone creating a new identity and a fake history. Apparently, he began running his own one-man shop in 2000, then closed it to start day trading in the stock exchange full-time in 2007 until he founded Blank Slate.

No phone number other than the one that matched Blank Slate Capital. A very private man.

The only office I found for Blank Slate was in La Jolla, but Baxter lived in Wyoming. Maybe Keenan Powell ran the day-to-day locally and Baxter flew in a few times a year to check in and wrangle new investors from the La Jolla elite. His preferred hotel being La Valencia. He was staying in the Sky Suite the night Shay was murdered, not Powell. I was sure of it.

The police must have already known that and they didn't seem to care. They had their man. Tunnel vision.

I was more convinced than ever that Chuck Baxter was Colt Benson. He stole $861,000 from June Sommers, faked his own death, then created a new identity that yielded little information for anyone to find.

And he had Shay Sommers murdered when she figured it out.

I needed a closer look at Chuck Baxter.

CHAPTER FORTY-EIGHT

THE UBER DRIVER dropped me in front of La Valencia at 8:50 p.m. I needed to get my eyesight back in a hurry, get a full-time paying job, or wait for San Diego's public transportation to spread out into the 'burbs, because Uber costs were bleeding me dry.

I tapped my way under the square arch, through the courtyard, and into the hotel lobby. The La Valencia lobby is actually on the seventh floor, even with Prospect Street, but higher than much of the property, which cascades down to Coast Boulevard facing the ocean in the back. The polished brick floor was slightly uneven under my cane and feet. Ahead to the right, I could make out a horizontal counter and a human form behind it. As I got closer, I saw a woman with long dark hair.

"May I help you?" Cheery young voice.

"Yes. Could you call Mr. Baxter in the Sky Suite and tell him Rick Cahill is here to see him on behalf of Shay Sommers' family?"

"Certainly." Movement, her hand to her head and she repeated my request, presumably, into a phone. Maybe ten seconds of silence, then her hand went back down.

"Mr. Powell will be down to greet you. There is a chair about ten feet behind you. I can guide you to it, if you'd like."

I was right. Baxter was staying in the Sky Suite and Powell was his toady. Another puzzle piece snapped into place.

"I can find it. Thanks." I turned, tapped over to the armchair, and sat down.

I was fifty-fifty on whether Baxter would agree to see me. But the Shay Sommers hook had snagged his attention. And concern. Powell, the front man, would be sent down to find out what I knew. Or find out if I knew too much.

I slipped my hand under the thin-fabricated blazer I wore and felt the cellphone in the breast pocket of my dress shirt. The voice-activated tape recorder app on my phone was turned on. I tested it at home in the same clothes and it worked perfectly.

I didn't have a well-constructed plan. I had my gut instincts and a tape recorder. Moira warned me about my gut in Idaho. She'd tell me anything that I taped would be inadmissible in court and I'd be subject to a misdemeanor conviction. That's why I didn't tell her about going to see Chuck Baxter. The man I was convinced was Colt Benson. The shot caller on Shay Sommers' murder.

Turk Muldoon was in the San Diego County Jail, unable to properly grieve the loss of his girlfriend and losing bits of his humanity an hour at a time. I had to do whatever it took to get him out of there.

If I got something incriminating on tape, I'd risk the misdemeanor and play it for Detective Sheets to get him to see the case in a new light. My light. Then I'd give a copy to Fenton. The recording wouldn't be admissible in court, but if I had something incriminating enough, the DA might drop the charges against Turk and set him free.

That was worth the risk.

Five minutes later, a figure approached me. Male. Five-ten, five-eleven. In decent shape by his outline. Aggressive aftershave. I stayed seated until he called my name. I wanted to keep my abilities hidden in my disability.

"Mr. Cahill?" Confident tenor voice. Pleasant. A business-man used to greeting people he didn't know. "My name's Keenan Powell. I'm here on behalf of Mr. Baxter."

Behind my sunglasses, I focused on Powell's face. All I could make out were a couple dark smudges for eyes. I couldn't tell if he was smiling, but I bet there was a forced one on his face.

I stood up and angled my head slightly to the left side of Powell like actors do when they portray a blind person. I stuck out my hand in the same direction and made him reach his own over to shake it. Firm, dry.

"Nice to meet you, Keenan. I guess you never got the message I left with your office last week to call me." I smiled.

"No, I didn't. Sorry." He lied convincingly.

"That's okay. I'm here to see Charles Baxter on behalf of Shay Sommers' family tonight. Are you going to take me up to his room?" Polite. We were still friends.

"I wish I could help you, but Mr. Baxter is still recovering from a recent health scare and is not seeing visitors right now." Calm as a psychiatrist with his legs crossed. "Why don't we go into the bar and you can tell me what you wanted to tell Mr. Baxter."

"I know all about health scares. I'm still recovering from one of my own." I took off my sunglasses, but still kept my head slightly angled away from Powell. "But I still like to stay active. Like the trip I just took to Bellevue, Idaho. It's important to stay engaged."

No noticeable reaction from Powell. At least none that I could see, but I'd bet he didn't give one. I thought of Kris Collins describing Powell as stoic while Shay Sommers was arguing with him at the Nine-Ten restaurant. I put my sunglasses back on.

"Beautiful country." Nonplussed. Powell was either very good or I was wrong about who was responsible for Shay's murder. "Let's go into the bar and have that talk."

A hand on my arm to guide me out of the lobby underneath a cement arch toward La Sala Lounge.

"If Charles Baxter wants to join us, fine. Otherwise, I'll pass." I stopped just above the stairs that led down into the lounge. "Shay's family wants to know what she and Baxter talked about the last night of her life."

I'd done my homework and found that Shay had distant cousins in South Carolina. I never talked to them and wasn't even sure if they knew Shay had been murdered or had had any connection to her at all.

"I'm afraid that's not possible, Mr. Cahill." Overly polite tone.

"Oh, I think it is." I matched his politeness. "By the way, the Hunter brothers at Smokey Mountain Ranch said to say hello." The next word wasn't so polite. "Billy."

"What do you want, Cahill?" The mask slipped. His eyes blotted darker and his voice had a sharp edge. "Is this some kind of shakedown?"

"Nope." I slowly shook my head. "Shay's family has some questions that need answering. I'm the first option. I'm sure they could go a more official route if I don't come through."

"Wait here." His hand went up to his chest, and he turned and walked through the lobby out of the hotel and disappeared into the courtyard. He must have grabbed his phone from his coat pocket. To call whom? His boss Colt Benson or his boss's henchman, the Invisible Man?

I kept my eyes pinned on the entrance to the hotel and my nose sniffing for Dove deodorant. No scent of a killer. Powell returned a minute later.

"Follow me." Powell walked past me to the right.

"Easier said then done." I could see his shape headed toward the elevator, but I wanted to maintain the façade of total blindness. I'd have the element of surprise if the time came to defend myself. My only advantage.

A grunt from Powell. He took a step back toward me and grabbed my arm. Hard. Hard enough to leave a bruise.

"This way. We're going to the elevator."

I let him lead me and tapped along beside him to the elevator.

We took the tiny elevator up to the tenth floor. I kept my eyes on Powell's hands. No sudden movements. The elevator came to a stop and the door opened without incident.

"This way." Powell turned right out of the elevator and led me down a carpeted hallway that changed to hardwood two-thirds of the way down.

He opened a door at the end of the hall and held it open for me to enter. "Straight ahead, Mr. Cahill."

I tapped inside, purposely boinking the rounded plastic tip of the cane off Powell's foot. I didn't apologize. A tall figure stood across the room to the right next to a dark expanse. A window with a view to the ocean. One of many. I scanned my eyes around the suite without moving my head. No one else in the room. No Invisible Man.

"Mr. Cahill, welcome." Baxter's voice languid and friendly. "Have a seat on the sofa to your right."

I turned to the right to match my body with where my eyes were already looking. Baxter came away from the window and sat in one of the two chairs across from a sofa. His gait sure and smooth. Not the movements of someone still healing from a "medical scare."

I tapped ahead toward the center of the room. Powell stayed behind me. There was something round and dark emanating from the floor right in front of me. The sofa was just to the left of it. I moved toward the dark shape in front of me and neither Baxter nor Powell said anything. A test of my vision. I bounced the cane against it, then shifted the cane to my left hand and felt below me with my right like I thought it was the sofa.

"Oh, that's an ottoman." Baxter's dulcet tone. "The sofa is a couple feet slightly to your left.

"Thanks." I followed his directions, tapped against the sofa, and did the feeling hand thing, then sat down.

Powell moved across the room and sat in the chair next to Baxter's.

"Keenan tells me that you're here on behalf of Shay Sommers' family. The pretty girl who was murdered by her boyfriend." Smooth, friendly. "Her murder is certainly a tragedy, but I'm not sure how I can help."

"Did you know that Keenan, here, knew Shay when she was a little girl and that they were cousins?" I kept my head pointed slightly to the left of Baxter, actor style.

"Yes."

"This question is for you, Keenan." I moved my head to the right so it was aiming between Baxter and Powell. "Did you know Shay quit a job she'd studied for in college, uprooted her life, and moved down here just so she could find you? What did you two talk about when she finally tracked you down?"

"She just wanted to touch base. And she didn't track me down. San Diego is a nice place to live. A lot of people move here. Does that about cover things, Cahill?" Powell.

"No. It doesn't." I leaned forward, my eyes, hidden behind sunglasses, darting between both men. "But I'm glad you brought up Shay's mother. That's the real reason Shay came to San Diego. To find the man who stole eight hundred sixty-one thousand dollars from her mother. Your uncle, her father, Colt Benson."

Baxter's and Powell's heads each turned toward the other. They were convinced I couldn't see. I maintained my posture; my head remained pointed between them.

Powell's head turned back to face me.

"My uncle's dead. He died in an automobile accident over twenty years ago."

"What happened to the money? Did he leave some to you? Shay didn't get any."

My phone silently vibrated a text in my pocket. I prayed it didn't interfere with the audio recording app.

"For all I know, he spent it all." Powell sounded relieved. Like he thought I only knew the story that had lived for twenty-plus years, not the truth that he and Benson had been hiding all that time. "The last time I saw my uncle was twenty-five years ago before he vanished with June Sommers' money."

"That's not true. You saw him one more time. When you identified his body in Mexico after the car crash."

"The last time I saw him alive." Unfazed.

"Well, I'm not sure why you wanted to include me in this little chat, Mr. Cahill, but it's time for me to get some rest." Baxter, still cordial. Untouched, in his mind. "Keenan can lead you back down to the lobby."

He and Powell stood up. I stayed seated, and not just to maintain the myth of my total blindness.

"Here's where you come in, Chuck." I fought the urge to turn and look directly at Baxter.

"Shay figured out that Colt Benson never died in a car crash. He used his nephew Keenan Powell to identify the body and ole Colt lived on under a different name. Something like *Chuck Baxter*. She even saw him with his wife one night while she was working at Muldoon's Steak House and called him a fucking coward."

Baxter and Powell sat back down but didn't say a word.

"She figured out that Chuck went back to Colt's stock market roots and started a hedge fund, relying on his clean biography to wrangle investors. I don't know much about hedge funds, but I know that prudent investors do their homework on the fund managers before they decide to invest huge sums of money with them. A good reputation is paramount to your success, isn't it, Chuck?"

"Of course." Nonplussed. "But the rest of what you said is nonsense."

I hadn't struck a nerve yet. I would soon.

"I guess she didn't press matters until she found out she was pregnant and wanted to give the life she was cheated out of to her baby." I turned my head a hair in Benson's direction. "Did Shay give you an ultimatum, Colt, oh, I mean, Chuck? Give her what was rightfully hers or she'd go to the press or your investors? Maybe even go to the police? Although the statute of limitations has already lapsed on the money you stole, there are no limitations on murder."

A confirming silence that I didn't need. Finally, Colt Benson spoke.

"You have quite an imagination, Mr. Cahill." Under control, but some of the coolness had evaporated. "You made some libelous accusations in your fabricated story."

"So, sue me. Let's go to court."

"I don't think that's what you really want, is it?"

"Why don't you tell me what I really want?"

"Money."

Jackpot. Consciousness of guilt. I was getting close enough for Detective Sheets to at least be interested. I hoped.

"Keep talking."

"You came here under the auspices of speaking for Shay's family, so I won't consider this a shakedown from a blind sleazeball private dick." The cool now all gone, replaced by a hard edge. "While none of what you just said is true, to refute it publicly could do harm to my reputation. So, on behalf of the Sommers' family, I'd be willing to give them a gift to help them deal with their grief."

"What kind of gift are you talking about?" I asked, waiting to hear the trap snap shut.

"Something with six figures. I'm assuming you would be responsible for delivering this gift."

"Of course."

"Keenan will contact you soon with the particulars."

"How soon?"

"In the next couple days." He stood up again. "Now get out."

CHAPTER FORTY-NINE

POWELL SILENTLY ESCORTED me all the way down to the lobby and out of the hotel to the sidewalk. I kept my eyes on his hands the whole time. Once on the sidewalk, his footsteps moved away behind me. I lost their sound and couldn't tell if he'd gone back into the hotel or just taken a few steps and stopped.

I didn't turn to look. Instead, I opened my phone to stop recording and to contact Uber, but remembered the text notification I'd gotten while I was up in the Sky Suite. I found my earbuds, plugged them into my phone, and listened to the text. I didn't want Powell to hear if he was close enough.

The text was from Kris Collins. She wanted me to call her. I started walking north on Prospect toward Muldoon's. I'd face-to-face her instead of calling. Footsteps behind me. Multiple. Voices from people out on Restaurant Row on the crisp winter night. I couldn't discern if any of the footsteps belonged to Keenan Powell. I stopped and turned toward La Valencia. If Powell was still on the street, he wasn't close enough for me to see him. Or close enough to hear me.

I called LJPD and asked for Detective Sheets. He was off until Monday, but I asked that he be given a message to call me ASAP.

I called Moira next.

"Now what?" A greeting I'd gotten used to.

"Make sure your home alarm system is armed tonight and that you are, too."

"What the hell did you do?" A high rattle.

"Talked to Colt Benson and Keenan Powell."

"Why the hell did you do that?" A sizzle.

"I wanted to try to get something incriminating on tape."

"You taped them?"

"Yeah. Made them think I was shaking them down. Got maybe enough to get Detective Sheets to take an interest."

"Are you insane?" A screech. "If they really are behind Shay's murder, you just put a target on your back!"

"They're going to contact me to set up a payoff. That's when they'll make their move. Of course, I won't show up. I'll take what I have to Sheets and see what he thinks."

"This is ridiculous! Shay Sommers was murdered in her sleep. They didn't wait for some stupid rendezvous site. You don't even have an alarm system on your house." Despite her continued insistence that I should get one. A precaution I never took while I was still in the game and an expense I thought I no longer needed after I quit playing. Except, now I was back in the game.

"I have an early alarm system. Eighty-five pounds of ears, muscle, and teeth."

"Where are you now?"

"About to go into Muldoon's to talk to Kris, then head home."

"Stay there. I'm in Mission Valley, but I can be there in a half hour."

"You don't have to do that.

"Shut up. You're staying with me until you talk to Detective Sheets. We'll pick up Midnight on the way over. And we're going to LJPD first thing in the morning."

"Okay, boss." Arguing would be fruitless. And staying with someone who could see and knew how to use a gun seemed like a good idea until I talked to Sheets.

I made it to the restaurant without incident. I was careful going down the stairs even though now I could almost make them out. Different levels of blur. Gravel-throated vocals backed by a gritty guitar riff assaulted me when I entered Muldoon's. My favorite kind of assault. Saturday was blues night in the bar at Muldoon's. I tapped down the hall to the hostess stand.

"Rick?" Kris. "You didn't have to come down here. We're swamped, but I would have called you back later. We have a party of twenty drunk women for a bachelorette party and a waiter called in sick, so I've been waiting tables and helping out a new hostess. I'm in the weeds, but will be free in a bit. I hope. You want dinner? It's on me?"

"No thanks. I'll wait in the bar."

"Let me find you a seat." She stepped in front of me and offered her arm. "I'm right in front of you."

"You're busy. I'll manage. Thanks."

"Come on." She grabbed my left hand and guided it to her right bicep. I let her lead even though I didn't need such hands-on help anymore.

We went into the bar. Mississippi blues bouncing off the walls led by the voice and guitar of Bob McKee, a San Diego blues legend. Short, squat with stubby fingers that pulled regrets out of your soul and ran them down guitar strings. A voice to match and a kick-ass five-piece band.

Kris sat me at a table against the wall to the right of the bar entrance.

"Would you like a beer? Ballast Point IPA?"

Kris still remembered my beer.

"No thanks." Beer went well with the blues but not for a blind man with a target on his back. "I'm good."

"I'll be back as soon as I can." Kris hustled out of the bar.

I settled in and listened to the music. Tried to get lost in it, but couldn't help but think of Turk as I sat in his bar in the restaurant where we first became friends and where, a dozen years later, he gave me a second chance at life. The music drifted into the background.

Memories flooded my brain of Turk showing me the restaurant ropes and convincing his father I deserved a raise after only a month working there. He knew my dad couldn't hold a job anymore and that my family could barely pay our bills. His father told me that Turk told him I'd earned the raise, but Turk never mentioned it to me. Eleven years later, he drove up to Santa Barbara to visit me in jail when everyone else believed I was guilty. A year after that, he gave me a job at Muldoon's knowing it would hurt business.

Now he was locked in a cage for a crime he didn't commit. Just like I'd been. I had to get him out.

The music had stopped. The lights were halfway up. The band was on a break. People moved past me to the bar exit. On the way to the bathrooms or outside for fresh air before Bob McKee and his band started their next set. A mass of fragrances, scents, and smells wafted by. Women's perfume, men's cologne, men's deodorant all commingling with human pheromones to give off similar, yet distinct smells. But no Dove deodorant.

A shadow appeared in front of me. Kris. She sat across from me.

"I'm worried about Turk." Her body slumped into the table. "He won't let me visit him in jail. He called me this morning to check up on the restaurant. He sounded awful. Like he's beaten. Like he's given up. Have you seen him?"

"Yeah. He's hanging in there." What else could I say? Kris was carrying the load of the entire restaurant, worrying about Turk, and grieving over the loss of her best friend. Why add to the grief with the truth. "How are you? Have you had a day off since he was arrested?"

"No, but Pat gets back from Europe in five days. I'm fine."

Her voice put a lie to her words. She was worn out.

"You need to take a few days off. Teach your best server how to close. You need a break."

"I'm okay. I owe it to Turk to make sure his restaurant is running smoothly when he's not here. I owe it to everyone who works here." A head shake. "Anyway, how's the preparation for the trial going? You're a part of the defense team, right?"

"Things are going well. Ellis Fenton is a good lawyer." I didn't tell her I'd been cut from the team. I was my own team.

"I feel so helpless with him sitting in jail. Is there anything I can do to help?"

"You're doing it by keeping the restaurant open and running."

"I started a GoFundMe page to try to raise money for bail." No optimism in her voice.

"Great idea."

"Well, we've only raised a few hundred dollars and some of the comments have been so vile that I had to turn off the comment function."

"The blessing and the curse of social media."

"Well, I'd better go tend to the drunk girls." She got up, but leaned toward me instead of exiting the bar. Spicy citrus fragrance mixed with feminine perspiration. Lips on my cheek. Then she was gone, her scent evaporating behind her.

People started to drift back into the bar. That's when I smelled it. A singular scent. One I'd smelled before. Three times. In one twenty-four-hour period. Men's Dove deodorant mixed with male musk. I snapped my head to the odor. A male form sat at a table across the entrance from me. Eight feet away. His head angled in my direction. A hand on his hip, elbow angled out. That's where he made his mistake. His underarm was exposed, leaking out his own unique stink.

The Invisible Man.

CHAPTER FIFTY

THE INVISIBLE MAN. He existed. And was within eight feet of me. Or was it an innocent civilian wearing the wrong deodorant like the old man at La Sala three days ago?

No. It was him. The mixture with the distinct musk whose absence I overlooked at La Sala. I knew it in my gut. I knew it in my heart. The person across from me was the Invisible Man.

Powell and Benson's assassin.

I turned my head toward the stage, but still watched the man through the corner of my sunglasses. He was a blur. I couldn't see his eyes, but his head was angled in my direction.

He'd followed me to Muldoon's from La Valencia. Just like he followed Moira and me when we met Turk. He was there later that night when Moira followed Shay to La Valencia. But how did he know to follow us to Turk's that morning? Only one way. A bug. Turk's girlfriend was making trouble for Powell and Benson. They were worried that she'd tell him what she knew. The Invisible Man must have bugged Shay's apartment and Turk's office or home. The bug picked up his phone conversations with Moira, and they found out that Turk hired her to tail Shay.

Had he bugged my house, too? The night I walked Midnight down Moraga Avenue. The person Midnight growled at coming from the direction of my house. The Invisible Man? Did he have time to get inside, plant a bug, and get out again? It didn't matter now. The assassin was eight feet away from me.

He'd tailed Moira and me the night of Shay's Maybach ride by the ocean when she overplayed her hand with Colt Benson in the Sky Suite of La Valencia. Maybe he staked out Shay's house while we were there and later saw Turk show up and the lights go on. He heard them arguing and waited for Turk to leave, for the lights to go out and enough time for Shay to fall back asleep, then he picked the lock and broke in. Incapacitated Shay with a punch to the face that fractured her eye socket, then used Turk's tie to strangle her. Maybe he saw the tie after he knocked her out or, earlier, when he bugged her apartment days or weeks before. Either way, Shay's dead and Turk's a patsy.

I might have been wrong about how everything went down, but one thing I was sure of. The Invisible Man worked for Powell and Benson.

And he murdered Shay Sommers.

And that very moment, there was nothing I could do about it. At least not until Detective Sheets listened to the audiotape of Baxter willing to pay me off. Until then, the police already had their man in jail.

I needed help and I couldn't get it from LJPD, yet. If they showed up now without the ability to arrest him, the Invisible Man would be in the wind and maybe lost forever.

But help *was* already on the way. Moira.

The band returned, so did customers, and the lights went down low. I kept my blurred vision on the Invisible Man through my sunglasses and the darkened bar.

Two minutes into my vigil, he got up from his table and left the bar. Shit.

I didn't know what to do. Was he leaving the restaurant or just going to use the restroom? Or going somewhere quiet to call his masters, Benson and Powell? If so, he'd be back in a few minutes and Moira would probably arrive by then.

Or was this a ploy to get me to follow him so he could get me isolated for the kill? Couldn't be. He and his bosses thought I was blind. How would I even know he was there to follow?

It wasn't a trap and he was getting away. The connection to Powell and Benson. If I lost him and he disappeared forever, Turk might spend the rest of his life in prison. I had to stay close until Moira arrived and could pick up the tail.

I bolted out of my chair and left the bar, my cane in hand but not needed. Through the opening to the right of the hostess stand, I saw a human blur going out the front door of the restaurant. I hustled after it, four seconds behind. I went through the front door and looked to the left and the staircase that led up to the street. Two figures, attached as one, coming down it. No one was going up. I looked to the right, under the blurred lighting of the restaurant's eaves.

A form. Male, moving away toward the lookout behind the restaurant with the view of La Jolla Cove or a right turn around the corner to the back door of Muldoon's and a staircase beyond that led to the second floor of the building. And multiple escape routes. If he went to the lookout, he'd have to come back in my direction to leave. If he turned right and went up the stairs, I might never see him again.

He turned right at the end of the restaurant.

Alone. Limited vision. No choice. I had to keep my eyes on him if I had any shot at getting Turk out of jail.

Instinct pushed me forward and I rushed along the walkway. Cane in front of me, not tapping, but moving it back and forth to give the illusion it was guiding me in case the Invisible Man suddenly reappeared. I needed to hide the capabilities I had left.

I hit the corner and turned. No one. A click of the door to the enclosed staircase closing forty feet ahead.

"I want to go look at the ocean!" A woman's slurred voice from behind, toward the front of Muldoon's. The couple I'd seen coming down the stairs.

I rushed toward the enclosed staircase. Twenty feet out.

"No, let's listen to some blues." Male voice from the same direction of the woman. Arguing about what to do.

Ten feet from the door to the staircase.

"I'm going without you." The woman's voice behind, in the courtyard.

I made it to the staircase door and whipped it open. Dark. Lights off.

A hard punch into my stomach. The air blew out of me. My cane rattled to the ground. I swung at the dark figure in front of me. My fist grazed his head. The fist in my stomach grabbed and ripped across my abdomen. Searing pain. Not a fist.

A knife.

"I guess you can see." A laugh from hell. "But not well enough."

I grabbed the hand on the knife to stop it from ripping me in half. Warm liquid enveloped my hands. I fought the knife out of my stomach. My guts shifted inside me. I wrestled the hand gripping the knife with both of mine. Pushed it up and back. Hands over my head, slick with my own blood. My body, fully extended. A slosh and sudden void inside my stomach.

Pain exploded my right temple. My head banged off the open door. I collapsed to the ground on top of my cane. My body half in, half out of the stairwell. The door wedged against my side.

Hands in my pockets ripping my wallet and phone free. I tried to crawl away in slow motion. A hand grabbed my hair and yanked my head back. The knife slammed into the left side of my neck just as I twisted and grabbed the cane under me. I thrust it up to my neck. The knife sliced and tinked off the cane. A scream stayed in my throat. Breath and blood and life gushed from my neck.

A woman's shriek.

Darkness.

CHAPTER FIFTY-ONE

Pain.

White coat.

Hand on my throat.

Blood.

Blurred face.

Mask on my mouth.

"Put pressure on the stomach wound!"

Clanking wheels. Jostled ride.

Lights blinking by overhead.

A hand holding mine.

"I'm right here, Rick." Moira, tight voice.

I moved my lips.

"Don't try to talk." Male voice.

"Invisible Man."

No sound came out.

Darkness.

Siren.

Poke in my arm.

Blurred face above me.

Male voice shouting medical terms I didn't understand.

Screeched stop.
Van door banging open.
Clanking wheels.
Lights passing overhead.
A forest of heads moving above me.
More shouted medical terms.
"Stat!"
Sharp left turn.
Abrupt stop.
Room. Lights.

Mask off.
Hand on mine.
"Don't' worry." Female voice. "Dr. Holt is a great surgeon."
New mask.
Darkness.

CHAPTER FIFTY-TWO

"Partially disemboweled. We had to remove seven and a half centimeters of his large intestine." Female voice. "He should make a full recovery, although he may not be able to speak for a couple weeks."

"Thank you, Doctor." Leah. "You saved his life."

"The paramedics deserve most of the credit, but even they couldn't have saved him if that woman hadn't seen him when she did. If she'd been even a minute or two later, he probably wouldn't have survived." A quick exhale. "Although, I may be selling Mr. Cahill short. He already had quite a few scars on his body. I checked his medical records after surgery. They show he's been treated for bullet wounds twice, but the scar on his left bicep looks like he might have been shot there, too. He's led a dangerous life. I hope he slows down after this."

"So do I." Leah.

My quest for the truth had put me in the hospital, near death, three times. I followed my own sense of justice. Every action I'd taken had led me to where I was today.

I'd survived, but Turk was still in jail.

* * *

"Mr. Cahill, it's Detective Denton from the La Jolla Police Department." I recognized her voice without the introduction. Even in my opioid haze. "Can you tell me what happened last Saturday night?"

Moira had kept me up to date on the investigation of my attacker. No one had gotten a good look at him. The woman who wanted to see the ocean and screamed and saved my life saw the Invisible Man as he leaned over me and tried to slit my throat. But she only saw the top of his head, then he was gone up the enclosed staircase. No one in the bar that night could remember the man sitting to the left of the entrance around ten o'clock. He truly was an invisible man.

"He's not supposed to talk, Detective." Moira, a machine-gun volley. She and Leah took turns watching over me. Unfortunately for Detective Denton, this was Moira's watch. "And he probably can't yet, anyway. The son of a bitch sliced his throat open and nicked his vocal cord."

The nurses had given me a whiteboard to write on in lieu of speech, but I was usually too doped up to make much sense. I tried to write "Invisible Man, Keenan Powell, and Benson/Baxter killed Shay," but I'm not sure if any of it was legible.

Moira interpreted, now fully onboard with my theory.

"Mr. Cahill's attack looks like a violent robbery." Denton. "I'm afraid nothing else."

"Someone's going to try to disembowel a man and slit his throat for a wallet?"

"His phone was stolen, too." Denton, unwilling to give an inch. As usual.

"Which LJPD pinged and found it in a dumpster a block away, right?"

"Yes."

"Why steal the phone then dump it?"

"Be—"

"Because he wanted to get information off the phone." Moira cut Denton off. "See who Rick had contacted, what he texted. Then he dumped the phone. This was attempted murder by someone working for Keenan Powell and Colt Benson, aka Chuck Baxter. I told Detective Sheets Saturday night that he needed to talk to them and get Baxter's DNA. The same night I told him Rick needed twenty-four-hour police protection, which LJPD refuses to provide. Powell and Baxter are the key to everything. Shay Sommers' murder and Rick's assault."

"Keenan Powell was murdered in his home. His housekeeper found him yesterday."

"When? Was he stabbed?" Moira asked the same questions that were in my head.

"We're not sure when he was killed, yet. Last Sunday or Monday. He was shot once in the chest and once in the face. Looks like a home invasion-type robbery."

"More likely Saturday night after Rick was attacked." Moira spat the words out.

I scrawled "Invisible Man Benson clean up" on the whiteboard and tapped my hand on it.

"We're not handling the case. That's the San Diego Police Department's jurisdiction, but they think it was a robbery."

I held up the whiteboard and pounded on it. Moira continued to explain what Denton refused to acknowledge.

After five minutes, both sides gave up.

"If you can think of anything else, let us know." Denton dropped something on the nightstand next to my bed. Probably a business card. "I'll check back in a few days when you're feeling better."

I pounded the whiteboard a couple more times, but she left without another word.

*   *   *

The next few days passed like a strobe light hallucination. In and out of opioid sleep. I tried to communicate on the whiteboard, but most of the time I was too drugged out to make any sense. Leah and Moira took turns holding my hand. Bandage changes, sponge baths, and doctor check-ins.

I gradually eased back on the medication, and my head started to clear after six or seven days, maybe ten. The days all ran together. I began to walk the halls. Each time a nurse insisted on holding my arm even though I had my cane and improving vision. I could make out Leah's eyes when she leaned in for a kiss. Sea blue. I'd missed being dazzled by their beauty.

During my recovery in the hospital, a neurosurgeon and my ophthalmologist confirmed what I already knew. My vision was coming back. Neither could tell me how much of it I'd permanently regain.

For once, I had more faith than the experts.

Finally, my discharge day arrived. Leah was outside with her car waiting to pick me up after I got my wheelchair chauffeured ride to exit the hospital. Moira went out looking for an orderly to expedite the process. She knew I had cabin fever and could barely wait another minute to be set free. I looked out the window and saw the outlines of medical buildings on the hospital campus. Sharp rectangle outlines, against the steel gray sky.

The world outside my sunglasses was coming into tighter focus.

I finally sat in the visitor chair next to the bed I was ready to burn and pretended to wait patiently.

A figure came into my room. Male. Blue clothes. Probably a suit. Calvin Klein cologne. Elk Fenton. I was surprised, but not surprised. Elk had jettisoned me from the defense team, but the grudge didn't go any deeper.

"Rick! I'm so glad you're getting out today." He moved toward me.

I eased myself up out of the chair. Pain and stitches grabbed at my stomach.

"Thanks for coming by." I stuck out a hand to cut off any attempt at a painful and awkward hug. He shook it.

"I visited you once, but you were under a lot of pain medication, understandably. How are you feeling now?"

I heard his last question, but didn't register it. Because I heard something else. Step, thunk, drag. Step, thunk, drag. Then a hulking figure appeared.

"Turk?" I strode to him and banged into a hug. We squeezed and held on. My wound screamed, but the pain made me feel alive.

A gasp behind Turk and a whiff of spicy citrus. Kris.

"He's free! He got out of jail this morning!"

Turk and I released, but kept our hands on each other's shoulders.

"What happened?" I asked.

"The DA dropped the charges without prejudice," Fenton piped up over my shoulder.

"Which means they can arrest me again if they want to." Turk, his red Brillo pad of hair smudged but visible to me. His eyes, dark circles.

"True, but very unlikely." Fenton. "The without prejudice is an attempt at face saving by LJPD and the DA's office."

"What happened? Why did they drop the charges?"

"We had Shay's fingernail scrapings sent to a private lab and the epithelial cells were mixed with a trace amount of cornstarch under a single fingernail that had unknown male DNA that they ran through CODIS and got a hit."

"Cornstarch?"

"Yes. Cornstarch has replaced talcum powder as a lubricant in some latex gloves." Counselor Fenton at his most comfortable. "Shay must have fought at the end and torn a hole in one of the latex gloves of the murderer."

"The fight in her kept me from spending the rest of my life in prison." Turk, emotion caught in his throat.

I patted him on the shoulder. "Did they arrest the guy? Who is he?"

"Well, no." Fenton's head tilted to the left. "The DNA belonged to Doug Breslin from Modesto, California. Born November 2, 1983. Died October 24, 2009."

"What? A dead man's DNA?"

"Yes. The district attorney knew that the DNA information, coupled with what you and Moira learned about Shay, her mother, Keenan Powell, and Chuck Baxter, would be, at the very least, too much reasonable doubt for any jury to convict. So, your unsanctioned investigation actually helped set Turk free." No bitterness or irony in Elk's voice.

"Wait a second. Somebody finally believes that Colt Benson and Chuck Baxter are the same person?"

"Yes, but we may never be able to prove it. Benson disappeared. Completely vanished. Left his wife, his business, everything behind."

"He's done that before," I said. "He had Powell killed so he couldn't finger him. Benson will show up again somewhere. His appearance will be altered again and he'll have another name, but he'll be wealthy and content spending other people's money. What do you know about the other dead guy who's alive, Doug Breslin?"

"He served in the Army for four years. Honorably discharged. Bounced around from job to job in central California. Was arrested twice. Once for shoplifting and then did time for felony assault. That's when he was swabbed for DNA. Did four years in Folsom State Prison and moved to Alaska in 2009. Worked on a crab boat where he was lost at sea later that year."

"Except he wasn't," I said. "Now he's someone else. He's murdered at least two people and he's still out there."

CHAPTER FIFTY-THREE

WE ALL HAD dinner at Muldoon's a few nights later—Turk, Fenton, Moira, Leah, me, and Kris, who couldn't stop herself from making the rounds of the restaurant, despite supposedly having the night off.

The dinner was in celebration of Turk's release from jail, but the mood wasn't celebratory. There were warm feelings all around and a few quiet toasts, but Shay's death hung heavy on the night.

Moira pulled me aside toward the end of the night and led me outside into the courtyard. San Diego winter had finally pushed through and I wrapped my arms around my coatless body. My stomach reminded me someone tried to kill me. With prejudice.

"You know this isn't over, yet." Alcohol on her breath. "That son of a bitch is still out there. He cleaned up Powell, whether on Benson's command or on his own. This guy's a pro. Two murders and one attempted. All different MOs. He's been at it for a while and you're not safe until he's arrested. Or dead."

"Neither are you."

"I've taken precautions, but you're target number one."

"You convinced Leah to take precautions, too. She had an alarm system put in my house while I was in the hospital. She also told me you guarded my room every night I was there." I wanted to give her a hug, but knew she wouldn't allow it. Besides, it would hurt my wound. "Thanks."

"I'm comforted that Leah knows how to use a gun. When is she going back to Santa Barbara?"

"I'm not sure, but I'll be fine when she does. You take care of yourself, Calamity Jane."

But I did know when Leah was going back to Santa Barbara. And I wanted to be alone in the house when she did.

* * *

Leah watched over me the next ten days, and I always accompanied her when she left the house. Even when she tried to convince me that I should stay home and rest. I didn't tell her I was on the lookout for anything out of place. Even with my improving but still worse than legally blind eyes.

* * *

Leah sat me down at the kitchen island the day she was to leave for Santa Barbara.

"I don't have to go." She held my hand between hers. The blue dazzle of her eyes visible to mine. "I can wait another week."

"I'll be fine. Your client's not going to wait forever. This job is going to change your life." I wanted her to stay, but I wanted her to go more. For her career, her future. And for my immediate future. "I'll get Moira to drive me and Midnight up in a week or so."

"You're my miracle. Twice. I don't want there to be a third." She kissed me. Long and soft. A tear brushed against my cheek.

Moira stopped by an hour after Leah left. Like they had it synchronized. The first thing she did when she entered my house was walk to the right of the door and check the new alarm system.

"Well, at least you didn't forget to turn the alarm on."

"I'm safe. All bunkered in."

"I still think you should make that bunker at my house."

"I'm good here. Thanks." I patted her on the shoulder, which I knew irritated her. "You did your check-in, you don't have to hang around."

"Doug Breslin, or whatever his name is, is still out there somewhere, maybe waiting for the chance to finish the job."

"There's no reason for him to stick around or worry about me. I can't identify him. He's already moved on to his next job and his next identity. He's in the wind just like Colt Benson or whatever he's morphed into now. I'm safe."

"No you're not. This guy's evil. Look what he did to you. Why not use a gun like he did on Keenan Powell?" A plead in her scattergun voice.

"Too loud." But I knew where she was going.

"He could have used a silencer. The knife was personal. This guy has been a ghost for over ten years and killed God knows how many people." Her staccato voice picking up speed and pitching higher. "And you sniffed him out. Literally. Some blind guy almost caught him. You damaged his ego. He wants payback."

"That's quite an assumption, Doctor Freud." I put my hands on her shoulders and gently turned her toward the front door. "I'll make you a deal and check in every morning so you know I survived the night."

"Asshole." She gently pushed me in the chest. "If that son of a bitch hurts you again, I'm going to kill him and then I'm going to kill you."

"Roger." I opened the door.

"Asshole." She left.

* * *

I waited until I heard Moira's car drive away, then contacted Uber. I stayed in the house until the driver arrived and had him pull into the driveway. The driveway where Leah's car had been parked the last couple weeks, now empty for anyone who was watching to see. The driver drove me to a pet store where I bought a large dog crate. I'd trained Midnight in a crate when he was a puppy but didn't move to a larger size when he outgrew it.

We made another stop at Von's where I bought two weeks' worth of groceries.

I didn't set the alarm when I got home. Or the next four nights. I locked all the doors like I always did and pulled all the drapes closed, but the alarm remained unarmed.

Leah called me multiple times a day, and Moira called late each night to check in and make sure I was still alive.

I didn't step foot outside the house except to throw the ball with Midnight in the backyard. He took to the crate even though his nighttime wanderings were now curtailed. I put the crate at the right foot of my bed, not the left, where he usually slept. I needed a free lane.

I put a thick spare comforter on the floor of the bathroom in my bedroom, as well as a large bucket of water that I kept full.

I'd gone to bed every night for the last six years with a Smith & Wesson .357 revolver in the drawer of my nightstand. Even when I couldn't see.

The last four nights it was on top of the nightstand.

CHAPTER FIFTY-FOUR

MIDNIGHT'S GROWL WOKE me from a restless sleep. I bolted upright and quietly shushed him. I grabbed the gun. The room was pitch black. My improving vision still needed light to see anything. I guided myself around the edge of the bed to Midnight in the crate. I brought my index finger to my lips and gave a quiet sshh, then silently opened the crate and let him into the bathroom six steps away with the soundproof comforter on the floor and the bucket full of three days' worth of water. More than enough if something went wrong.

I bent over and kissed Midnight on the forehead then left the bathroom and quietly shut the door behind me.

Midnight was my alarm and would fight to the death to save my life, but I wouldn't put him in that situation. I'd prepared. I was ready.

Ten steps to the bedroom door. The house, still a black cave. I squinted down my eyes and listened to the night. Silence.

Fifteen silent steps to the staircase. Both hands holding the gun in front of me in a perfect shooting platform. I took one hand from the gun and grabbed the railing at the top of the stairs to situate myself. Slowly, I knelt down to the floor, then proned myself out on my stomach, arms out in front. The pain from my stomach wound heightened my senses.

I waited.

A blurred narrow beam of light in the kitchen. He'd picked the lock on the back door. The light moved around the kitchen, the living room, and shot over my head to the second floor. I kept the gun pointed at the source of the light. Still too far away to zero in on.

The light moved across the living room toward the staircase. Each step silent. I had just enough time to bolt back into my bedroom, lock the door, and call 911. The killer would probably flee and I'd be safe. For tonight. But what about tomorrow or the next time I left my house. The home alarm wouldn't do me any good out in the world.

The source of the light reached the bottom of the staircase. The beam rose six inches with each silent step. Closer and closer to my face and outstretched arms at the top of the stairs. Step six. Two more and the target light would find me.

I aimed just below the light and whispered, "Rory."

The light shot up. I squeezed the trigger. Yellow light flashed the stairway as three explosions rocked the house.

Two from my gun, a silenced one from his.

"Umph." A thump, then tumble down the staircase. The beam of light bounced down the stairs and came to rest at the bottom. Pointed at the human mass next to it.

I sprang to my feet and scrambled down the stairs. My gun pointed at the body below me as I counted off each step in my head above the ringing in my ears. I knelt down and picked up the gun the light was attached to and pointed it at the man gasping below me. The gun had a long, thin suppressor screwed into the barrel. The man was dressed in dark hospital scrubs and something was covering his shoes, probably plastic booties. His hands, dark, encased in latex gloves. The uniform and weapon of a professional killer.

I pointed the light-mounted gun at his head. He was bald now. No more brown hair that the woman who screamed saw the night he stabbed me. But I could smell the Dove deodorant mixed in with his

musk even with the metallic stink of smoke and the coppery scent of
blood in the air.

The Invisible Man had already changed his look and, no doubt, his
identity. For the final time. In the light I could just make out his face.
His mouth was gaping like a fish out of water.

With my gun still aimed at him, I used my left hand to find his
wounds. Two in the upper chest. I put pressure on them as best I could
with one hand. The man's breathing grew more ragged.

"Did Benson tell you to kill me or is this on your own?"

"I . . . I . . ." A death rattle and he was gone.

*　*　*

Another square white room. I'd been in too many of them the last
fifteen years. This one belonged to the San Diego Police Department.
My second time in it in the last three days. Fluorescent lights overhead. Bright enough for me to almost make out the features of
Detective Skupin sitting across from me. We had a history. Not as bad
as I had with most cops.

"I'm trying to help you out here, Rick, but you got to meet me
halfway."

"Whatever you need, Detective."

"What I need is an explanation that doesn't come off as you lying
in wait for Doug Breslin and cold-bloodedly shooting him."

"Kind of hard to lie in wait in my own home. The guy broke in,
shot at me, and I shot him."

"I'll tell you what you did and didn't do, Rick." He thrust out a
hand. I could barely make out his fingers as he unwound them. "You
didn't call 911 when you heard an intruder in your house. You didn't
arm your home alarm, which was in working order. By the way, I

checked with the alarm company and they said you hadn't had the alarm on for four days. How do you explain that?"

"I've been forgetful since someone stabbed me in the stomach and tried to slit my throat. A lot of painkillers."

"The facts of the crime scene don't correlate with your story. I'll give you a chance to change it right now. No harm done."

"I'm not sure what you mean."

"You could not have been standing up when you shot Breslin. The angle would have been more downward. Plus, the bullet from his gun went into the ceiling right above the staircase, like he'd already been shot and was falling backward when he fired his gun."

"I might have gotten where he was standing wrong when he raised his gun to shoot me and who shot first. It all happened pretty fast."

"That's another thing. You're legally blind. How could you tell he had a gun and not just a flashlight?"

"A reasonable assumption considering that he did have a gun."

"And you were willing to bet his life on an assumption?"

"No. I wasn't willing to bet mine."

EPILOGUE

DETECTIVE SKUPIN HAD me down to San Diego PD headquarters two more times. At Elk Fenton's insistence, I took him with me for both. Skupin didn't charge me but never completely bought my story, either. That didn't matter. The press had already anointed me a hero.

Again.

I declined all interview requests.

* * *

Four months after Doug Breslin tried to kill me, the second time, Turk requested Moira, Kris, Elk Fenton, and me to meet him at the Mount Soledad Veterans Memorial one night. The memorial sits under a forty-foot-high cross and has a 360-degree view of La Jolla and much of San Diego all the way to Mexico. I'd spent many a solemn evening up there with my dad as a kid and alone as an adult. And it's where Turk saved my life and took a bullet that changed his own.

Turk had us gather on a patch of grass below the cross that had a spectacular view of La Jolla. Night or day.

"Thanks for coming tonight." Turk held a letter-size piece of paper in front of him with both hands. "I know it was an odd request. This place was special to Shay and me. We used to drive up here about this time of night, look at the view, and talk about our future together."

Turk's voice wavered. Kris rubbed his shoulder and he took a deep breath then continued.

"Anyway, I'll get to it." Another deep breath. "Shay had a safe deposit box at her bank that I didn't know about. No one knew about it. Anyway, her cousins in South Carolina ended up with the contents, which wasn't much, but they sent me a letter Shay had written that was in it. I wanted you to hear it, because no one here but Kris knew the kind of person Shay was. In fact, because of me hiring Moira and Rick to spy on her, the three of you probably didn't think too highly of her. This letter says who she really was."

He handed the letter to Kris. She held a flashlight on it and read it out loud.

Dear Turk,

I know things have been difficult lately. That's my fault. I haven't been truthful with you. I've lied about what I've been doing after work and I think you can tell. I'm sorry. It hurts me deeply to know I'm hurting you. I don't know if I'll ever be able to explain what I've been doing or even show you this letter, but I hope I have the courage to soon. I know you put me on a pedestal and I hate that you might think less of me.

Before I met you, when I lived in Portland, I took an ancestry DNA test for fun. I found out that my cousin, Keenan Powell, lived in San Diego. The man who helped my father fake his own death.

You see, my father is still alive. He's changed his name and is now the CEO of a hedge fund. I'm sure he started it with some of the money he stole from my mom. It's probably some sort of scheme to steal money from more people. He's an evil man, but I don't think the police can do anything about what he did to my mom now. I know he cares about his fake reputation, though, and I'm using that against him. I'm not proud of what I'm doing, but it's the only way to get back some of the money he stole from my mom. From my future. From our baby's future.

I know things aren't great with the restaurant and I want to pay you back for all the money you've given me for rent. This money will give our child a chance to have a fair start in life.

I hope that, if you read this, or find out what I've done, you'll understand why I did it and still want to raise a child with me.

I came to San Diego to find my cousin who I hoped would lead me to my father. He did.

But what I didn't expect was to find, and was blessed to find, was you. You're the best man I've ever known and I want to spend the rest of my life with you.

I love you with all my heart and can't wait for us to start a family.

Love,

Shay

Kris' voice caught at the end, but she made it through. Turk had his head down. Moira went over and hugged him, then wiped her eyes. I wiped mine and hugged him, too.

"She was flawed, like the rest of us." Turk steadied his voice. "But her heart was in the right place. If only I'd known what she was doing, I . . ."

"You can't do that, Turk." I put my hands on his shoulders and looked him in the face. "I've been down that road and there's no good end to it. You were the best man she knew and you loved her. You did the best you could. That's all anyone can ever do."

* * *

Sixteen months after losing my eyesight, I now only wear sunglasses outside. The prescription matches the glasses I wear indoors. My vision seems to have dead-ended at 20/200, but lenses correct it to 20/20. I can see. Well enough to work cases without having to rely on my nose and my ears, which have regressed to normal with my corrected vision. Tradeoffs.

Leah is living in Santa Barbara full-time. We take turns spending weekends together there and in San Diego. With Midnight as my traveling companion. Family.

Turk, Kris, and I sometimes share a drink or two after closing time at Muldoon's and talk like we used to seven years ago. Friends.

I finally had plastic surgery to repair the bullet hole in my face. It's not perfect. There's still a scar. Fits about right.

My office is booth four at Muldoon's again.

I work cases. I follow my gut. I do the best I can.

PUBLISHER'S NOTE

We hope that you have enjoyed *Blind Vigil* by Matt Coyle. This is the seventh novel in the Rick Cahill series. If you have not read the previous novels, we'd like to give you a brief recap.

Yesterday's Echo is the first book in the series. Rick Cahill had been a Santa Barbara cop until he was accused of murdering his wife. Never convicted—but never exonerated, either—he now manages a restaurant in La Jolla. When a beautiful, young TV reporter, arrested for murder, comes to him for help, Rick is pulled into her case. But things go desperately wrong, and he, too, becomes a suspect.

Night Tremors follows when an old nemesis asks Rick for his help to free a man from prison, a man he thinks is wrongly convicted of murder. Scared from the past, chased by nightmares, Rick jumps at the chance to save an innocent man—by uncovering the truth only the real killer knows—what happened one bloody night eight years earlier.

Dark Fissures is the third Rick Cahill novel. Rick, now a struggling private investigator, is hired by a beautiful country singer to prove her husband's death was not suicide—but murder. This case pits him against the La Jolla Chief of Police—again. This time Rick is out of time—with no place to go—

Rick Cahill had long feared the truth about his blood, the blood of his father, coursing through his veins. In *Blood Truth*, the fourth in the series, Rick faces head-on the truth. After opening a long hidden safe, he embarks upon a quest to redeem or doom his late father's disgrace. As he uncovers layers of clues, he encounters powerful forces intent on keeping the past buried.

The fifth novel in the Rick Cahill series is *Wrong Light*. Rick has been hired to protect a sexy nighttime radio show host, who's prey to a demented stalker. But can he escape his own past long enough to intercede?

Lost Tomorrows is the Rick Cahill novel that directly precedes *Blind Vigil*. While attending the funeral of his former partner in the Santa Barbara Police Department, Rick discovers she may have been murdered. Following clues leading to her murder, he discovers the truth about the tragedy that ruined his life—his wife's murder. Consumed by revenge, Rick plots his course, leading to the consequences you find in *Blind Vigil* . . .